A
THE MISTLETOE

ADDISON FOX

KAREN WHIDDON

Recycling programs for this product may not exist in your area.

ISBN-13: 978-0-373-00988-6

A Hunter Under the Mistletoe

This edition published by arrangement with Harlequin Books S.A.

For questions and comments about the quality of this book, please contact us at CustomerService@Harlequin.com.

HARLEQUIN®
www.Harlequin.com

Printed in U.S.A.

Praise for Addison Fox

"An intricate, action-filled plot and steady pacing create an engaging read."
—*RT Book Reviews* on *The Royal Spy's Redemption*

"This is the kind of story that true romance readers, like myself, love and have a hard time putting down till you read the last page."
—*Fresh Fiction* on *The London Deception*

Praise for Karen Whiddon

"I love how this book is a sweet romance but also manages to be an action-packed story that...keeps you on the edge of your seat."
—*Aussie Bookworm* on *The Wolf Siren*

"A nice backstory and exciting plot make this a must-read."
—*RT Book Reviews* on *The Wolf Siren* (4.5 stars)

"*The Lost Wolf's Destiny* is action-packed with a lot of twists and turns that lead the reader on an amazing ride."
—*Fresh Fiction*

About the Authors

Addison Fox is a lifelong romance reader, addicted to happy-ever-afters. There's nothing she enjoys more than penning novels about two strong-willed, exciting people on that magical fall into love. When she's not writing, she can be found spending time with family and friends, reading or enjoying a glass of wine. Contact Addison at her website—addisonfox.com—or catch up with her on Facebook (addisonfoxauthor) and Twitter (@addisonfox).

Karen Whiddon started weaving fanciful tales for her younger brothers at the age of eleven. Amid the gorgeous Catskill Mountains, then the majestic Rocky Mountains, she fueled her imagination with the natural beauty surrounding her. Karen now lives in north Texas, writes full-time and volunteers for a boxer dog rescue. She shares her life with her hero of a husband and four to five dogs, depending on if she is fostering. You can email Karen at KWhiddon1@aol.com. Fans can also check out her website, karenwhiddon.com.

CONTENTS

Dear Reader,

Welcome to the world of the Helios, a sexy race of phoenixes descended from a powerful Greek god. Although the Helios keep their true selves hidden from the world, their secrets don't keep them from active, engaging lives in their chosen city, Las Vegas.

The Stavros family, one of the oldest descendants of the Helios, settled Las Vegas nearly a century ago and now runs one of the city's most glamorous hotels, The Archangel. Currently helmed by entrepreneur Rafael Stavros, the hotel-casino is preparing for one of their busiest times of the year—the holidays and New Year's.

Rafe is a man on the brink. His seasonal regeneration has come upon him early, catching him out in the open at the moment he's consumed by his fire of renewal. But he's spotted by the casino's head of horticulture, Evangeline Kennedy, before he can hide himself.

Evangeline's determined to uncover the reality behind what she saw—but she's not prepared for where that journey of discovery will take her. Or the bright, vibrant man who will make her fall in love.

I hope you enjoy Rafe and Evangeline's story as well as Karen Whiddon's story about Rafe's brother, Gabe. These are two sexy men ready to do battle to keep their secrets—and their people—safe. Is there anything better than a protector like that?

Wishing you a wonderful holiday season of your own. May it be filled with precious time spent with the ones you love.

Best,

Addison Fox

ALL IS BRIGHT

ADDISON FOX

For Carly

An editor's job is made up of many parts—
active cheerleader, gentle guide, creative steward
and, *always*, stalwart champion. You do each of
those things with amazing aplomb
(and really awesome gifs).

This time you also brought the understanding.
Thank you.

Prologue

Evangeline Kennedy was superstitious enough not to tempt fate and practical enough not to care when she did. So after firing two team members who'd taken it upon themselves to give some friends restricted access to the employee entrance of the Archangel Casino where she worked, she'd estimated it was safe to assume her day couldn't get worse.

Until that night when she saw a man consumed in a ball of orange flame.

She wasn't even supposed to be working, but the holiday installations needed to be finalized and there was simply no way she could go home and leave them unfinished. Which was how she found herself on her knees in the dirt, on the grounds beside the infinity pool that served as the property's lone—and wildly popular—topless destination.

The sun worshippers had long vanished for the day, trading their golden glow for an evening among the restaurants, bars and gaming tables the Archangel prided itself on. Evangeline sat back on her heels and took in the mix of ivy, poinsettia and lights she'd spent the better part of eight hours planting, irrigating and arranging. She'd been cultivating the poinsettia on her own in the property's large greenhouse, unwilling to miss out on the color palate she wanted by the possibility of someone else's carelessness. Poinsettia color was a tricky thing, after all.

And oh, wow, did it pop.

Even in the nighttime lighting that flooded the grounds, she could see the reds, creams and marbled pinks she'd been aiming for, with a well-placed burst of orange mixed in. The wash of vibrant hues would catch the eye, just as she planned. Even better, the installation—a layered structure guests would pass from their rooms near the pool and on into the casino—would match the look, feel and tone she'd built across the property.

As the Archangel's horticultural architect, Evangeline had full range of the grounds, the only mandate that she continue to use wild explosions of color and unexpected installations of flowers to resemble a walk through an artist's canvas more so than a Las Vegas casino. And damn it, she thought with no small measure of pride, she did it well.

She wiped a bead of sweat that worked its way down her temple toward her cheek and admired her handiwork. Those two slackers, Troy and Victor, could bite her. Even if it was three in the morning, she hadn't eaten since noon and she was due in for a presentation with the casino brass in another five hours, she could sit for a minute and admire her handiwork.

The poinsettias had been a gamble. The plant was fairly hardy in the subtropical climates that had been its origin, but the Nevada soil was tricky, the desert climate something that required continued overcompensation.

Sort of like you.

Evangeline shook off the strange thought and stood.

While she didn't regret her earlier choice in firing two members of her team, the harsh words she'd had with Troy and Victor had left an unpleasant aftertaste that had tinged the edges of her thoughts while she worked.

Loosen up. What's the big deal? No one cheated or anything after we let them in.

The big boss is so busy earning money and overcharging people for food and liquor he's not going to notice a few guys in the back door.

You're a bitch of a boss, anyway. Who wants to spend all day with some compulsive, anal need to plant some stupid flowers?

It had been the last that had struck with surprisingly sharp claws. She'd believed herself in tune with her employees, enjoying a relatively easy camaraderie and kinship over their work. From Troy and Victor's abrupt exit interview, it sounded like she needed to rethink that perspective.

Perhaps she needed to rethink a lot of things.

With one final look at her handiwork, Evangeline resolved to shake off the malaise and the unpleasant memory. Careless employees didn't matter. Her work spoke for itself. And if she needed to think about getting a hobby or find a way to spend more of her personal time off the Archangel's grounds, then she would think about that in the New Year.

She wrapped her tools in the oversize canvas bag she carried everywhere, the heavy, jangling weight a comfort and reassurance as she walked down a small, nearly hidden curved pathway toward the greenhouse. She'd stow her things, grab her purse and would be home and asleep in less than half an hour.

The late November air wafted over her skin, a cool breeze that refreshed more than it chilled. Although the season was limited, Las Vegas did experience winter. The sunny days usually compensated for any cold, but the desert lost its warmth at night, here on the floor of the Mojave. Evangeline slipped into the button-down shirt she'd tied haphazardly at her waist, juggling the thick canvas holding her tools.

It was only when she came around the last corner, the hothouse in sight, that she came to a sudden halt. A wall of heat washed over her, the blaze searing in its intensity as it reflected off the floor-to-ceiling windows of the greenhouse.

Fire!

She instinctively stepped back, the heat blanketing her in another wave as she searched for the source of the blaze. Bright orange flames rose toward the sky, the heat immense even as she tried to focus on the source. The fire seemed…contained. Oddly still, even.

Was it possible?

The lawn appeared untouched, as did the building. Standing her ground and forcing herself to take stock of the blaze in order to understand how to fight it, Evangeline's gaze swept the wide-open lawn, the two-story greenhouse, the rolling flower beds that edged toward the rim of the property.

It was only when she turned her attention once more toward the fire that a scream rose up in her throat.

As the orange and red snapped their fangs, forming and reforming in that strange, isolated blaze, she finally understood its shape.

And saw a man trapped in the flames.

Shit, hell and damn.

Those and several other, more inventive curses floated through Rafael Stavros's mind in the few seconds before he lost consciousness, an image of the lovely Evangeline Kennedy imprinted in his thoughts.

He'd pushed it tonight, allowing a meeting to run long. Which meant he hadn't made it to his rooms before the fire came upon him.

Before that lone moment in his pristinely ordered world when he lost control.

Chapter 1

She'd nearly called in sick the next day. Even with a frantic scramble to find hotel security and a solid belt or two of whiskey when she got home, Evangeline couldn't shake what she'd seen.

A man on fire.

She'd been unable to move, shocked when the flames that had warmed her all over suddenly vanished as if they'd never been, the air and grounds once again still. It was only once she'd moved closer to the sight of the blaze, the grass untouched and still cooled by the night air, that she'd run for help.

Security had come with her to the site, then reassured her over and over there wasn't anything wrong. It had only been her insistence to watch the security feed that had finally sent her home in a puzzled haze.

Mac, the lead on duty, had replayed the tapes of that quadrant of the grounds. She'd watched herself come around the corner. Had even seen the look of shock paint her face. But when she stared at the space where the burning man should be, the grounds looked as calm and peaceful as a baby sleeping.

But damn it, she'd *seen* him. His long, powerful form had been consumed by the fire, and the wall of heat shot off by the flames had felt like the combined power of ten furnaces. She'd never felt anything like it.

How could something so strong and powerful remain so contained? How hadn't it spread? And why the hell wasn't it showing up on the security cameras or in the spot where the fire had been?

"Miss Kennedy." The office admin nodded to her. "They will see you now."

Evangeline smiled at the woman, a perfect complement to the powerful outer office she found herself in. Thick, plush carpet muffled the noise of her steps and a soft, gentle hum of elegance pervaded the air.

Had she ever looked that perfect? From the artful makeup, to the stylish hair, to the trim jacket that stopped at the woman's hips, the admin to the great and powerful Stavros family was perfection and grace personified.

"Thank you." Evangeline scrambled to her feet, inwardly acknowledging that, no, she'd never managed that look. She was a woman who preferred dirt to pearls and comfortable, baggy cargo pants to a skirt any day. The outfit she'd managed for her meeting—a plum silk shirt and a trim pair of black slacks—was about as dressy as she got.

"Thank you for the tree." The woman pointed toward the towering pine in the corner of the office, immaculately decorated in a wash of red and white. "I understand you managed the decorations throughout the property. They're way better than what we had last year."

The primary reason she'd snagged the job, but Evangeline didn't say anything. Instead, she nodded. "Thank you. I have a supplier I've used for several years. His trees are the best."

"No arguments here." The admin held open the door to the inner sanctum of the Archangel's brass, a secretive smile playing about her lips. "Knock 'em dead."

Before Evangeline could attempt to respond, she was through the door, staring down the two brothers who ran the Archangel.

She'd met them before, of course, and had seen them around the grounds, but the wall of masculinity that greeted her was something to behold. Gabriel and Rafael Stavros, sons of powerful casino mogul Michael Stavros, were an impressive sight. Dubbed The Archangels by the press, they were as easily found in the business news as the gossip pages.

In fact, Evangeline amended to herself, their bachelor status ensured they occupied those gossip pages with shocking regularity.

She thought them both attractive—and had yet to meet a woman on staff who didn't—but something about Rafael Stavros had always drawn her more intensely than his brother. With the dark hair that shagged a bit too long around his neck and the piercing gray eyes that always reminded her of a winter storm, he was a study in contrasts.

Delicious contrasts, the small voice in her head that kept her perpetual company whispered.

Shaking off the fanciful that had no place in a business meeting, she shifted her portfolio to her other hand and shook the outstretched palms before her. After the standard pleasantries, it was Rafe who spoke first. "It's lovely to see you again, Evangeline."

"You, as well."

"Gabe and I took a look at the installation at the infinity pool this morning. It's good work."

"Thank you."

The gray eyes that had occupied more than a few of her fantasies hardened. "Work you did yourself, I understand?"

"It's nothing I—"

"It's good work." Gabe spoke over Evangeline, stilling any further comment. "And as I understand it, we're well rid of the two men on your team."

The focus on two employees who shouldn't have mattered a whit to either man was a surprise and she tried to remember there was little that happened in their casino either of them missed. "I spoke to Human Resources immediately after it happened, Mr. Stavros. Troy and Victor were escorted from the property, their photos circulated in Security immediately."

"Which is how I found out about it so quickly." Gabe's eyes twinkled, his smile broad and far more inviting than his brother's.

So why did her gaze keep darting to Rafe?

"Why don't I leave you two to the discussion at hand and I'll go make sure those photos have, in fact, been circulated to the staff." Gabe leaned in and pressed a quick kiss on her cheek. "Enjoy your meeting, Evangeline."

A small frown lit Rafe's face and she scrambled to understand why he'd be upset. Troy and Victor were her responsibility and she could dismiss a member of her team for infractions.

"I apologize if I overstepped with the employees. I caught them—"

Rafe stepped forward, his large form seemingly even larger in the fitted cut of his black suit. "You think I'm mad about that?"

"You don't seem happy."

"You were forced to finish the infinity pool installation all on your own."

"It was fine. It's my job."

"I don't expect you to work at three in the morning."

"But that's what was required to—"

Once again, he cut her off, his frown carving deeper grooves in his cheeks. "It's not required and it isn't healthy."

Although her role as lead of the horticultural program at the Archangel was the pinnacle of her career thus far, Evangeline had worked her way up to the position, taking jobs up and down the Strip since moving to Las Vegas shortly after college. She'd spent her career working long hours and had never once been reprimanded for it.

An image exploded in her thoughts—the burning man on the grounds. She'd briefly forgotten him in the tempting testosterone of the Stavros brothers but the strong memory hadn't lain dormant for long.

Did Rafe know? Was that why he didn't want her working late? Curious, she pressed him. "I'm perfectly capable of seeing to my responsibilities."

"Your responsibilities don't require you to keep a schedule of eighteen straight hours of manual labor. It's neither healthy nor good for you."

"I manage just fine."

"It's dangerous work if you're tired."

"Yes, well the holiday season comes once a year and leaving beds of empty dirt all over the property where plants should be is hardly festive. I'm not a slacker like your former horticulture lead and I'd think you would appreciate the effort."

"It's not a matter of appreciation."

"So maybe you should say thank you and we can move on." Evangeline waited for the inevitable result of her bold words—narrowed eyes and a small layer of shock at her frankness—before she pressed her advantage. "Or perhaps you'd like to tell me why there was a burning man on the property at three o'clock this morning?"

Rafe had to give her credit—Evangeline Kennedy was crafty. Able-bodied and brassy, she'd come into the Archangel like a whirling dervish and almost eleven months later hadn't slowed down. She fascinated him, with her long, coltish gait and thick, curly hair that was perpetually piled atop her head.

But it was her eyes. A rich brown the color of the finest dark chocolate. Every time he looked at her, he could swear she saw him to the very depths of his soul.

She had old eyes. Ancient eyes. Just like the curse he bore upon his body as surely as it was the greatest gift he possessed.

She'd intrigued him immediately, the woman who'd stood on his property, giving hell to the former horticulture expert they'd had on staff. Although Don Casey had a strong reputation throughout Las Vegas, Rafe and Gabe had soon discovered the man's penchant for the bottle had dulled his artistic sensibilities to be virtually nonexistent. He'd been on the hunt for someone new when Evangeline took matters into her own hands.

Presumably visiting the property one evening on a stroll down the Strip, she'd seen Don butchering an installation, designed to look like a heard of African elephants marching in a row through the lobby. She'd berated Don, then ripped several tools from his grip. Evangeline was on her knees, patting a thick hoof into place in the lobby when Rafe had come upon her.

Gabe had quickly ushered Don away, saving what small amount of pride the man had left, leaving Rafe to deal with the dirt-stained harpy in his lobby. He'd nearly yelled right back at her until he saw the small, frustrated tears that filled the corners of her eyes.

And damn it to hell, if she hadn't caught him by the balls in that moment, and all the moments since.

"I'm waiting, Mr. Stavros."

Images of those big brown eyes, swimming with the lightest sheen of tears, faded in the face of those same eyes, alight in banked fury. "What are you talking about? If anything was burning on my property beyond the couples on the dance floor at Spark, I'd know about it."

"Last night. The property outside the greenhouse. I saw a man burning."

"Impossible."

Rafe knew just how possible it was, but he held his ground, unwilling to break his gaze. "I am aware of all incidents that happen on property and nothing burned last night."

"Then explain to me what I saw."

Rafe folded his hands behind his back and stared down at her. He only had a slight height advantage and estimated her around five-nine or -ten to his six-two. "A late-night hallucination after pushing yourself for eighteen hours?"

"I know what I saw."

"And I know what goes on here at the Archangel. We had no fire last night."

The slightest tilt of her head was the only sign she mulishly didn't believe him, but she was all business when she next spoke. "I brought the designs you requested."

"Let's get to them." He gestured her to a seat at the long conference table that dominated the far wall of his office.

In moments, he had visions of a forest glade rising in his mind, scattered with wood nymphs, centaurs and sprites as she walked him through her designs. "You want an evil queen, too?"

"She has to be there." Evangeline tapped on the edge of the layout, the paper equivalent of the west side of his lobby. "It's an enchanted forest, drawing the guest from an inviting jaunt past the fairy glade farther and deeper into the installation. Once they realize they're in the queen's clutches, it's too late to turn back."

"And you can do this in a week?"

"With your approval my team will start construction of the basics this week. We'll create the forms off-site and bring them in for the final installation just after the New Year."

"No rest through Christmas?"

He wasn't sure why it bothered him so much, the idea that she took no time for herself. He was no stranger to work, the casino business a twenty-four-hour-a-day job.

"I wasn't aware the casino closed during the holidays. And I've made provisions in the timing to accommodate everyone's reduced vacation schedules."

"And what about you?" He laid a hand over hers. "Will you be taking some vacation?"

Her hand stiffened beneath his, but Rafe was intrigued to see she didn't remove it. "I have no need of vacation time now."

"Nor have you taken any since joining the Archangel?"

She slipped her hand from his, folding the large architectural rendering into a roll. "What's this sudden interest in the hours I work?"

"I'm a concerned employer. All work and no play makes one dull and uninteresting."

A small smile tugged the corner of her lips. "I spend my days doing what I love. Vacation is unnecessary."

Rafe stilled, the security review he'd conducted at five that morning—post-recovery—filling his thoughts. "I love what I do, as well. It doesn't negate the need to change the scenery every now and again. Do something simply for myself."

She inclined her head ever so slightly, but didn't back down. "As is your choice."

"These designs are approved."

The rapid change in subject had the desired effect, her eyes hazing over briefly as she sought to keep up. "Approved? Just done?"

"Yes."

"No one else has to see them?"

"Who else would?"

"Right."

When that cute look of confusion continued to stamp itself across her face, Rafe added, "I know quality when I see it. I also know an idea that will bring people into my casino, potentially enticing them to stay and play. Your fairy glade and evil witch will be a perfect enchantment once the holidays are over."

"Thank you."

"I only have one question."

"What's that?"

"What happens when they get past the evil queen?"

Evangeline tapped the rolled paper on the table, all confusion gone from her eyes. "It's all up to the guest."

"Oh?"

"They can turn right back the way they came. Or they can push past her and straight on through to the other side and try their luck in your casino."

"Cowardice or greed, Miss Kennedy?"

"I'd say it fits most people to a T."

He couldn't say why his conversation with Evangeline unsettled him, but three hours later Rafe was still restless as he prowled the casino floor. He'd spent a few moments glad-handing the high rollers, thanking them for their business and ensuring they were comfortable with all the Archangel's accommodations. As three of the five individuals he met with had been back several times, he took it as a noteworthy sign his staff was exceeding expectations—as expected.

After the floor visits he moved on up to Security. The command center was the heart of the property's sophisticated security system and the high-tech room boasted a setup as slick as NASA, only with newer equipment. He and his brother had maintained his father's practice—all technology was upgraded annually.

The Archangel was their business and their sanctuary and they were committed to it staying profitable and safe. As a result, the security team was handpicked and compensated handsomely for seeing to both.

"Floor's looking good today." Charlie, the husband of one of Rafe's multitude of cousins, greeted him. The grizzled ex-marine had shoulders like a linebacker and eyes as flat as a cobra. And two pictures of his one-year-old twin daughters dotted his console, both decked out in frilly pink.

"No issues with the weeklong bachelor party in quadrant six?"

"Nope. All of 'em already moved on to their rooms, the decidedly overt flirtations of a group of conference goers reassigning their priorities." Charlie shook his head. "Casino hormones. Nothing else on earth as powerful."

"Except how cute Alexis and Andie are."

Those flat eyes warmed immediately, Charlie's gaze flicking to the photos of his girls. "They're amazing. And will be locked up in roughly two decades to avoid the same sort of business that recently went down in quadrant six."

"No casino hormones for them?"

"Over my dead body. And any men who dare to touch them."

A thoroughly unpleasant image filled his mind's eye at the clear promise in those words as Rafe patted Charlie's shoulder. He was about to head to Gabe's office when something caught his eye on the pool cams. "There." Rafe pointed toward the top row of screens. "Zoom in on the west pool."

Charlie moved quickly over the console, the image transferring to a larger viewing screen in the center of the room. "This what you want?"

"Yep. Zoom in on the area in front of the greenhouse."

Charlie did as he was asked, but his tone was speculative as he manipulated the image on-screen. "Busy part of the property. I hear the night crew spent quite a bit of time on this sector last night."

"Son of a bitch." Rafe shook his head, another more inventive curse following his first. "Damn fool woman."

Although Charlie's shift to the big screen in the center added breadth and depth to the image, Evangeline was just as unmistakable on the smaller screen. She moved over the area in front of the greenhouse, her steps slow and plodding as she retraced the night before.

But it was the moment she knelt and bent toward the earth, her hands roaming over the exact spot where he'd burst into flames, that had Rafe out of the security room and headed for the far side of the Archangel.

Chapter 2

Evangeline traced and retraced her steps, searching for anything that might prove there was a fire in the area in front of the greenhouse. Yet no matter how hard she searched, each blade of grass was as pristine and green as the one next to it.

She knew horticulture. And the earth. And how the soil nurtured what grew within it. Fire was a natural form of renewal, even with the immediate destruction it left in its path.

But she also knew herself. She trusted her instincts and she sure as hell trusted her eyes.

And last night she saw a man burning in this very spot.

Yet Rafe Stavros stood there this morning, plain as day, and told her nothing had happened the night before on the property.

Was he hiding something? She'd spent her life in Las Vegas and was well aware of the city's more seedy reputation. More than a few had lost their souls in the desert—

gambling was a gateway to any number of crimes. While she'd always believed she worked for one of the more honest and upstanding employers on the Strip, it was always possible the Stavros family was into any number of poor practices.

"What are you doing out here?"

Evangeline popped back on her heels as the low voice washed over her from behind. "Checking the grass."

"For?"

She thrust her chin out and stared up at him. "Signs of burn marks."

"Find any?"

"No."

It shocked her how defeated she felt. She knew what she'd seen, damn it. A man stood in this very spot the night before, on *fire*. People didn't just imagine those things.

Even if your mother had?

The small voice whispered through her mind, as scary as it was real. Her memories might be that of a child's, but Evangeline could still remember the sleepless nights as her mother descended into madness.

"Come with me." Rafe stood above her, his hand extended. She took in those long, tapered fingers, the strength in them evident as she accepted what he offered.

"Where are we going?"

"For reasons that elude me, you seem offended when I suggest you're working too hard."

"I most certainly am no—" Her words—and the corresponding tug of her hand against his—were cut off as Rafe pulled her against his body.

A reply died in her throat as she took in the hard, firm lines of Rafael Stavros. Absorbed them, really. Although she'd—reluctantly—had more than a few thoughts about that body pressed against hers, she couldn't deny the raw power she felt in the thick musculature beneath that finely cut suit.

Oh, what would it be like to simply stay there, wrapped in the protection of that large, powerful body? He channeled it well, his physicality. Wielded it as easily as he wore five-thousand-dollar suits and several generations of Stavros wealth.

Rafe moved through the gentle swish of electronic doors, the cool, refined air of the hotel wafting over them. His feet echoed on the thick marble floor, a sound of purpose and power, while her sneakers thunked and squeaked beside him. It was only when they reached the entrance to the spa that Evangeline registered their destination.

"What are you doing?"

"You need some rest and relaxation. As luck would have it, I can provide both."

"I'm not going in there."

"You afraid of a little massage oil?" The question was flat—bland, even—but Evangeline didn't miss the unholy light that flared in his gaze. The normal storm-cloud gray had turned a liquid silver, tempting and oh so tantalizing as they stood in the entrance of the spa.

"I'm not afraid."

"Then after you."

He gestured her forward and she had the choice to stay stubbornly still or nod and move forward.

"Mr. Stavros." The woman who headed up the spa—Madelina, Evangeline remembered—came up to them immediately. Her gaze showed nothing but Evangeline couldn't quite squelch the urge to hide her dirt-stained hands behind her back. "How can I be of help today?"

"My friend here needs the full spa package."

Madelina's gaze shifted to assessing, scouring Evangeline head to toe, before she gave a solid nod. "Hot stone massage. Ninety minutes. Facial. Manicure. Pedicure. With paraffin, of course."

"Of course," Rafe added, his voice solemn, even if that light in his eyes remained stubbornly, wickedly, bright.

"I don't need any of this. And I certainly don't need goop on my fingers when all I'm going to do is shove them right back into the dirt."

She held out her hands proudly, trying to prove her point when Madelina's elegant fingers wrapped around hers, stilling Evangeline's movements. "Then it's all the more important to protect your greatest asset."

"Call me when she's finished." Rafe bit out the edict before turning on his heel.

Although it nearly killed her, Evangeline threw her last card. "I don't have the money for this."

Rafe barely gave her a backward glance. "Then it's good you know the owner. I've got plenty."

Rafe flipped through the file he maintained on Evangeline. He managed the materials himself, unwilling to go through the security team on the details of her or her background.

Orphaned at seven.

Bumped to several foster homes before declaring as an emancipated minor at sixteen.

Worked multiple jobs after that, including a flower shop in Henderson, a crummy little casino barely making it down on Fremont, and wedding bouquets for a nearby chapel.

"Doesn't let any grass grow under her feet," he muttered, an image of her doing just that filling his mind's eye. She wasn't going to give up on her supposed man on fire and he damn well knew a few hours of spa time wasn't going to change that.

Rafe continued scanning the file, his careful notes an

accompaniment to the various pieces of intel he'd gathered over the past year. Her background had been surprisingly easy to uncover, even with his ability to get details on most anyone he wanted. There was easy and then there was *easy*, and Evangeline fell into the latter category.

And what he'd learned during that investigation had stopped him cold.

Her father had been a Hunter, focused in and around Las Vegas for the legion of Chaos-seekers who hunted Rafe and his people, the Helios. Their age-old enemies, the Hunters believed eradicating the Helios would unleash their master—Chaos—on the world.

As with most things with the ancients, life was never that easy, and modern times brought modern challenges. There was plenty of chaos in the twenty-first century world, and Rafe doubted some epic battle with a band of zealots would change that much.

None of it changed the fact he and his people were hunted. Plotted against. And constantly under threat.

Was it possible Evangeline was one of them?

The bio had been straightforward and bleak—Hank Kennedy had drifted in and out of jail throughout his late twenties and early thirties before turning his skills and his loyalty toward the Las Vegas area's corps of Hunters. A suspicious fight in the desert late one night hadn't ended well for Hank or a fellow addict and he'd left his wife and child alone and destitute.

Nothing about the intel had sat well and Rafe had kept a purposeful distance from Evangeline over the past year, in favor of watching and monitoring her. Other than their bimonthly meetings to discuss the property, he avoided contact with her.

And had been more than surprised to see she kept to herself, worked like she had no life outside the casino and generally flew under the radar.

Until last night.

Damn, why had he waited when he knew his Rejuvenation was upon him?

Rafe's head snapped up at the hard slam of his door. Gabe crossed the plush carpet soundlessly, even as his large frame quivered in agitated, restless motion. "You burned in front of her?"

"Excuse me?"

"Don't screw with me. Last night. Evangeline Kennedy saw you? Midtransformation?"

He never lied to his brother, but the anger and frustration laser-focused on him was barely an adequate mirror for his own shame and embarrassment. Hell, he hadn't lost control like that since he was fourteen and coming into his power.

"Yes."

"Mind telling me why you were hanging around, full well knowing you were running hot?"

"I had a meeting that ran late."

His brother slashed a hand through the air. "No excuse."

"It is when you're courting three foreign whales with several whale friends back home."

Gabe snorted, clearly unconvinced, even with Rafe's argument about squiring several high rollers around the property. "It's careless and unnecessary. Since when are you the only one who can court high-end guests and build relationships?"

"I needed to check them out. See for myself. We know Hunter activity increases near the solstice, and something about the one guy's backstory didn't check out."

"So you went in alone?"

"I'm never alone in here and the high-roller room has more attention than most."

"The private villas don't." Gabe dug his phone out. "It's careless."

"It's necessary."

When Gabe said nothing, Rafe knew he'd hit a nerve. Rafe trusted his brother, more than anyone in the world, but he couldn't stand by and ignore an opportunity to get the upper hand on a band of Hunters, especially so close to the solstice. The possibility of a rogue with money would be a danger beyond measure.

Besides, his damn Rejuvenation wasn't supposed to happen then. It was nearly a month until the winter solstice and he'd been rejuvenating like clockwork since puberty.

Vernal equinox, summer solstice, autumnal equinox, winter solstice. His body regenerated *then*, not nearly a freaking month early.

"Guy ultimately checked out?"

Rafe shook off the lingering discomfort of his early change and gave Gabe his full attention. "Yeah. Charlie texted me the moment he had confirmation the guy was legit. I glad-handed him a bit more, offered him an extra night in the villa and hauled ass out of there."

"You didn't haul fast enough."

No, he hadn't. He'd considered letting himself into the villa next door and waiting out the burn but they were full up, the Archangel's reputation ensuring all the rooms were accounted for. He and Gabe had taken their father's life's work and upped the ante. The hotel rooms were spoken for nearly every night and they had a list of high rollers the rest of the Strip envied.

Who would have believed success was so damned inconvenient?

"We've gone this long without discovery. Your life—all our lives—are worth more than one more high roller wasting his fortune at our gaming tables."

Rafe rarely apologized but his brother hit a nerve. A fair one at that. "Look. I get it and I'm sorry. I've been tired and the moment hit me hard. I thought I had more time."

A small grin finally curved his brother's lips. "Losing your control, big brother?"

A few choice expletives bubbled to the surface but Rafe opted against the grain. He'd managed to blow over his brother's bad mood, he might as well use it to his advantage. "You talk to Pop lately?"

"He and mom are still lounging around the Côte d'Azur and last I heard he was raising hell with the management at Monte Carlo's casinos."

"They let him back in?"

"Some sort of royal decree. I suspect the prince is sorry he got suckered in by the charms of one Michael Stavros."

"Once a gambling man…" Rafe left the words hanging there, an image of his father giving instruction on the latest security protocols falling on some severely irritated Monegasque ears.

"Old man's not settling into retirement well."

"Are you surprised?"

"Nah." Gabe shuddered. "Claims he'd be better at it if he had grandchildren."

A wholly unexpected image of Evangeline rose up in his mind's eye. She was absolutely unsuitable—she was an employee with a highly suspicious lineage—but Rafe couldn't fully ignore the hot rush of need that accompanied the vision. "He can keep wishing."

"You put Evangeline off?"

"Not dropping this one?"

Gabe smiled, the grin bordering on feral. "Not a chance."

"The woman knows her mind and isn't willing to be put off. I've got her down in the spa now, giving her the royal treatment and attempting to convince her she's been working too hard."

"Having any luck?"

"We'll see in about two hours after Madelina's team

works on her." Rafe stood from his desk, tapping the file folder that had already worn around the edges. "Of all the damn people."

"Why?"

He and Gabe were as close as brothers could be, but he'd kept this from him. Kept the quiet knowledge to himself about Evangeline's background and parentage. On a hard breath, he snagged the folder and handed it to his brother.

Gabe took the offering, his ability to quickly assess a situation more than evident when he snapped the folder closed a few moments later. "She's a Hunter?"

"The daughter of one."

"We've had a freaking Hunter on property for damn near a year and this is the first you've told me?"

He rarely second-guessed himself, but one look at Gabe's face had Rafe reconsidering. "I've been watching her."

"We could all have been watching her. Or better yet—" Gabe threw the folder on the desk. "We could have let her go on her merry freaking way and avoided hiring her in the first place."

"She's good. Her installations alone have increased foot traffic by thirty percent."

Gabe stiffened up at that, straightening to his full height. "First the whales and now this? This place is our sanctuary. Have you forgotten that?"

"I've forgotten nothing."

"Then how can you ignore the fact the woman's dangerous? To us. Our way of life. Our people."

An image of that long, lithe form curled up inspecting the grass outside filled his head. Was she seeking proof? Attempting to set a trap? Or was it something else?

Rafe hadn't sensed malice in her. More, she had an aching vulnerability about her that called to some strange, empty place deep inside of him.

Orphan.

Emancipated minor.

Workhorse.

None of those images matched with the sullen, disillusioned cadre normally drafted into the Hunters' midst. Chaos thrived on the weak-minded and the easily swayed.

Evangeline Kennedy was neither.

"We got the intel on the two men she fired yesterday."

Rafe knew his brother and there was no way he was dropping the subject of Evangeline anytime soon. But there was something underneath the comment that slashed through Rafe's thoughts. "And?"

"They're Hunters. My team's tracked them back to a flophouse on the outskirts of Henderson. I'm headed there tonight."

"I'll join you."

"Save it. You need to keep your focus here."

"You won't keep me out of this."

"Then get your damn head in the game. She comes from the line of people determined to expose us and slaughter us all."

"The Hunters are minions of Chaos. We've yet to narrow in on a leader. We've dealt with them before and we'll deal with them again."

"He's here. I can feel it. Know it. There's been too much static lately. Too many close calls." Gabe dropped onto the edge of Rafe's desk. "Don't tell me you can't feel it?"

Rafe shook his head, suddenly unwilling to put voice to the feeling. He understood Gabe's point—had felt the same raw energy swirling around the casino and their people—but kept pushing against it, unwilling to act rashly.

He was the methodical Stavros, while Gabe had their father's brash, devil-may-care attitude in spades. They complemented each other—they always had—so why were they so far apart on this? Rash action threatened their secrets, but so did ignorance. And it was time he remembered that.

Especially now that Evangeline had seen him take his true form.

And, by all accounts, was determined to understand what it all meant.

While she was still irritated at Rafe's heavy-handed behavior, dragging her from the lawn and pushing her into a series of spa appointments, Evangeline had to admit the man had a point.

A great point.

If she could put together a coherent thought to remember just how great his point really was.

Relaxation! That was it. He'd been on her, stressing the importance of taking some time for herself and not working too hard.

Firm hands slid up and down her spine, kneading muscles and loosening knots she didn't even know she had. The massage was the coup de grâce in an afternoon full of rest, relaxation and a significant amount of pampering. A facial. A manicure and pedicure. And some amazing thing with hot rocks that should have burned like crazy but instead, managed to loosen her muscles even more than they already were.

Why didn't she do this for herself?

The question began as an abstract cloud, floating through her mind, but something about it stilled, expanding in her thoughts.

Why didn't she do this more often? She wasn't poor any longer. Far from it, in fact. The Archangel paid her a generous salary for the work she did across the property. She didn't live extravagantly, her one-bedroom apartment more than enough room for the amount of time she spent there. And working on-property gave her a discount on the spa services.

So why not do this for herself?

Instead, she hoarded her hard-earned income as if she were still shivering and cold, hoping her parents would stop fighting or—worse—praying for the noise when their apartment got so quiet she could hear her own breath. She'd huddle in those moments, her parents' normally volatile state hushed by whatever drug her father had managed to score that day.

"Miss Kennedy?"

The soft voice pulled her from the dismal memories, the hand on her spine gentle. "Hmm?"

"The treatment is complete. Feel free to stay and relax a bit longer. I've left some water on the counter."

"Thank you."

Hesitant to let the dreamy state end, Evangeline lay there a few more moments after the door clicked on a quiet close. Try as she might, she couldn't fully bring back that delicious dream state. Instead, those memories of her parents peeked in, pressing against the edges of her memory with all the finesse of an attack dog.

Her father's addiction. Her mother's equally helpless outlook on life. And the loss of both of them by the time she was seven.

"Miss Kennedy." The knock was soft, yet insistent and Evangeline sat up, pulling the sheet tight around herself.

"Come in."

Madelina bustled in, her elegant form somehow softened in the muted light and calming music. Where she'd initially seen a militant effectiveness shining in the woman's eyes before, Evangeline had to admit three hours of pampering had softened the edges of her vision. Madelina had gone from dragon to fairy godmother and she gave her a big smile. "Hello."

"It looks like my team did their job."

"They were wonderful." Evangeline glanced down at her toes where her legs swung against the table. "I even have red toes."

"Enough to drive a man wild."

"I'm not… I mean."

Madelina patted her arm. "It's always good to be prepared."

The woman seemed to understand she had nothing to say and bustled on. "Have you had your water?" When she eyed the glass still on the counter, she picked it up and marched it over. "It's essential to hydrate. Drink up. Then you'll come with me."

The cool water, tinged with the refreshing taste of cucumber, was fresh on her tongue as she drank.

"You enjoyed the treatments?"

"I did." Evangeline set her glass of water down, abstractly wondering if she'd ever tasted anything so good.

"Excellent. Because I've made a standing appointment for you monthly."

"I don't—" Evangeline broke off, not sure why she was arguing. She'd had a similar thought herself, so why be irritated when someone else did the kindness for her? And yet…

"Mr. Stavros has added it to your employment package."

That urge to argue flared once more, even if Madelina was simply the messenger, but the woman held up a hand to forestall her.

"Mr. Stavros insists. Spa treatments aren't simply a frivolity. You're a woman who works with your body on a regular basis. It's important to keep it finely tuned."

"I can pay for it myself."

Madelina cocked her head, those eyes sharp. Once again, the fleeting image of a dragon floated through Evangeline's mind before vanishing. "But why do so when your employer presents you with such generosity?"

"It's frivolous."

"There's nothing wrong with that, either." Handing over a fresh glass of water, Madelina pointed to the door. "Drink this, then join me in the salon. Berta will direct you once you leave the room."

Evangeline watched her go, the conversation unsettling on several levels. She wanted the treatments—had thought that very thing as she lay there, soft and warm and boneless from an awesome massage.

So why complain when it was offered as a job perk?

An image of Rafael Stavros filled her mind's eye, in clear answer to the question.

Tall and dark, the man was a walking, talking version of sin in the flesh. Mercurial gray eyes. Thick, dark hair. Chiseled features and a body that made her fingers itch. She'd never been a woman to ignore her body's needs, but she'd also never understood the extremes people went to for attraction.

Rafe Stavros tossed that thought right out his penthouse window. The man was lethally sexy and equally formidable in his business. His father had established a successful casino whose business he and his brother had only shot into the stratosphere. From high-end restaurants to Broadway shows to a casino floor that boasted just enough winners to keep the tables packed, the Archangel had become a must-see destination on the Strip.

And she was part of it.

Draining the rest of her water, Evangeline hopped off the table and stretched like a cat. She hadn't felt this loose-limbed in oh…about forever.

"So what are you complaining about?"

As she caught sight of herself in the small mirror over the treatment room's sink, Evangeline had to admit to herself she had no answer.

As the original founder of the Archangel, Michael Stavros had a firm policy. Hire good people and leave them alone to do good work. If you found a gem, you had to respect their genius and leave them alone to do their best work in their own way. Alternatively, if you ended up hiring someone who was lazy, stupid or worse, both—fire their ass on the spot.

Although he and Gabe hadn't adopted every practice their father employed in his own brand of management, some rules of business were immutable.

Hiring good people was essential.

It was why he'd been so drawn to Evangeline. Her work—and her passion and enthusiasm for that work—had stood out above all else. It had him hiring her on the spot and it had been the thing that kept her on staff even after he discovered her past. If the woman was a Hunter, she was a damn fine actress.

Because in nearly a year, all he'd ever observed was a woman obsessed with the look and feel of his property and very little focus on anything else.

Madelina interrupted his thoughts. "Mr. Stavros. The things you requested are ready."

"And Evangeline?"

"She'll be out momentarily." Madelina hesitated for the briefest moment—at odds with her normally tart tongue—and Rafe's gaze sharpened on her.

"Yes?"

"She enjoyed the day. Told me as much."

That hesitation remained and Rafe couldn't resist probing further. "But?"

"I believe she's a bit perturbed at the generous monthly addition to her compensation plan."

"Is she now?"

Madelina only nodded, and he couldn't hide his broad smile, already anticipating the battle that was sure to ensue.

"Madelina!" Evangeline's voice echoed from the other side of the door to the interior of the spa moments before the thick oak swung inward. "What is this?"

Evangeline blew through the door, a goddess in full pique, her hands full of dresses. Her hair was pulled back from her face, sticking up at odd angles from the massage. Her face glowed a high pink—heightened by her anger but still rosy from her facial—and the sexiest toes he'd ever seen peeped out from beneath a long spa robe.

"You look well."

Evangeline shook the dresses at him as Madelina slipped out through the still-swinging door. "Where are my clothes?"

"Laundry, I presume."

"They were nice clothes. And clean."

"Now they'll be cleaner."

Evangeline tossed the handful of silks onto a nearby couch. "I am perfectly capable of dressing myself. Taking care of myself. Sleeping when I want, working when I want. I do damn fine living my life."

"What's wrong with someone showing you some kindness?" Rafe asked.

"Kindness is a day off. Not spa treatments and expensive dresses." Evangeline bent down and snagged one of the dresses. The move tugged the bodice of her robe ever so slightly and Rafe got a glimpse of tanned skin, tapering into the slope of one breast.

Catching his eye, she snapped the robe closed as she tossed the garment his way. "This is a thousand-dollar dress."

He shoved his hands in his pockets, his gaze flicking briefly to the fabric before taking in the thick, schlumpy fit of the robe. Even covered in acres of terry cloth, she was a vision. "I don't see a tag."

"I've seen it in the boutique window for a month. I know how much it costs."

"So you like it?"

"It's gorgeous."

"It's yours."

She shook the dress at him. "What is wrong with you?"

"We have a strict dress code at Flame. Since we've got reservations this evening I figured you'd like something to wear."

"I have clothes. Good ones that are more than acceptable for Flame. And—" She broke off, her eyes narrowing. "I'm not going with you to the casino's steak house."

"We've got business to discuss."

"Then we can go to your office."

"I'm hungry."

"You're mad."

"And you're the strangest woman I've ever met." Rafe moved in, the lingering wash of lavender and jasmine from her treatments assaulting his senses. "Most women like spa days. And new clothes. And nice dinners."

"As a date, maybe. Not with their employer."

"I can't show you gratitude for the work you've done?"

"A thank-you is fine."

Rafe took another step closer, those scents fading as something distinctly Evangeline rose up through the lingering effects of a day of pampering. Something earthy and natural, like the air after a rain or the bright scent of rebirth after he regenerated.

With gentle movements, as if a sudden motion would startle her, he pressed his lips to her ear. "Well, then. Thank you."

Chapter 3

Rafe wasn't sure what had gotten into him. First the misstep the night before during his Rejuvenation and now this focused, deliberate sensual assault on Evangeline Kennedy. It was dangerous and very out of character.

Yet he couldn't seem to help himself.

A year of watching Evangeline from afar was suddenly not enough. Ignoring that strange tug of attraction that gripped him each and every time he saw her moving around the property had grown tiresome. And leaving the lingering question in his mind if she'd come to the Archangel to undermine his people was no longer tenable.

He wanted answers.

And damn it, he wanted her.

There was no reason he couldn't have both.

It was a simple idea, formed as he'd marched from the security center to the lawns where she'd been determinedly seeking out scorch marks. But it had grown as she whiled away the afternoon in her spa treatment. He was going after the answers he sought.

If he could seduce them out of her, then the process would be that much more enjoyable.

"Say it," he whispered against her ear once more, pleased she hadn't yet pulled away.

"Say what?"

"Yes."

His overt meaning was dinner, but something in the question stuck with him, searing his thoughts with images of the two of them, naked and locked in each other's arms.

Would she say yes to sharing his bed?

A possible Hunter?

The thought was enough to jar Rafe from the tempting interlude and he stepped back and reached for the dress that had fallen next to his feet when she'd tossed it. The pale silk slid through his fingers and the stubborn ache that had settled in his chest subsided as his focus narrowed on his plan.

"It's just dinner. Wear a pretty dress. Join me for a meal."

Indecision painted her features in sharp relief, the heightened pink glow from her spa treatments fading as she considered his offer.

For reasons he refused to think about too closely, he held his breath, awaiting her response. And was more than a little surprised when she finally answered.

"Yes."

For a woman who'd always prided herself on her unassuming life and the easy, simple comfort of her home, Evangeline couldn't quite figure out why it felt like the walls were closing in. She'd returned home from her afternoon at the Archangel with several hundred dollars' worth of spa treatments still coating her skin and a dress worth twice that in a small bag with silky string handles.

And she had dinner plans with Rafe Stavros.

Had her brains leaked out of her head somewhere between the facial and the hot stones?

She was a woman who worked in the dirt, for Pete's sake. Her life—her own personal harmony—was never more in balance than when she was wrist-deep in the earth, planting any number of flowers and plants. So what was she doing?

A glance down at the bag—and a quick peek through the tissue paper—told her *exactly* what she was doing.

She was contemplating a date with her boss.

"You went way past contemplation when you said yes." The self-admonishment fell flat as she stood in the middle of her living room, her voice a harsh clanging in her own ears.

So just why had she said yes?

Unwilling to think too hard on the real answer—because she wanted to—Evangeline marched to her bedroom and unpacked the small bag. She laid the dress out over her bedspread, then traced a finger over the silk.

And oh, wow, was it gorgeous.

The silk was dyed a pale lavender, barely registering in the purple spectrum. She suspected it might even appear a grayish-silver in muted evening light. Dying to put it on, she quickly stripped out of her clothes and pulled on the dress. The material slid over her skin with a cool caress and her mind immediately snapped to Rafe as her body gave out an involuntary shiver.

Thank you.

Such simple words, meant to convey gratitude. Yet on Rafe's lips they were a sexy promise, encouraging her to take a firm step closer to him.

Where had it come from? This sudden, immediate

dance between the two of them. She'd presented to him before, the quarterly design meetings with him placed on her calendar like clockwork. Yet something had snapped this time.

Turning to the mirror, she gave a small spin as the material hugged her body. Her year-round tan and natural coloring complemented the dress and something budded to life, pooling in the very depths of her being.

She felt feminine.

For the longest time, she hadn't felt anything. A few dates here and there—fewer romps to bed to scratch an itch—but other than that her life was her work. Work that made her happy and satisfied, but over the past year it had become everything.

Why not go out and enjoy this evening? Even if something about it felt the slightest bit wicked.

Evangeline gave one more spin, enjoying the way the material gently caressed her thighs. But it was the moment she imagined Rafael Stavros staring at her as he got his first look at her in the dress that had her pulse racing. It was time she accepted the truth.

She had a date with her boss.

Flame Steak House was a joint effort between the Archangel and one of Rafe's cousins, a world-renowned chef, Rocco Stavros. It had taken a considerable amount of persuading to get Rocco to come around and put one of his restaurants in the Archangel—the bastard had wanted a higher-than-average cut of the profits—but the decision had paid handsome dividends.

The food was exquisite, the steaks some of the finest cuts of meat in the world, complemented by an array of appetizers and sides that would make the most critical foodie sit up and take notice.

And take notice they had.

Reservations typically booked out six months in advance and for the holidays, some people had been waiting two years for their chance to dine this evening. Tonight was no exception. Rafe used the walk to his table to make discreet inquiries of his staff as well as to glad-hand some of the high rollers visiting this weekend.

Everything kicked up a notch over Christmas, and the casino business was no different. The hotel rooms were in demand, as were the gaming tables, the reservations and shows.

Rafe swirled the last of his whiskey, ice cubes clinking against the thick crystal of his glass. He'd arrived early ready to welcome Evangeline and was surprised by the shot of nerves that lined his stomach.

And then he forgot everything—nerves, her background, hell, he damn near forgot to breathe—as Evangeline walked through the entrance of the restaurant.

Pale silk sheathed her body, flowing over her breasts, waist and hips like a sexy waterfall. Unbidden, thoughts of Sirens and rocks came to mind. And while Evangeline wasn't singing, Rafe could practically swear he heard music. Rachmaninoff. Or no, Puccini.

She stilled when she spotted him, the silk still shimmering around her like a halo, before a soft smile painted her lips. Strangely, it was the smile that calmed his nerves and had him moving toward her.

"You look beautiful."

"Thank you."

Rafe pressed a light kiss to her cheek, his fingertips drifting over her elbow. The urge to press his hands to her spine was strong but he held back, unwilling to break the subtle spell that wove around them both. The she-cat from earlier had vanished, replaced by a kitten-like softness he was loath to mar.

"Shall we?"

She nodded and they followed the tuxedoed host, who stood waiting discreetly nearby.

"It's still so busy." Evangeline's voice was low, but her gaze assessed the room as they were escorted to his table in the back.

Although he knew his father preferred being front and center—all the better to see the action while being seen in the process—Rafe preferred something out of the way. And where he could keep his back to the wall and his gaze fully on the room.

Things had changed since his father's time. His grandfather had been one of the first Helios to settle the area, enjoying the relative anonymity and distance from their natural adversary, the Hunters of Chaos.

Hunters still believed the legends—that the Helios guarded the gate of the ancients. Gain access to the gate and the Hunters' master—the god of Chaos—believed he'd possess the knowledge contained within.

Rafe knew it wasn't quite that simple. While his people did help secure the gate, knowledge had been leaking out for millennia. The world had changed, yet Chaos still acted as if it was the dawn of time.

His father had followed in Grandfather's footsteps, enjoying his position as a mover and shaker in Las Vegas and ignoring the increasing signs the Hunters were making inroads. The occasional attack was chalked up to luck, nothing more.

While he and Gabe appreciated all their father had built, they practiced a far more cautious approach to their role as hotel owners and purveyors of a good time.

And always kept their backs to the wall.

Life had changed, inside and outside the Archangel. Technology had radically transformed the casino business—the games, the rooms and the security most of all—but it had also honed their enemy's skills. Recruitment through social media, transmissions through bounced mobile devices and a watchful eye that knew how to disguise itself.

"Enjoy your evening."

The quiet murmur of their host pulled Rafe's attention back to his lovely companion. Was it even remotely possible she was in league with the enemy?

He held a chair for Evangeline, careful to keep his expression neutral and his hands solicitously on the wood rail. Even with the restraint, the urge to touch her clawed at him, the dress she wore nearly knocking his breath away.

Once seated he no longer had a view of her exposed back and long, long legs, but he found himself distracted by toned arms and impressive chest. She was firm and fit, an athletic beauty that made him think of sun, sand and wrestling.

Naked.

"Rafe? Are you all right?"

Her dark brows slashed over equally dark eyes and he fought the urge to reach out and smooth the slight crease. "Of course."

"You look upset."

"Just keeping an eye on business. And cursing my cousin."

"For?"

"My cousin Rocco is the owner and creator of the restaurant. Bastard keeps asking for a raise and much as it pains me to give him one, I can't argue with a roomful of happy people enjoying their meals."

The set of those slim, fit shoulders sagged slightly as she relaxed. "I had no idea your cousin was Rocco Stavros. I should have known by the last name."

"You know him?"

"I know of him. And it's hard to miss the loud sighs

that flutter in his wake every time we're in here managing the flower installations."

"They're beautiful, by the way." He shifted his attention back to his companion. "But pale in comparison to you. You're glowing."

If the frank appreciation bothered her she held back, a smile ghosting her lips instead. "I'd hope so. The torture experts in your spa exfoliated me back down to the skin I was born with."

Rafe ran a finger over the back of her hand. "They exfoliated everywhere?"

She slipped her hand away but her gaze remained firm on his. "A woman deserves to keep a few secrets."

"I suppose it's a wise strategy. It gives a man something to work toward."

"To work toward what?"

"Uncovering them."

Those expressive eyes widened, a million emotions flaring in their depths. He reveled in that look, recognizing he could use the confusion—and the underlying attraction he saw as well—to his advantage. What he hadn't accounted for was the heady sensation of being in her company.

The woman was a vision. More than that, she was an interesting companion. They'd already discussed the property on their walk through the casino to dinner, her questions and insights astute and thoughtful, several of them tinged with a biting humor he'd not have expected from her. She was also sweet, waving and acknowledging by name several coworkers as they'd made their way to dinner.

Their waiter gave a discreet cough as he came to their table, effectively ending round one. From the besotted look in the man's eyes as Evangeline greeted him, Rafe mentally added the man into the woman's legion of fans.

And avoided the small kernel of doubt that attempted to invade the moment.

She knew people. Knew the property and what went on across the grounds. Was the warmth and kindness all an act? Was it possible she was plotting and planning to help her fellow Hunters?

The doubts came fast and furious, disturbing in their intensity. He'd always considered himself a strong judge of character but for some reason, in spending time with Evangeline, he couldn't be sure. Worse, he increasingly questioned if he could be objective when it came to her.

Evangeline waited until Ross departed their table before she pushed her full attention toward Rafe and wondered—not for the first time—where he'd gone. Oh, he was sitting there, the fine cut of his suit making for an impressive—and incredibly attractive—dining companion.

But he wasn't *there*.

Instead, he'd drifted in and out of their conversation since they'd met up in the hotel lobby.

If she'd believed him indifferent to her she might have chafed at the behavior, but his too-warm gaze and awareness during the moments he was present told a different story.

And then there was his touch. Hot as a brand and twice as powerful. Evangeline had never felt anything like it. Or been as tempted to let the fierce need that had settled in her chest have free rein.

She wanted him.

A simple emotion with the most complicated set of outcomes.

He was her boss.

He was a wealthy, powerful man who could have anything he wanted.

And he was hiding something.

The first two might be overcome or even ignored in the pursuit of pleasure, but the last was what held her back. She hated secrets, equating them to the same lack of power and control that had ruled her childhood.

She'd vowed to herself long ago never to be that helpless again. Her choices had made for a quiet life, full of a solitude she'd never planned on, but at least she was safe. Protected.

And if that protection had also become something of a cocoon, well, then, she'd live with that.

She didn't do secrets. Or omission. And she'd be damned if she was going to accept a bald-faced lie.

Rafe might be charming, but he'd continually denied answering her questions about the burning man on the property. And lest he think a few hours in the spa and a fancy dinner would erase what she knew she'd seen, she now had to figure out a way to get answers.

But first, she'd play the role of ingenue for the evening and flirt a bit with the temptress routine. Stone-cold bitch certainly hadn't done the trick.

"This is quite a place you and your family have built."

"Thank you."

When he said nothing more, she pressed on. "This hotel isn't more than a decade old, yet your father and grandfather have legendary reputations in Las Vegas."

Something almost imperceptible flashed in his gaze and if she weren't watching him so closely she'd surely have missed it. "We purchased this property years ago but this end of the Strip wasn't nearly developed enough for our needs. The original Archangel was over on Fremont and the Stavros family managed joint ownership or backing in other properties here on the Strip until we were able to bring our vision fully to life."

"That's all rather patient of you."

"A trait my family has in spades."

The sommelier arrived, effectively pausing their conversation and Evangeline took a small, unobtrusive pull of air through her nose.

Patience? Planning? Perhaps bit of world domination tossed in for good measure?

Who did she work for?

She'd taken the job on a whim, circumstance driving the decision more than an overt hunt for employment. She'd seen a need—the poorly managed grounds—and had pushed and poked her way into the Archangel. When she'd seemingly been accepted at face value, she hadn't questioned her good fortune.

So why was she now?

A small, predatory light filled Rafe's gaze, perhaps indicative of her sudden discomfort and uneasiness.

Their sommelier departed, two glasses of red wine left behind in his wake, and Evangeline lifted her goblet in response to Rafe.

"To patience." Rafe clinked his glass against hers. "And all the dividends it inevitably pays."

"Cheers."

She took a sip of the wine, an exquisite explosion of taste on her tongue as she drank the rich red. The spa. The dress. Now the dinner. Rafael Stavros did nothing by half measure.

"Lovely."

"As are you." Rafe inclined his head before he settled his glass on the table. "What about you, Miss Kennedy? Are you a Las Vegas native?"

"I think so."

The words were out so fast there was no way to retrieve them, even as the answer was far more honest than she'd ever have intended. While Rafe waited for her to continue, she weighed the merits of sharing her past.

How did one share the details of a wretched childhood

that began in an abusive home and ended in the cold, airless confines of foster care?

And why did she even care?

"My pedigree isn't nearly as well established as yours."

Rafe's eyebrows did lift at that, a mix of humor and affront painting those gray depths. "Are you suggesting I'm some sort of purebred dog?"

"No, but I definitely have strains of mongrel." She took a sip of her wine, fortifying herself with the burst of flavor and obvious quality of the drink. While certainly not necessary, it did make the telling a bit sweeter.

"My parents were rather poor at their jobs. Both had drug problems, my father especially."

Where she'd braced for sympathy, something more akin to anger morphed in the swirling depths of his gaze. Oddly, the unexpected reaction encouraged her, allowing her to push on. "The tale's not new, but Vegas certainly doesn't provide a helpful backdrop for those battling addiction."

"No, it doesn't."

"I was young at the time, so there's quite a bit I don't remember. But one day my father just stopped coming home. My mother ranted and railed about it for months, falling deeper and deeper into her own abyss and then one day, it all stopped and she was gone, too."

"You remember?"

"Some days."

"And others?"

"I remember how I survived. Learning places to hide. Understanding how to read moods and body language and whatever else went on in a room. And finding my own solace in the small patches of dirt outside our apartment, the hardscrabble something I could make beauty out of."

"A flower in the desert."

"Perhaps."

"There's no perhaps about it. You clearly found a way

to triumph over unfair circumstances no child should ever have to experience."

"It's why, you know."

"Why what?"

She'd never been one to avoid or evade when she could simply go for what she wanted. It had been like that in foster care and she'd carried the trait on into adulthood. Hell, it had earned her a place at the Archangel.

Yet in this moment—at this time—she nearly backed down. Almost walked away in the light of that anger that still burned in his gaze.

Anger for her.

Evangeline felt it. *Knew* it, on a deep, visceral level. The story of her past had upset him. Angered him with a primal rage she could read in the set of his broad shoulders and the tight grip he had on his wineglass.

But a lifetime of loss and of looking out for no one but herself had more gravity than the rather new sensation of sitting opposite a champion.

"It's why I won't forget what I saw. Or stop looking for answers as to why there was a man burning to death outside the greenhouse last night."

Chapter 4

White-hot flames licked at his soul, a dark, dangerous fire Rafe struggled to keep in check. He prided himself on his control—he knew who he was and what he was capable of—and always held himself—and his needs—in a firm grip.

Until Evangeline.

She was incendiary, a bright, vivid match to the flames that already consumed him.

And she was more dangerous than she ever could have imagined.

Damn it all to Hades, he'd intended to leave the subject of last night alone. He'd foolishly believed a day of pampering and seduction would turn her mind away from the impossible.

Or what should have been impossible but which was very, very real.

Evangeline Kennedy was too smart—and far too intuitive—to leave the subject alone. Even with all the efforts of Gabe's security team, working to divert and dissuade her from what she'd seen, she was unwilling to be put off.

None of it changed the fact she'd also done them a massive favor by getting rid of the bumbling Troy and Victor. Their idiocy and obvious desire to infiltrate the casino was the reason she'd still been on the property at such a late hour, working without two team members.

Was it really possible she had no idea the men were agents of the very organization seeking to bring down Rafe and his people? Did he dare ask her?

Or more to the point, was he willing to deal with the consequences if she hid the one secret he feared?

His gaze roamed over the delicate lines of her throat, her tan honing her skin to a fine shimmer. The steady throb of her pulse reflected in the hollow, deep and rich, and he could see the light movement of her flesh where her life force beat. If he were closer to a Rejuvenation, he could even hear it, those first moments of renewed life always a trauma to the senses.

Was it even possible she was one of the monsters who hunted him and his people in service to Chaos?

"You won't find anything."

"I have to try." Her dark eyes sheened with tears, the response as surprising as it was unexpected. "I can't live with myself if I don't. That sort of violence and pain. How can you expect me to ignore it?"

What if I told you it wasn't violent? Wasn't painful? Instead was filled with the richest sense of renewal and fresh life. It was the antithesis of pain. Of suffering. Of our mortal tether to human life.

But he said none of those things.

Instead he reached for his glass of wine and sat back in his chair, a bastard of the first order who wouldn't break or bend, acquiesce or yield.

He was Helios.

And his secret was not to be shared or entrusted to another.

* * *

Gabe finalized preparations for their evening plans in the security center, his gaze on the screens that captured all the action down at Flame. His brother had been there for some time, his beautiful companion seated across from him, and the two were deep in heated conversation.

Normally, he wouldn't have given a shit if Rafe had a date. His brother's chosen arm candy for the evening always lit up a room—always drew attention to their perfect faces and even more perfect figures—and he'd grown used to the steady parade. What had become something of a family joke, his brother's refusal to go anywhere near the merest whiff of settling down, had a certain sort of comfort to it.

A predictability Gabe had never really appreciated.

Especially when now faced with Evangeline Kennedy. As stunning as every other woman Rafe had ever escorted, there was something else. Something *more.* The woman was unique, her vibrancy extending beyond the simply physical.

And she was the first of any of their acquaintances to put them at risk. Add on Rafe's recent Rejuvenation—totally out of pattern—and something didn't sit well with him.

Gabe had gone back and reexamined the file, Evangeline's sad past coming to life in each and every word. Despite his wariness, he hadn't been unaffected by what he'd read. Or what he knew needed to be done. Hell, he liked her himself. She'd done wonders to the property in little less than a year, ran a tight ship, and the woman knew how to take care of herself. She was impressive and intriguing and he admired her.

If only…

The woman was a risk to them all. If she was a Hunter, she had far too much access. If she wasn't, it was more than possible she could still lead the Hunters straight to their door.

Troy and Victor had been perfect examples. Both had checked out—Gabe had examined their employment files, too—yet both were on staff, plotting to do worse. Evangeline had dealt with them, but was it all an act? A show of camaraderie that would soften them up and assume she wasn't in league with those who sought to destroy them?

He and Rafe had done everything in their power to make the Archangel a haven. They knew how to cloak and shield their existence, both from determined prying eyes and from the world around them. Add on the standard measures of security and caution required to run a world-class casino hotel and they had believed themselves safe.

Protected.

Was it an illusion? And had they really led the wolf straight to their door?

"Gabe!"

Charlie ambled up to the security station, leaning forward as he zeroed in on the image of Rafe and Evangeline. "Who is that? Wait—Evangeline?"

"Yep."

"Rafe's dating her now?"

"He's watching her."

Charlie leaned forward once more. "Damn right he is. She cleans up well."

Charlie's reinforcement of the scene playing out on the restaurant cameras did nothing to calm his spiking ire and Gabe tapped a few keys on the console, changing the main display. "Heard she had a tussle yesterday with a few of her employees."

"Didn't Trevor walk you through it?"

At Charlie's narrowed eyes, Gabe pressed him. "I'd like it from your point of view."

"She followed protocol to a T. Kicked both of her employees straight off the grounds for poor conduct and possible endangerment of hotel guests. Was pretty steamed about it, too, but she called Security and let us manage the removal of badges and escort off property."

Gabe let Charlie talk, his matter-of-fact recap of events reinforcing what he already knew about the incident.

"Heard you were going to investigate them tonight yourself. Looking for company?"

"I could use an able body or two."

"I'm in. I'm always up for a little Hunter ass-kicking."

Reject, deflect. Parry, thrust. Like an endless dance, she and Rafe kept going round and round throughout dinner over the burning man on the hotel grounds. Oh, he'd done a good job of changing the subject, but each and every time she directed the conversation back that fruitless dance started once more.

For reasons she couldn't quite name, that disappointed her most of all.

She liked him. When she wasn't irritated at his obtuse behavior, she had to admit he was a charming and enjoyable dinner companion. And while he was way more than a little easy on the eyes, his appeal quickly extended beyond the physical.

It made whatever secret he was hiding that much more difficult to bear. And Evangeline wasn't sure whether she was ready to back off or hunt down the police and the gaming commission in one fell swoop.

She knew what she'd seen. No amount of refusal or denial on Rafe's part was going to change that. What *had* changed over the past two hours was her need to understand the reasons why. Why there was a burning man in the first place. Why she couldn't see any evidence on the ground. And why nothing—absolutely *nothing*—showed on the security cameras.

Where she'd been initially wary that the Stavros family was hiding something illegal, or worse, committing crimes of their own, her time in close company with Rafe had shifted her direction. Her instincts might be on high alert, but increasingly it seemed there was a mystery afoot that had nothing to do with crime or greed or anything else.

The problem was, what sort of mystery would surround a man who burned to a crisp and left no detail, residue or ash behind?

Trying desperately to shake off the endless questions and keep her wits about her, she brought herself back fully to the moment. The two of them walked down the marble expanse that led from the restaurant to the indoor gardens, their steps slow and measured as Rafe asked her questions about the internal installation she'd proposed that morning.

"You think you can do this installation fully in two days?"

"Of course. We'll start early the day after New Year's and be done by the end of the next. Forty-eight hours, tops."

"And when will you sleep in all this?"

Evangeline stopped at that, turning to him fully. "What is it with you and my work schedule? This benefits you. Your hotel. The experiences your guests will have when they visit. I'd think you'd appreciate a timely schedule and a plan of attack."

"Not at the expense of your health. Your well-being."

"It's not like I'm doing anything else, anyway."

The words flew out before she could stop them and the congenial dinner companion morphed right there on the spot. The stubborn, hardheaded man who refused to share any of his own secrets almost seemed to surge forward as he leaped to understand hers.

"What's that about?"

A healthy blush crept up her neck, spreading toward her cheeks. "No holiday plans this year. It's not a problem."

"Will you be alone?"

A sudden chill swept up her bare arms, at direct odds with the embarrassed heat, and Evangeline fought the urge to rub her upper flesh. "It's no big deal."

"Forgive me if I don't agree." Rafe moved closer, his large hand closing around her empty one, devoid of her small clutch. "The holidays should be full of family and fun. The chance to make memories."

I have plenty of those and none of them are good.

The words had nearly left her lips—*nearly*—before she caught herself. "I'm ready to make memories. The moment I watch the guests of the Archangel walk through the interior gardens in wonder and awe."

"That's not what I'm talking about."

"Why not? If it makes me happy, makes me satisfied that my work brings pleasure to others, what's wrong with it?"

"Nothing. It's just that the holidays are a time for family. For being together. For celebrating."

The banked embarrassment flared to life once more before it shifted—transformed, really—into whip-quick anger. Evangeline tugged her hand from his, taking a step back in determined self-preservation. "Not everyone celebrates. And not everyone has a family. More to the point, not everyone wants one."

"You don't want a family?"

"Of course I do. At some point." And she did. It was her fondest wish, something she wrapped close to her heart each night as she lay down to sleep. Her lack of one haunted her as she worked the property, watching couples walk arm in arm or families laugh as they traversed the Archangel.

She *did* want a family.

But the very last thing she wanted was to discuss that here, *now*, with a rich Greek god who practically owned Vegas.

"You don't seem in any hurry to make one." The words shot back before a small corner of her brain—the one not short-circuited out by the impressive presence of Rafael Stavros—warned her not to talk to her boss that way. But it was too late.

"I have a family. A large, loud one who is up in my business each and every day, pressing me on that very question." He leaned forward, a predatory smile painting his lips in a wolfish grin. "Are you sure they haven't hired you?"

Lingering anger and loneliness and that weird heat that suffused every single nerve ending each time she got within ten feet of Rafe flared to life once more. She remained still, even as the urge to reach out and brush her fingers over the lush lips that still quirked in that naughty grin had her fisting her hands, one on her clutch and the other by her side. "No."

"Then why bring it up?"

"It's no secret you're one of the city's most eligible bachelor playboys."

"A dubious honor at best."

"You wear it well. You and your brother."

"So you watch out for Gabe's love life, too?"

With the evidence her words had been twisted once more, Evangeline stilled.

Stop talking. Immediately.

The order echoed over and over in her mind, at direct odds with what wanted to spill from her lips. Questions. Observations. And that continuing wonder at what secret he hid over the man who'd burned to a crisp on Archangel grounds.

Rafe reached out and dragged the tip of his finger over

her cheek. "It's okay if you do, you know. It's nice knowing someone is watching out for me. Caring."

"I don't care."

His eyebrows shot up before a slow, lazy haze seemed to mist over that enigmatic gray gaze. "Of course you don't."

The pad of his finger drifted from her cheek down to her jaw, painting a line over the delicate bone before moving on down to her neck. His large hand settled at the base of her neck, the tips of his fingers curling around her nape before he drew her close.

"What are you doing?" The question fell from her lips, a breathless whisper that sounded like it came from someone else. Someone sexier. Someone used to this sort of blatant seduction.

"Isn't it obvious?"

"No."

"Then let me show you instead."

Rafe's mouth pressed to hers, an insistent brush of lips that worked a magic all its own. Firm and persistent, in moments he had her mouth open, his tongue delving inside to explore secrets she didn't even know she possessed.

But somehow he knew.

He seemed to know everything as his lips and teeth and tongue wove masterfully over her mouth, drawing a response that was both tentative and strong, timid and powerful all at once.

She wanted him.

It seemed like such a simple notion, steeped in the increasingly urgent needs of her body and the attentions of the man opposite her.

But for her, it was a novel thought, unexpected and deeply, crazily potent.

"Rafe!"

The heavy, baritone shout seemed to come from outside

herself, an abstract thought that took shape and dimension as Rafe lifted his mouth from hers.

"What is it?" His words were clipped, with a gravelly edge that seemed to match the thickness that filled her own throat as Evangeline came back to herself.

Oh, no!

Her first thought was to cover herself, the power of Rafe's kiss surely branded all over her exposed skin in the revealing dress. That thought was quickly followed by another. Gabe was standing there, his focus fully on Rafe as if he barely even saw her.

"We have an appointment this evening. I believe we discussed it earlier? You mentioned wanting to take part in the meeting."

Something loud—even though it was completely unspoken—arced between the brothers and Evangeline came fully back to the moment. Embarrassment at being caught kissing Rafe in the lobby vanished as she attempted to decipher what neither was saying, even as their silence spoke volumes.

Rafe spoke first, his gaze flicking to hers before returning to his brother. "I'll be ready to leave shortly."

"I'll meet you in the security center."

Gabe marched off as fast as he'd arrived and she had the distinct impression he'd left an uncomfortable Rafe in his wake.

"I'm sorry to end our evening early."

"It is nearly midnight." She stilled, their earlier exchanges over the burning man at odds with the liquid desire that still muddled her veins like a thick, delicious milk shake. "An odd time for a meeting."

"The casino business never closes."

"So true." She glanced around the atrium, currently filled with a holiday theme she'd spent endless days developing and refining. "Sort of like the flower business. We do what we must, when we must."

With that, she took a step back. The desire to follow him and his brother was strong, but the unceasing eyes that followed everything happening in the hotel would no doubt capture her if she attempted it.

So she'd retreat. Review what she'd learned. And reassemble her arguments tomorrow.

"Thank you for a lovely evening." She ran a hand over the skirt of her dress. "A lovely day, as well."

With that, Evangeline turned on her heel and left him standing in the midst of her flowers. The urge to look back was strong, but she kept moving forward.

And wondered how she was going to uncover the secrets he hid.

The large black SUV rumbled, silent as a wraith, through one of Las Vegas's poorest neighborhoods. Apartment houses had the look of the abandoned or the damned, and the few souls who loitered in front suggested both. Rafe fought an inward shudder at the evidence of such poverty and despair. He wasn't immune to the plight of those who lived mere blocks from the Archangel and they had several programs in place to ensure they didn't further contribute to such problems.

But none of that stilled the inherent frustration that such horrible conditions existed next to the opulence and refinement of the Strip.

"Strange place, our hometown."

Gabe's comment was a funny mirror to his own and Rafe shifted his attention from the street. "I was thinking along similar lines."

"Beauty and horror, wrapped up in one big package."

"The universe does love balance." Rafe murmured the words, and Gabe picked up on them quickly.

"Dad's preached yin and yang for years. Nothing exists alone."

"Just like us."

The thought lingered in his mind, emotional ballast he was never fully able to shed. Even during each period of renewal, when his thoughts should be on rebirth and rejuvenation, he was innately conscious of the weight and responsibility that rested on his shoulders.

Their father had seen to that. For all his joviality and easygoing nature, Michael Stavros had always impressed upon them their duties and their responsibilities. Their people guarded the gates of the ancients. And while the Stavros family had made their life in Las Vegas, acting as protectors in the human world instead of taking up arms at the gates, they knew the path to the ancient world.

The Stavroses understood their destiny wasn't the Archangel or Las Vegas or even the lives they'd live to the fullest. Their legacy was the fire they carried inside, born of the earliest times and entrusted to them by the very gods that ruled over the heavens, the earth and the lower realms.

"Are you prepared if there are Hunters in here?"

"Yes."

"Your Rejuvenation came early."

"And?" He shot his brother a dark look, the subject still a sensitive one.

For his part, Gabe ignored the attitude and plowed forward—his style since birth. "Any ideas why?"

Rafe had no clue and that nagged nearly as much as the fact that it had come upon him so early. They were creatures of the earth. Driven by the cycles of nature as surely as the moon and the tides. Yet instead of his Rejuvenation at the winter solstice, it had come upon him with unexplained prematurity.

A few days here and there were normal. Shedding one's mortal form through the most ancient of fires took time, and pending overall mood, health, age and attitude, the process could take a few days. But nearly a month early?

Hell, he hadn't been so misadjusted since puberty.

Gabe pressed on, oblivious—or uncaring—of the lack of response. "You haven't said much about your date. Were you successful in persuading the beautiful Evangeline that she saw nothing last night?"

"No."

That lone word hovered there, shimmering in the air between them as vivid—and lethal—as his own fire.

"What are you going to do about it?"

"I'll be damned if I know."

"No, you'll be damned if you don't do something about this."

The dark snarl in his brother's words matched his mood and Rafe had no interest in another lecture. They'd been down this road already. Hell, he knew the stakes and knew what was at risk. He didn't need a freaking lecture to boot.

"Gabe—"

"We don't know this woman. She's a possible threat and now she's bound and determined to nose around because you couldn't be bothered to take care of yourself."

"Lecture me one more time, little brother, and I'll—"

The words died in his throat as Rafe stared at the flophouse before them. Enormous flames licked the walls, spiraling toward the sky as people spilled onto the lawn, disgorged from the smoke.

"What the hell?"

"The fires of hell, more like." Rafe watched the flames as they crawled up walls, something seeming to pulse in the atmosphere around the degenerated apartment. A light, sickly-sweet scent on the air caught his attention and before he could check the impulse, Rafe was out of the car and across the lawn.

A woman and her children limped from the home, a

baby squalling on the woman's arm as two kids hovered around her legs. Snagging the children under each arm, he screamed to the woman, "Run!"

Fear and exhaustion painted her features, yet in that moment, he saw understanding.

"Now! I've got them!" Rafe held the children beneath his arms, their screams echoing in his ears as smoke filled the air around them. The smaller child, a little girl, kicked hard at his leg but he ignored the stab of pain, moving—always moving—away from the house.

Noise, great and hulking, hovered in the air around them, but it was the transitory moment of silence that had him taking his next move. On a hard push, he pressed the children into their mother, a few paces in front of them, then leaped on top of the family.

The air nearly rent in two as the apartment house exploded behind them. A great cracking sound filled the air the briefest second before heat engulfed them in thick waves. Rafe channeled his own inner fire, the move as natural as breath, and used the power in his own frame to press back against the wild conflagration behind them.

Power poured from him, thick, wild waves of fire that pressed back on the demonic blaze that continued to eat the apartment house. Smoke billowed everywhere, choking the air, and still, Rafe stayed where he was, his body a living cover for the shaking woman and her children beneath him.

Slowly, he felt the atmosphere shift, the immediate danger fading as the initial explosion died, the rapidly disintegrating building giving less and less fuel to keep the blaze aflame. The woman beneath him shifted, her eyes going wide as she caught sight of an area over his shoulder.

"But…you're on…fire!"

Rafe shook his head, using her disorientation and fear to his advantage. Pressing her face to his shoulder, he let his own power fade, only letting go of her when his fire had fully winked out. "Shh. It's okay."

The woman scrambled from underneath him as Rafe sat back on his heels. Smoke still filled the air, but other than the soot that covered all of them, his clothing was intact.

"I don't understand." The woman scrambled up, her fear fading as curiosity and determination lit her features. "You were on fire."

"It was behind us."

"No. You—" She broke off as her crying children tugged and pulled at her, their keening wails diverting her focus. Rafe used the momentary distraction to his advantage, waving over several paramedics.

Gabe followed close behind, his hand extended to pull Rafe up, his face dark.

"Not here."

His brother shook his head. "My thoughts exactly."

It was only when they were back in the car that Gabe spoke. With a hard toss, something thick and metallic thudded into the SUV's cup holder.

Rafe eyed the piece, a brass token with the distinctive marks of a swirling sky, wrapped around an all-seeing eye. "Son of a bitch."

"I'm not sure which is worse. The Mark of Chaos or the fact you flamed up in front of a fucking lawn full of humans."

Chapter 5

Rafe turned the small medallion over and over in his hands, the noise of his office flat-screened TV filling the air in the executive suite with a steady drone. The flat disc about the size of a silver dollar practically burned in his palm, a physical embodiment of all his people fought against.

There were Hunters in Las Vegas.

And if the medallion were any indication, the ones here were more than the simple, bumbling fools usually impressed into service on behalf of the great and all-powerful equalizer of the universe.

Chaos.

Oh, no. These would be well trained. Well funded. And far more lethal than the typical minion who wreaked havoc and discord.

Images of the fire still filled his thoughts, the physical imprint of that family still pulsing against the nerve endings of his chest. And that smell, its thick, sweet redolence filling the air moments before all hell broke loose. The news claimed it was a tragic outcome of a meth lab gone wrong, but he knew different.

The lab was the overt cause, the production of the dangerous drug coating the house with a lingering miasma that led to the explosion. But it was the power beneath it—the sickly fingers that had directed it all—that was the real and true danger.

Rafe crossed to his office safe and tapped in the ten-digit code. A small light flicked to green before a light hiss of air opened the thick metal door. He reached in and pulled out what lay hidden—protected, really—behind the reinforced metal wall of the safe.

The thick wood was heavy in his palm, an icon from another age. A spoke from the wheel of Helios's chariot, nearly as powerful as the immortal hand that had crafted it.

The spoke was his family's own personal talisman, entrusted to them from the dawn of the Stavros line. Though not immortal like their great ancestor, they were imbued with his power and his wards of protection.

And with that power and authority, they willingly protected the race of Phoenix that called Helios for their first ancestor. Rafe and Gabe, and their father before them, understood the responsibility—had lived with it since birth—but a battle had always seemed distant. Separate, somehow.

But no longer.

An image of Evangeline shimmered to life, her delicate features never far from his thoughts. Was she the source? The root cause of what was steadily rising to life? He'd have hardly believed it, but now found it hard to deny the evidence.

She was the child of a Hunter. And she had unfettered access to the Archangel. Was it possible she'd been the Trojan horse, delivered in a spunky, fiery package designed to distract even as it laid the groundwork for their ultimate demise?

He didn't want to believe it, but the previous night had left him with a layer of anxiety he'd never felt before. His skin crawled with a strange energy, as if it recognized the seething, writhing threat that hovered nearby. He and Gabe had gone to the apartment house with the intention of finding Evangeline's ex-employees, Troy and Victor. Instead, they'd found destruction and a very clear message in the planted medallion.

They'd also missed their targets. The meth lab explosion had left significant destruction in its wake, including two apartment residents who didn't make it out alive, but the bumbling members of Evangeline's team weren't accounted for in the dead or the living.

Which only forced the additional question of just how bumbling and stupid Troy and Victor really were.

He and Gabe had argued the point until early morning, going round and round without answers. Gabe wanted to exorcise Evangeline from the property and Rafe continued to press for her to stay. His overt argument was so they could watch her. If she was a channel for the Hunters, she was far more useful to them nearby than from a distance.

And if a small part of him fervently wished she was oblivious to the threat that swirled, he'd live with that. Their stolen moments in the corridor downstairs had been some of the sweetest of his life and he refused to believe he was simply thinking with his hormones.

Even if he knew damn well they played a role, too. He wanted the woman. The razor-sharp claws of desire had dragged at him for days—hell, since she started at the hotel, if he were being honest—and something in spending time with her had only made that need more intense.

More urgent.

And far more potent than if he'd continued to deny his interest and stay away.

None of which answered the lingering questions that swirled around the subject of Evangeline Kennedy. Was she the reason for his early Rejuvenation? He'd felt the change coming on for a few days, but in those moments in the high-roller suite, hosting their potential clients, he'd been nearly overcome. Hell, he'd practically stumbled from the high-end villas across the back of the property.

And then he'd fully regenerated, practically in front of her.

Was it possible she had a hand in his early transformation?

He crossed to his desk and picked up the flat disk once more. The thick metal was warm to the touch, a strange, heavy counterpoint to the wood he held in his other hand. Power seemed to pulse between the two objects, that yin and yang his father was so determined to preach.

That strange, precarious balance that dictated their lives more succinctly than any plans or goals they set for themselves.

Rafe tightened his fingers around the objects before crossing back to his safe and relocking both firmly behind the metal door.

It was time to get some answers.

Evangeline let out a heavy breath as she took in the row of sculptures, set at odds among a bright, vivid infusion of flowers. The installation was a centerpiece of the Archangel's entertainment corridor, an effusive welcome as casino patrons moved past several restaurants and bars.

And someone had craftily positioned two statues beside each other in flagrante delicto.

Where was Security when you needed them?

And worse, why was her mind immediately filled with impressions of Rafe?

Shaking off the erotic image of his mouth trailing along her skin, she desperately tried to focus on the problem. And *off* all the delectable places Rafe might put those lush, gorgeous lips.

The Archangel's curator, Arturo, was bound to throw a fit when he saw that his prize sculptures, on loan through the New Year, had been tampered with. Worse, the insurance risk was enormous. She'd done a cursory scan of the marble to see if she might be able to move it herself or secure help from her crew, but there was no way around the problem. She'd have to call Arturo down from his lofty perch in the hotel's third-floor art museum and get him to put a specialized team on repositioning them.

She dragged out her phone, already preparing herself for the inevitable shooting she'd receive as messenger, when she caught sight of security. Waving down the large, beefy figure, she continued to pace around the sculptures after catching his eye.

How had someone managed this unnoticed? She'd been there when the statues were set in place. Each easily weighted at least three thousand pounds, the Italian marble hewn into the erotically lusty figures that now stood before her. Where their original placement had suggested a sensual feast, sexy nymphs lounging or traipsing through the lush garden she'd wrapped around them, the new placement suggested raw sex and something decidedly dirty.

Like a public shaming. Or the ravages of original sin.

The ringing of the phone in her ear ended, replaced with Arturo's clipped voice as his voice-mail message rattled off in her ear. Unwilling to linger, she ordered him down to the lobby and shoved her phone back in her cargos. Like she had time for this.

Just like she didn't have time for dates or kisses or erotic images of Rafe.

The guard she'd motioned for still stood at the opposite end of the hall and she waved him down once more, adding a wolf whistle for good measure. Was the guy blind? And what was taking him so long? He'd be in trouble enough for leaving the statues in the first place, but to ignore a direct request?

"Why, Evangeline, I had no idea you'd planned such a fascinating display for the promenade."

The dark voice, rich as sin, seemed to float over the back of her neck like a brand. The erotic images she'd fought against rose up once more, a tantalizing replacement for the side of beef who continued to ignore her from the opposite end of the corridor.

Turning on her heel, Evangeline went into damage control mode. "I did no such thing!"

"I'm not saying I don't like it."

"You shouldn't like it. Someone's tampered with the sculptures and I can't seem to find Arturo and security's gone MIA."

The litany was enough to draw his focus off the sexy art and Rafe's brows lowered. "Where's security?"

"I have no idea. I've been flagging that hulk down there for the past few minutes and he's ignoring me." Evangeline glanced over her shoulder, surprised to see the end of the corridor empty, the mountain of a man nowhere in sight. "I… Where is he?"

"Where's security?" Rafe's gaze sharpened, his dark eyes sweeping the breadth and depth of the corridor. "Where's anyone, for that matter?"

"I don't—" She broke off, a strange, insistent pounding in her ears in direct counterpoint to her confusion. Where *was* everyone?

The Archangel lobby was rarely empty, although traffic dimmed considerably during the overnight hours. But it did *not* vanish in the middle of the morning, nor did the air hum with a malevolent sort of silence.

"What's going on?"

"How long have you been here?" Rafe's question was sharp, at odds with his subtle steps as he moved closer toward her.

"Only a few minutes. I wanted to refresh some of the flowers in here and then I found this." A wave of embarrassment heated her skin, creeping up her neck toward her cheeks. "It's not how they were originally placed."

"Not at all."

"But how could someone move them unnoticed?"

"You could."

Those two words were spoken in quiet tones despite the accusation that screamed from each of them. "They're too heavy. I couldn't even push one."

"Directed your team, then?"

"No!" The pounding in her ears grew thicker, adrenaline drumming a hard beat through her body. "Someone snuck in here and moved these. A group of guests, maybe, who thought it was funny. Or someone on Arturo's team. I just found them."

"Of course."

Memories from long ago spiraled through her mind and she was once again a helpless child, at the whim of the adults around her. When in one of their moods, her parents had accused her of any number of childish crimes she'd not committed, and those memories braided with Rafe's dark, endless stare. Fear wrapped around her throat with tight hands, nearly choking off her breath.

I didn't do it. It wasn't me. No!

Forcing air into her lungs, she lowered her voice. "What are you trying to say?"

His eyes narrowed, a hard, storm-cloud gray that indicated he wasn't persuaded by her response.

Did he honestly believe she was responsible?

Something swirled at her feet—a hard tug, really—that had her glancing down. The moment she did, a heavy gust of wind blew through the hallway with all the force of a hurricane. The tug at her feet became a hard drag, sucking at her shoes like cement while thick winds buffeted her. A scream crawled up her throat at the hard press of air that pushed against her bones with brutal force. The immediate urge to seek shelter was foiled by the large hands that wrapped around hers.

"Hold on to me!"

Rafe's grip was tight but it was a solid match for the invisible tether that gripped her feet.

"I can barely move."

"What?"

"My feet. It's like I'm stuck or something." Evangeline tried to lift her leg, straining against the force holding her down. She managed a few steps but a hard ache gripped the muscles of her thighs.

Rafe shifted his grip and bent at the waist, pulling at her leg. "Try once more. Match my movements."

She ignored the tingle of electricity that ran the length of her calf where his hands gripped her body. On his mark, she lifted, him pulling in unison. Her muscles strained against the weird force attempting to hold her still, but his added strength was enough to get them moving. The moment she sprung free from the sucking vortex, Rafe had her on the move. "Come on!"

The long corridor seemed to flatten and stretch out, all at the same time. What was about one hundred yards of shops and restaurants shifted before her eyes into a long tunnel that she could barely see the end of.

"What's going on?" Her question flew into the ether,

cut off by another hard gust of wind, this one stronger than the first as it slammed against her chest with bone-crushing force.

"I don't know." Rafe's grip was tight as he pulled her along, his expensive loafers sliding over the marble floor of the Archangel. Designed for interior beauty, not exterior gale-force winds, the two of them slipped and skidded toward a small alcove on the wall.

Were they under attack?

Although she paid it little mind, she knew Las Vegas—especially the small cities that basically made up each casino—was vulnerable to terrorists. Had some group targeted the Archangel?

But with what? Some drug? Maybe that was what distorted perception, making the hallway look and feel like an endless corridor to nowhere. She smelled no smoke and saw no fire, yet that weird wind seemed to fill the space around them, pressing in on both of them. Where were the other guests?

She saw no one. Instead, it was only her and Rafe as they huddled, breathing hard against the wall.

"You okay? Are you hurt?"

"No."

"Can you stand upright?"

She tested her weight against the wind that still swirled when he spoke again, a hard shout in her ear. "Try to take a few steps against it."

Evangeline pushed herself off the wall, moving forward against the full-body press of air. It wasn't like before—her feet moved this time—but the wind was a harsh taskmaster. "Yes, but—"

Her words vanished along with her breath as a hard, supernatural hand seemed to slam against her chest, shoving her back against the wall.

Rafe's arms cushioned the blow, but even with his full

strength holding her, the violent shock of the attack seemed to echo through her midsection, her ribs vibrating like a pair of cymbals. What the hell was going on?

The fear of an explosion or fire never materialized, the air blessedly free of the acrid tang of smoke. Instead, there was that continued wind—harsh and unyielding.

Rafe's urgent voice echoed in her ear, loud enough to be heard over the howling wind. "We need to get out of here. Whatever it is, it's purposely blocking us here in this alcove."

"It?"

The anger she'd seen only moments before had vanished fully from his eyes, replaced with something fierce and urgent. And careful.

Too careful.

"I think it's targeted us."

The lack of answer to her question was even more unsettling than his response and for the first time real fear choked at her throat.

"I need you to hold on to me. We need to get outside. Out in the open."

"The door's too far away."

"That's why I need you to push forward. As hard as you can. We're making a run for it."

She nodded in assent, the wild, raging wind swallowing the last of his words. Before she could blink, Rafe had her hand in his, pulling her out into the raging vortex of air. Once more, that hard, screaming wind wrapped around her, a violent storm of molecules forming and reforming, punching every inch of her body.

Evangeline focused on putting one foot in front of the other, Rafe's hand around hers in a reassuring grip. The wind fought them, but the two of them fought back, their forward momentum a mix of their own combined strength as well as raw, purposeful motion. Whatever this was—

and she was increasingly convinced there was a real, tangible force behind the assault—it wasn't going to beat them.

Step by step, they moved down the corridor. Where they'd initially hovered along the wall, the force they fought quickly used that thick barrier as the immovable half of its wallop, so Rafe pulled them into the center of the corridor, forcing the wind to reform around them.

"The door! We have to get it open. It pulls inward."

Rafe moved behind her, positioning himself as a shield for her to drag on the thick mass of glass. With both hands on the ornate brass handle, she positioned herself against the door, bracing her feet. A hard spear of wind pressed against the door, an opposing force to her strength. On a hard breath, Evangeline doubled her strength and tried again.

Only to have that reinforced burst of wind rise up and slam against the door once more.

She turned to Rafe, panic and terror choking the words in her throat. "We're trapped."

"We're—" His words were cut off by another shot of air, a sly sort of agreement seeming to wrap around them.

His gaze narrowed, the briefest moment of confusion stamping itself in his gray eyes before he seemed to come to a decision. "We're going to try this one more time."

"It's not working."

"Once more. On my mark."

When she didn't move, Rafe placed his hands over hers, his palms warm against the backs of her hands. He leaned in, his lips hovering over her ears, his voice full of encouragement. "You can do this."

Although it was a far cry from the accusation he'd levied mere minutes before, Evangeline took heart from the clear, unwavering support. On a hard nod she focused on the door, absorbing his strength through her skin. Willing the heat of his body to infuse her rapidly evaporating strength.

"We'll do this together."

She nodded, a heavy ache settling in her arms as she fought to hold on amidst the continued bluster behind them. Nothing about the past ten minutes made sense, from the sculptures to the wind to Rafe's unexpected arrival. Yet something deep inside her relished his presence and his added strength.

Together.

For the first time in her life, she wasn't alone. And that knowledge ceased the trembling in her limbs, instead suffusing her with a deeper strength—one born of determination and an unwillingness to let him down.

"Okay. Together."

"On my mark. Three. Two. One."

His hands tightened on hers as Evangeline pulled, the door springing free beneath her efforts. Cool, late November air rushed in and she took a large breath, free of the hard press of the hallway. Rafe's hands dropped from hers and she turned to pull him forward just as a large wave of heat rose up behind them.

Time slowed, the already-surreal moment giving way to something unearthly.

Unimaginable.

Rafe stood before her, immersed in a wash of flame.

Chapter 6

Air, fresh and sweet, surrounded them as Rafe pushed Evangeline out onto the grounds of the Archangel, his fire winking out in a flash. The heavy doors closed behind them, effectively trapping whatever was left in the corridor back inside the building. The urge to radio Gabe was strong, but the bright, near-hysterical glint in Evangeline's dark gaze took priority.

The corridor that had trapped them opened straight onto a walking path to the property's pools, and he refused to stop until they'd put a good bit of distance between themselves and the building. With each step Evangeline's panic seemed to rise, her eyes darting between him, his torso and somewhere in the distance behind him as he marched them farther and farther away from the casino.

"What? Why? How?"

Her words were barely intelligible at first, but quickly coalesced into a steady litany of questions.

How?

The what he knew. Even the whys of it. The how was always what tripped him up.

How did you explain what you were? His people had stopped trying long ago.

"We need to get to a quiet place."

"I'm not—" Her protests increased as he sped up, the greenhouse in the distance his intended target. "No way."

When she continued to drag her feet, tugging against his hold on her hand, he stopped and faced her. "Please. Can you give me that much?"

Whether it was the urgency of his words or the "please," Rafe didn't know, but he wasn't going to question his good fortune. Whatever it was had been enough to get her moving forward in lockstep with him.

The heat of the greenhouse surrounded them as he swiped his access badge at the door and he ushered them inside. The thick air enveloped them immediately, along with an innate calm he couldn't fully describe.

Something lived here. Plants and flowers, dirt and decay. And from that decay came something real and alive and welcoming. Bright blooms and lush, exotic fronds. Fruits of the earth, each and every one giving back life to the world around it.

If he were prone to the fanciful he'd have said it was the same feeling he'd experienced the night before with Evangeline wrapped in his arms.

With her, he felt welcome. A sense of belonging he'd never known. And here, inside her world, he felt welcome, as well.

"You owe me an explanation." Those thoughts of welcome vanished under her thunderous expression. While he struggled with what he was about to reveal, he couldn't deny the time had come.

Finally.

"Okay."

"What are you? And what was that in the hotel? And were you the one out on the lawn? The one on fire."

"First things first." He shrugged out of his suit coat and undid his sleeves, rolling the cuffs up to his forearms.

"Why aren't you burned? You were on fire." She rushed forward, snagging his suit jacket from the worktable he'd laid it on. Her hands roamed over the material, seeking some evidence of the fire he'd used to beat back the wind, staving off its impact so they could get through the door. "And why is this untouched?"

"I'll explain everything. But first I need something from you."

She dropped the jacket and took an abrupt step back. "I have nothing."

Something twisted in his gut at the fear that replaced the bravado in her deep brown gaze. "What did they do to you?"

He hadn't even realized he'd spoken the words out loud when those same eyes widened, instantly shuttering all emotion. "No one did anything."

The urge to press her was strong but he didn't push any further, instead he used her wariness to his advantage. "I don't know what that wind was inside the hotel. Nor do I understand where all the guests went, but I have an idea I need to run by Gabe."

"Want to run it by me first?"

"I don't think anyone else saw or felt what we did."

Whatever reassurance he took from that thought was lost on Evangeline. "You can't be serious."

"But I am. There's no force on earth that could summarily vanish the roughly fifteen thousand people currently in my casino and hotel. Yet none of them filled the hallway. None passed by us. None could hear the commotion of hurricane-force winds."

"Maybe they're hurt."

"Then where are the bodies?"

"But—" She broke off, her gaze brightening. "You think no one was hurt."

"I certainly hope so. But the more I evaluate it, I think I'm right. Gabe will need to confirm." Rafe dragged out his phone, not surprised when there wasn't anything from his brother. "Nor has he contacted me, which adds further support to my theory. No one saw it but us."

"So if no one else saw it, then what happened back there?"

"I don't know." Rafe hesitated for the briefest moment before he made his decision. He made a vow—his entire family had—but Evangeline had a right to know. Her life now depended on it. "But I have an idea why it happened. I think it's connected to you and me."

"Me?"

"What do you know about your parents?"

Her parents?

Rafe's question hung there, in the middle of the thick, wet air of the greenhouse. What could her parents possibly have to do with weird winds and a crazy fire that kept consuming people with no discernable trace of damage?

"What are you?"

She'd asked the question a myriad of ways, but she wasn't waiting any longer for an answer. If they were both involved in this—whatever *this* was—she had a right to know.

That mercurial gray of his eyes seemed to change before her, even as his gaze remained steady on hers. From a cloudy storm gray to an almost gunmetal blue until finally morphing to an electric silver that sent heat winging through her veins.

Nearly as inopportune as that wash of heat she'd felt near the inappropriately placed statues.

What sort of spell did he have her under?

Whatever she imagined, it was nothing compared to the deep breath and mysterious words that fell from his lips. "I am Helios."

"Heel-y what?"

"Helios."

"What is that? Are you a man? And if you're not, what are you?" Although her words were not intentionally designed to be hurtful, she didn't miss the quick flash of embarrassment in his eyes at that question before he waved a hand.

"I am very much a man."

A weird, achy relief slammed her in the chest with nearly as much force as the hallway tornado. How odd that relief could provide as strong an assault as an F5. "If you're a man, then what is a Helios?"

"I'm a descendant of the Greek god of the sun, Helios, who drives his chariot each day, bringing light to the world."

Vague memories of high school English did battle with the words Rafe spoke. She remembered mythology—had enjoyed it even—but never had she believed it to be anything more than stories designed to explain lack of modern human understanding.

Was Rafe possibly for real? And did he honestly believe what he was saying?

Even as she thought it, she had to admit the fire had been real. Two nights ago she'd seen a man in flames and just now, she'd seen the same phenomenon.

"Do you worship him? Like a cult?"

"Not exactly."

"So what would you call your attachment to him?"

"Mythology would call what I am a phoenix. In my family, we prefer the more historically accurate depiction as

I explained it. We are descendants of Helios and we carry his gifts within our life essence."

Phoenix? No freaking way. She'd seen *Harry Potter* and had even read beyond the Greeks when it came to mythology of ancient cultures. But he couldn't possibly be serious.

Even if it did give some explanation to a fire that burned, yet didn't consume.

"But phoenixes are birds."

"In some cultures, that's the accepted mythology."

"Yet you're a man."

A wry smile painted his lips and it took her a moment to register the steps he took to narrow the gap between them. "You seem rather hung up on that aspect. Would you care for a demonstration?"

Need—raw and primal—rose up in answer to Rafe's question and she quickly back-stepped, slamming her hip into the long worktable that dominated the center of the greenhouse. A hard *oof* escaped her lips before she tumbled over herself. His strong hands reached out, steadying her. "I'm not going to hurt you."

"You haven't been truthful with me."

"I don't have a right to protect myself? My family? You know the world we live in. The danger of being different. You'd begrudge me my privacy and my right to live free of public scrutiny?"

His arguments were so simple and, if she were honest, more than fair. She knew what it was to be different. To be seen as the outcast wherever she went. That was simply based on her lack of parents. But to be…other. It not only went against the grain, but it caused irrational fear.

And with fear came violence. Pain and suffering. And the dark agony of force and aggression.

She knew fear. Knew what it did to a person—to how they saw the world and how they saw the people around them. Her parents had lived in fear and had transferred that panic to her. She'd spent her childhood locked in a nightmare of abuse and neglect, unable to see there was any other way of living.

Her father had seen to that and her mother had been dragged along in his wake.

The hazy images that usually accompanied thoughts of them faded, Rafe's earlier comments flaring front and center. "What of my parents? What do they have to do with this?"

"Your father was a Hunter."

"My father?" She shook her head, the sad reality of Hank Kennedy's life something she'd accepted long ago. "My father was a drug addict and a criminal. If he'd hunted anything, it was his next fix."

"No, you misunderstand. Your father was a Hunter. The souls who seek my people for the god Chaos. Hunters are the sworn enemy of all Helios."

"You're not making any sense. My father wasn't part of anything. The man could barely keep his family together. You think he was some sort of member of a secret army?"

"That's exactly what he was."

"It's not possible."

"It's entirely possible. Your father has been on a list of known enemies for a long time. I put it together after you started here."

Cold fingers scraped over her spine, plucking each vertebra like piano keys. "You looked into my background?"

Once again, those enigmatic eyes flashed; only this time, she was unable to read the specifics. She didn't miss the cool tone of his voice. "A background check is normal on our employees. Your job application stated as much."

"My father died when I was six. My mother a year later. That shouldn't show up in any standard credit check."

"We do more than run credit checks on our employees. Especially when a familiar name pings in our database."

Those cold fingers squeezed, their grip brutal. "You knew? I've been here nearly a year and you knew this whole time? Have you been watching me or something?"

"Keeping tabs, yes. I had a right to keep my home and my people safe."

"And what about my rights? My privacy. My family. My everything."

The god of Chaos leaned against the bars of his prison and fought to maintain his strength. His vision blurred but the scene he'd seen through the eyes of one of his minions was still a crystal clear memory.

A casino.

Full of hordes of imbeciles so wrapped up in their stupid games and their vacations and their pathetic lives they had no idea the power that shimmered in the air around them. He'd channeled his power through one of his weaker Hunters and set his will against Stavros and the woman.

Woman? What rubbish. Evangeline Kennedy was a child. Worse, she was a descendant who had no idea or understanding of the forces that had made her. Shaped her. *Created* her.

She understood none of it, content to while away her time planting flowers and trees, tending to them like a busy little bee who never settled or rested.

What a waste.

Her father had been a waste of skin, but he'd served his purpose. When he wasn't strung out, the man was a true zealot, committed to the cause of taking down the descendants of Helios. Those pristine chosen ones, who instead of taking their rightful place in the Pantheon had elected to live amid the riffraff of human souls.

It angered him, that abdication of power.

And now he had to contend with Evangeline, as well.

Their subtle attempts through the years to recruit her

had all been for naught. His Hunters were born but their retention of free will ensured they made the choice to become one of his followers. The occasional boyfriend who campaigned for her attention was summarily brushed off, unable to sway her. Potential friends, impressed into service to lure her to a new way of thinking, ultimately dropped. Even her previous employer hadn't been effective in destroying her spirit—she simply took on more until she'd been successful in finding employ at the Archangel.

Damon Frost had been completely ineffective in swaying her way of thinking, his attempts at drawing her into a relationship ineffective. He'd now exact a price, but even punishment—while allaying a small measure of his anger—couldn't fix what was now set in motion.

Troy and Victor hadn't helped, either. Frost's bumbling henchmen had been ineffective from the start. The trouble with minions was that their lack of motivation worked in two ways. They were easily swayed to the cause, but not easily persuaded to do the required work.

A flaw he'd found far too many humans possessed in abundance.

But not Evangeline.

She'd been impressive. The wind was a particular favorite of his, the sensory overload on the recipient a thing of beauty to watch. Yet she'd stood firm.

Oh, what he could do with her. Even Frost wasn't talented enough to compare to the bright, agile mind and lithe form of Evangeline Kennedy. He need only find a way to channel it properly.

Of course…

The thought flared to life in his mind, simple. Elegant. Perfect.

Stavros had led her wrong from the beginning. And despite their ability to work together in the hallway, there was no way she trusted him. Nor did Rafe trust her.

And he could use that.

He did a quick evaluation of his crew, mentally selecting who he might send in as an initial line of attack. Keeping Rafe and his brother off guard would be necessary, now that he'd tipped his hand to Stavros that he could find his way inside the precious halls of Stavros's domain.

He didn't have much time.

Of course, neither did Rafael Stavros.

Evangeline walked the length of the worktable and back, her hand trailing over the dirt-stained top. She'd been in here steadily for the past week, repotting endless sets of poinsettias for the holiday installation. She knew this room. Knew the worktable and the tools arrayed at each end. Hell, she could even point out where her own tools had left scratches over the past year.

So why did all of it look so different now?

The room that had provided comfort, emotional shelter and a gloriously open work space suddenly felt stifling and much, much too small.

Because he was here.

A phoenix? No, she amended herself. A *Helios.* A direct descendant of the sun god of Greek mythology.

Those thoughts layered over and over in her mind, at times screaming the news, at other times quiet. But always there.

Her new reality, bound up in a world she didn't understand. Worse, it was a new reality that included her parents.

"My father died of a drug deal gone bad."

Rafe glanced up from his phone. He'd already spoken to Gabe and had tapped away at the smooth face ever since. "Yes."

"So that's true, then? He did die that way."

"I'm afraid so."

"If that is the case, how could he be some messenger of

evil? The man I remember was deeply broken. An addict who couldn't stay away long enough from his next fix."

"Then he fit the bill perfectly." Rafe pocketed the phone, his steps purposeful as he came around the worktable. "I'm sorry to tell you that he was a tool. A blunt instrument for Chaos to do its work."

"Chaos? You said that before, like it's a person."

"That's where Hunters come from. They're a creation of the god of Chaos. A counterforce to the power Chaos believes my people were imbued with."

"But you are powerful."

"Yes." Rafe nodded. "In many ways we are. But not in the ways that typically matter to a god. I'm not immortal. I don't take up arms in battle unless directly threatened. I'm not even enmeshed in Pantheon politics. My people have chosen to coexist quietly among humans, living our lives."

"You're serious about this."

"Of course I am."

Just like her questions earlier, probing if he really was a man, she sensed something beneath his response. Sadness? Embarrassment? She tried both on but neither fully fit.

"Do my questions bother you?"

"No." His response was fast and clipped and she knew it for the lie that it was. It was only when Rafe exhaled a deep breath and moved a few steps closer that she took a deep breath of her own. "Yes, on some level, your questions do bother me."

"Why?"

"Isn't it obvious? Yesterday you were kissing me and today you're afraid of me. Worse, you think me some sort of freak."

"I don't—"

"I'm a man, Evangeline. My blood runs red and I have needs like any other. I eat. I sleep. I make love. All of it as necessary to my life as anyone else's."

The words ripped from him, as if cleaved out of a large block of ice. She wanted to be immune—wanted to believe it was simply for show—yet something primal responded to what she heard beneath his words.

Loneliness.

She knew the emotion—had lived with it daily for her entire life. And she understood what it was to be "other."

"You have your family."

"Yes, all as isolated as I am. Do you know what it is to be hunted for what you are? To be ever on your guard, focused on protecting what is yours? We're a closed people and we don't let many in. Few even know we exist."

The life he spoke of was hard to understand. For all the opulence on the surface, that never-ending wariness had to be exhausting.

"And you're not immortal?"

"No. Helios live exceptionally long lives and we're generally free of pain and disease, but we aren't immortal. Just as each day must end with Helios's chariot descending across the sky, so do our lives."

The formality in his tone intrigued her. "You speak of him with reverence."

"He's the source of my power. My life. The fire that burns inside of me comes from him."

"Which means it was you? On the grounds the other night?"

Rafe remained silent for long moments, his focus somewhere else. "That was a mistake. I don't normally Rejuvenate in front of others. Nor do I lose control in public."

"Are you ill?" The idea that something was wrong with him stabbed at her, filling her with a dread she'd not have thought herself capable of even hours earlier.

"I don't think so."

She might have been inclined to believe him if he hadn't hedged. The response was a surprise, especially from a man who always seemed so in control of his surroundings. "What aren't you telling me?"

"This typically happens at each solstice and each equinox."

Evangeline did some quick math, well aware of the earth's cycles around the sun and its impact on her work. "And the winter solstice is still more than three weeks away."

"The timing varies slightly, but my entire adult life, I've regenerated near those windows. From the first, really."

"From the first what?"

"The act of Rejuvenation doesn't happen prior to puberty. Helios must be fully adult before their body regenerates."

Clearly Mother Nature had as much of a sense of humor with supernaturals—was that what she should call him?—as with any other human. Puberty was hard enough but at least she'd made it through without bursting into flame. She was nearly two decades past it and she could still remember the seemingly endless tears followed by near-manic melancholy that had ushered her fully into adulthood.

What did intrigue her was Rafe's comment about "from the first." "You've had that famous Rafe Stavros control from the beginning. Interesting."

"Excuse me?"

"You're known for it. That stony face and stiff back. You're sort of a tight ass, truth be told."

"I'm a what?"

She couldn't hold back the smile at the flush that crept up his neck. "It's a compliment."

"Hardly."

"It sort of is. The entire staff is afraid of you. It's one of the reasons I had no problem firing Troy and Victor. They were a bit more vocal than others about how the Archangel is run. I figured we were well rid of them."

"A move more intuitive than you think."

"I don't need slackers on my team. Add on a bad attitude and bad-mouthing the boss, and it's not something you can fix."

"Evangeline—"

"The way they spoke to me." Even now, the memories of their attitude and their parting shots—the "bitch boss" slur, along with mocking her compulsive need to plant flowers—still stung.

"Evangeline." Rafe finally broke through her thoughts. "They're Hunters. Both of them. You did more by firing them than simply removing poor performers. You saved us from a far darker threat."

"You think they were here to hurt you? Some sort of advance warning system?"

"Without question. Troy and Victor were here to discover our weaknesses so a group could breach the hotel."

Chapter 7

Rafe wasn't sure of the exact moment when the air between them had shifted, but something had. What had been fraught with tension and fear when they walked into the greenhouse had changed—altered, actually—into a wary sort of camaraderie. His mother would have said it was a result of them sharing a near-death experience in the lobby, but Rafe wasn't that fanciful.

Nor did he believe it was some cosmic force pushing the two of them together, which his mother would be all too quick to endorse, as well.

No, it was something else. Something that went far deeper than attraction or lust or even survivor's guilt. It all rested with her childhood. The very thing he'd feared would make her a likely asset to the Hunters had done the opposite. Dealing with the tragedy of her family life had made her strong beyond measure, forging a deep wellspring of grit, moxie and honor.

Evangeline Kennedy was no more working against him than Gabe was.

But was he prepared to work with her? He'd hidden so much of his life for so long, the idea of sharing who he was with another was more frightening than facing an entire band of Hunters.

Did he have a choice?

"You still haven't explained why you Re—" she hesitated before pushing forward "—Rejuvenated early."

"I don't know why. Gabe's asked me the same thing and I don't have any answers for it."

She moved forward and laid a hand on his arm. His skin tightened under the gentle outreach before a wave of awareness shot through him. He could smell her—that potent combination of flowers and earth that was uniquely Evangeline—and he was captivated. "Were you feeling badly? Have you been sick?"

"No."

"What are other reasons you might regenerate early?"

Her questions were the same as Gabe's, yet from her they held the distinct notes of concern. His brother's tone held far too much accusation for his liking. Which was monumentally unfair to Gabe, his long-standing partner in protecting their culture and their family.

Brushing off the tension, he had to acknowledge there were several reasons he might Rejuvenate early, yet none of them seemed a fit. Age or illness could have an impact, as could excessive travel between time zones. His body was hearty and resilient, but as he'd tried to explain, he wasn't immortal. The fire that burned beneath his skin held many properties, most of them healing, but it took a lot of energy to maintain.

The problem was, he had experienced none of those things.

Which left sexual attraction.

He'd been honest when he'd explained that he had the same passions as any man. He lived a hearty life and he enjoyed women. But he'd also learned long ago to control himself and a few weeks without sexual release wasn't likely to harm his body or throw him out of kilter.

Deep-seated sexual attraction was a different matter, but he'd be damned if he was going to share that tidbit. Especially since he hadn't been in the throes of unfulfilled attraction when his regeneration came upon him.

You're feeling a bit different now.

Something sly and unfailingly honest whispered through his mind. He was attracted to Evangeline—hell, he had been from the moment she'd walked on the property—but even her arrival hadn't altered his quarterly rebirth.

"Will you change again? When the solstice comes?"

"No. I should be good until spring."

"But you Rejuvenated nearly a month early. Won't that change your next regeneration cycle?"

"My body knows how to regulate itself."

If she were skeptical of that news, she hid it, instead focusing on a row of tools at the edge of her work space. The items that had been left out in haste she now placed in neat holders, all specially marked. She kept her gaze on her task instead of on him when she finally asked one more question.

"What is the purpose? Why do you do it?"

"It's a rebirth of sorts. Not that much unlike normal human cell regeneration, but with even more pronounced benefits. The speed with which it happens is sort of a full-body protection."

"And the outcome of that?"

"I'm stronger. Faster. My reflexes and senses are superior." As if to prove his point, he snaked out a hand, effectively capturing the small pair of needle-nose pliers she was already reaching toward.

"Hey!"

Rafe turned the pliers around, then handed them to her. "Just making a point."

"So how do you die?"

"The same way as anyone else. Age, mostly. Killing blows are another. There's no amount of Rejuvenation that can effectively alter a bullet to the heart or brain or a killing strike to a major artery."

"And the fire? It's not just when you Rejuvenate. You used it back there when we were under attack."

"My fire has its own properties to heal. It can also repel danger and protect me and all I can place in my aura. I can control its heat and its power as long as I have enough time to focus."

"So a surprise attack is the worst thing that could happen to you?"

Her questions were all fair—a mix of curiosity and what he sensed was a desperate desire to make some sense of what had happened—but there were some things he couldn't answer. Or wouldn't. He might accept Evangeline was part of what was going on, but even he couldn't bring himself to share with the daughter of a Hunter all the ways to make it easier for him and his people to die.

When Evangeline walked out of the greenhouse a half hour later, she wasn't sure if she'd fallen down the rabbit hole or been absorbed by an alien spacecraft. All she did know was that she'd been in the dark for much too long about her parents and her childhood and it seemed as if Rafe Stavros was the key to unlocking that mystery.

Add on the steady buzz and hum of an attraction she couldn't deny, and she had the makings of a full-blown life explosion.

"Which is pretty much your life in a nutshell." She muttered the words to herself, surprised when Rafe moved closer, his hand at her lower back.

"Everything okay?"

She'd suggested they make a quick stop at an area behind the greenhouse she was developing for outdoor events and he'd agreed. On some level, it felt like a reprieve—before they had to go back to the formality of their work lives—and she sensed a slight easing in him as they wove around the brick path toward the small enclave.

Even with the relative calm, Rafe was so focused on any possible threat around them she was surprised he'd heard her.

Oh, yeah, right. Superior reflexes and senses. Damn man could probably hear a dog barking over in Henderson.

"I'm fine. Just processing all you told me."

He'd already put his jacket back on and the material spread across his shoulders in a straight line. "I understand."

"No, I don't think you do. You seem to feel like my questions are designed to make you feel less than, and that's not my purpose."

"I don't—"

Evangeline whirled on him, effectively blocking him from walking any farther. "You don't what? You say you want me to be comfortable, yet *you* don't seem comfortable when I ask questions. I'm curious, Rafe. I want to know more. To understand what shapes you and makes you who you are. I have a right to want to understand, especially since you were the one who brought my parents into things."

"Of course."

Since she saw Contrite Rafe, oh, about never, she took the moment to enjoy herself. The man was a vision. His dark silk suit was immaculate and expensive, and the crisp white of his shirt, open at the throat, only accentuated that aura of power and wealth. Add on the chiseled jaw, dark-as-sin hair and lips a sculptor would weep for and you had the makings of a rather impressive package.

On impulse, she ran a long finger down the line of his jaw. The barest hint of beard stubble against her fingers. "I do have a right to want to understand."

"You do." His hand shot up, holding hers in place. "You also need to understand I don't share this part of me. This part of my life. With anyone outside my family."

"Then I guess it's a big day for both of us."

"In more ways than one."

Before she could sense his movements—and in this case she was hardly going to argue over being the object of those whip-quick reflexes—he leaned in, his mouth pressed to hers. The moment their lips met, something warm and amazing speared through her.

Attraction.

Desire.

Life.

She'd been living in darkness for so long she'd barely realized what she'd been missing, but Rafe brought light and need and a renewal of her spirit.

Her work comforted her. She was driven by it and by her love of horticulture, but if she were honest, it had become a refuge, as well. Being in Rafe's arms pushed her to be more. To take more.

To take all.

She ran her hands over his shoulders, weaving her fingers through the hair at his nape. Corded muscles bunched at the top of his spine and she allowed her fingers to drift there for the moment, enjoying the strength she felt beneath all that warm skin.

He was a man, just as he'd claimed. One with the form and the musculature of a human male, but now she knew there was something more, as well. Even as she tried to get her head fully around what he was, she couldn't deny the appeal of what she felt wrapped up in him. Broad, thick shoulders. Firm, sensual lips. Slim hips that pressed against her with an insistence that set her on fire.

Oh, yes, he was a man.

Heat and fire suffused her body, having nothing to do with Rafe's physical traits and everything to do with how he made her feel. Desire, like liquid gold, filled her up with a delicious fullness that made her body throb with longing. Oh, how she wanted him. The quiet strength and the overt arrogance, the subtle grace and the oft-unconcealed conceit—all made him who he was. A powerful man with an even more powerful secret.

And he'd shared it with her.

He'd let her in and that meant more than she could ever describe.

Her abstract thoughts faded as he pushed them both further. His tongue swept through her mouth, the hard thrust against her mimicking what was surely to come between them.

What she knew, she could no longer deny.

She wanted him.

His hands roamed over her body, hot and dangerous, traveling a sensual path from her waist to her spine and over her rib cage, his thumbs teasing the underside of her breasts. She sucked in a hard breath; the teasing probe of his thumbs—so close to her nipples, yet not touching her in public—a delicious torment.

Evangeline tried to surface from the sensual depths but each time she attempted it, Rafe pulled her back down. The man was a master, somehow soft and hard all at once, as he coaxed responses she didn't even know she possessed.

A light breeze whispered over her skin and she had the abstract thought that they were standing on a public walkway, in the middle of the hotel property. It might be a secluded area, but anyone could still see them. Guests. Security cameras. Her staff.

So why was she finding it hard to care?

One more element of her personality Rafe had managed to change simply with his presence. She wasn't sure how it had happened, but he'd found a way in.

And she never let anyone in. Ever.

Past boyfriends. Fleeting friendships. Even the few extended family members who'd tried looking out for her after her parents died. She'd kept them all at arm's length, never allowing anyone a chance to get close.

Yet all of that had changed with Rafe.

Not only had she let him get close, but she wanted him even closer. Desperately so.

The thoughts that kept her company throughout his sensual assault dimmed as she sensed more than felt a fleeting change in him. Before she could fully register what was happening, he dropped his arms, then pushed her behind him, just as a high-pitched giggle filled the air.

She stared over Rafe's shoulder, her height giving her enough advantage to see who, or what, had him acting with such speed.

"I'm so sorry to interrupt." The words dripped from a nasty grin that had her skin crawling.

"Somehow I doubt that." Tension lit up Rafe's frame from head to toe, and once again Evangeline was fascinated by the warrior that lived beneath the refined, elegant suits. The barely leashed violence she'd sensed at different times was on full display and there was no mistaking the power that lived inside of him.

Although there was a light breeze, the Nevada sun shone high and bright in the sky, warming the air. She couldn't believe it was anything more than a fanciful notion on her side, but the sun seemed to add to his strength, elongating that frame even more as Rafe stood at his full height.

"You've been nosing around in business that's not yours." A gun appeared from behind the man's back, waving and glinting as it caught the sun. Hair stuck out from his head at spiky angles and his eyes darted from her face to Rafe's and back again. The man practically danced on the balls of his feet as he delivered his pronouncement, the erratic, back-and-forth swaying of his limbs a sure sign of his depravity and general instability. "Saving damsels and kids in fires. Saving this pretty lady from the power of my master. The hero routine has drawn some attention."

"So it was Chaos's hand inside the hotel."

"He's everywhere."

Those solemn words fascinated and repulsed as Evangeline took in the odd sort of reverence that limned the attacker's face with a beatific light. Without warning, an image of her father filled her mind's eye. She hadn't thought about this moment in years, yet the instant she did the memory came back, fully formed.

"Sit here, my Evangeline." She ran to him, anxious to sit on Daddy's lap. He rarely invited her to do so and she loved the way it felt to lean her head against his big chest.

She settled where he patted his knee, surprised to feel a lot of bones at her back when she attempted to nestle in. He didn't feel at all like the large daddy she remembered, but she hadn't sat on his lap in a long time, too. She must be forgetting what it felt like.

"I want to tell you a story."

At the offer she nodded and ignored the sensation of bones cradling her. This was her daddy and he wanted to hold her and talk to her and tell her a story. Even if he felt hot and sweaty and smelled sort of sweet, like cherry cough syrup. Ignoring that slight sense of discomfort she focused on the moment. With him. "Tell me the whole thing. No stops."

He laughed at that before tightening his hold. "No stops. I promise.

"In all the earth, over all the lands, there lives a force. It lives inside of us and outside of us and it's the most powerful force in the universe."

"Do you mean God?"

Her question had him stumbling, his arms squeezing around her. She felt squished and at his firm "no" she held back the other questions that bubbled to her lips, just like the way the water bubbled in the fountain at school. This was his story and she'd better remember that.

"Okay."

His squeeze relaxed and he began to tap his fingers on the side of his knee near her legs. "The force is Chaos. And it's more powerful than anything you can imagine."

"Chaos." She whispered the word, rolling it over her tongue. It sounded okay but there was something in her daddy's voice that wasn't okay.

It was the same sound he had when he talked to her mom about a "score." She had no idea what that was, but every time he talked about it he sounded different. Like there was something else inside his mouth, wrapping around his words.

Which was dumb.

But it was still true. She knew when things sounded different. She knew when her parents would have a fight because their voices would get weird just before. And she knew when the seasons were going to change because she could hear the grass and how it sounded different in spring and summer and fall. And in winter she didn't hear it at all. She was a good listener and she spent more of her life listening than talking because talking could get her in trouble. Like asking about God.

"Chaos, Evangeline, is more powerful than anything.

It can divide people. Countries. The world and beyond. It is the source of all power."

"Okay." She nodded, wanting him to believe she understood, even if it seemed like a silly thing. Dividing countries was what led to war. She heard about it on the news that her mother always had droning in the background. Even though she didn't like the stories, she always felt bad when she saw the pictures on the TV.

"Repeat my story back to me, sweetheart."

Daddy's voice pulled her out of her memories. "Tell it back to you?"

"Yes, like a game."

"Your story is about Chaos. And how it's the most powerful force in all the world."

Pride had spilled from his gaze that day, along with a maniacal fervor she could still remember. A hard shiver gripped her spine and she kept her hands at Rafe's waist where he'd placed them.

Chaos.

The opposing force that Rafe and his people battled. She might still be processing Rafe's explanation of who he was and where he came from, but she had lived with the knowledge of what Chaos did to people, its—his?—bleak, miserable influence on human lives a dark blight.

Whatever she'd believed—and there was still a small part of her that hadn't wanted to accept it all—there was no denying what her father was. He'd carried an addictive personality that had been manipulated and used against him. While she couldn't fully forgive him for his choices, she wasn't immune to the injustice of it all.

A man with inherent weakness, enslaved by the manipulation of those weaknesses.

"You two look awful cozy for a pair that was fighting in the lobby a little while ago."

Evangeline wondered how the man knew what had transpired. "How'd you know something like that?"

"I got eyes."

"Full of crazy and drugs." She spat the words back, unable to contain them. When the man amped up the bouncing on his feet, the gun shaking even more in his palm, Rafe laid his hand against hers in silent warning. Belatedly, she remembered his instructions on how he could be killed, but the words were already out of her mouth. Too bad she'd never been all that good at taking orders. "You're just some little minion, doing someone else's business. If Chaos is so all-important, why'd he send you to do his dirty work?"

The narrowing of their assailant's eyes indicated she'd struck her mark. Clearly this minion had never considered his place in the pecking order.

Or the raw power Rafe Stavros could wield to take him down.

"Thanks for the assist, darling."

Before she could levy any additional taunts, Rafe lashed out, fire expanding from his arms with the simplest flick of his wrist. A terrible cry went up as the flames reached the Hunter, his hands flying up to shield his face. The move was enough to distract him and Rafe used the moment to leap on the guy and disarm him of the gun that still wavered in his hand.

The wicked-looking piece fell to the ground and Evangeline watched it, her gaze darting between the gun and the struggling men on the ground. Rafe had the physical advantage, but the Hunter likely had addiction and a quick high on his side. He fought like a demon—even if he wasn't fully imbued with one's power—and scratched and clawed at Rafe as they rolled on the ground.

Sparks flew off of Rafe's body, a clear sign he looked for another opportunity to unleash his fire. Where she'd been protected when pressed up against him, she suddenly sensed she might be in danger if the two of them weren't touching. Which was likely the problem with the Hunter. As long as their bodies touched, Rafe's fire couldn't harm him.

She needed a distraction.

With a loud war cry, Evangeline leaped for the gun, scrambling around the two men through the finely mowed lawn. She reached, stretching for the gun, wrapping her fingers around the heavy piece. The metal was warm in her hand and slightly wet from the other man's sweat. Shaking off the urge to scream in disgust, she focused on maintaining her grip. The handle fit to her palm, a fit that instantly brought back memories of her childhood. Bad people had come to her parents' door, their own guns in hand, demanding any number of things.

She'd always believed the gun was the signifier that they were bad and she hadn't necessarily changed her opinion since.

Backing away, she focused on Rafe and off the weapon. The moment she was free of him, she screamed her position. "Rafe. I'm away. Do it now!"

His gaze briefly connected with hers before he pushed the man off with a thick grunt. Those broad shoulders bunched with effort and he kicked with his legs, using his body's full momentum to push off the threat.

The moment Rafe was free, he ignited, his entire body a wash of flame. Evangeline watched—captivated—as that fire stole over his opponent in a wash of reds and oranges.

The blaze consumed the captured man, who was screaming in agony as Rafe's fire coated his body. It was only when Rafe stumbled back, his hand extended for the gun, that Evangeline understood what he wanted.

She checked the safety, concerned she was handling things properly. Unsure of the exact protocol and afraid to injure Rafe, she bent and tossed the gun lightly across the grass, the muzzle pointed away from him. It landed with a soft thud and without going off.

The flames ceased immediately, vanishing as if they never were. The blaze that consumed the Hunter vanished as well, even as the fire left an imprint on his body. Without second-guessing himself, Rafe retrieved the gun and ended the screams with a lone, merciful shot.

The gun fell from his hand, its thud on the ground considerably harder than hers. Before she could even question it, Rafe turned from the dead man and pulled her into his arms. "I'm sorry. I'm so very sorry."

"Rafe, it's—" He pulled her close, pressing her head against his chest.

"It's not okay. You shouldn't have seen that."

"Rafe, I'm fine."

Hard shudders racked his body and she ran her hands over his back, making circular motions across the broad expanse. The motions didn't soothe as much as gentle, his heaving chest slowing beneath her ministrations.

"I'm sorry."

"Are you okay? You're so shaken."

"I'm… It's not." He stumbled over the words, the reaction so unlike the man she'd observed for the past year Evangeline had to wonder at the transformation. "It's not okay."

"He was trying to kill you."

"My fire isn't for killing. It's not meant to torture another."

"Rafe. He was going to hurt you and he clearly felt no remorse."

Rafe bent his head, pressing his forehead to hers. "I couldn't let him hurt you. There were other ways for me but I couldn't let him touch you."

"Shh. Shh, now." She continued to rub those circles

over his back, desperate to soothe the remorse that now gripped him. The minutes passed and she became aware of a buzzing around them. Gabe's voice was louder than the rest as he gave out orders to several people, his security team descending en masse. She assumed they worked for him as she recognized a few on the staff quickly covering the body before lifting it onto a gurney.

"That was close."

Rafe lifted his head but kept his arms tight around her. "How did he get on the property?"

"We don't know."

"And earlier? The demonstration in the lobby?"

Gabe frowned, his lips pressing into a narrow line before he spoke. "We don't know that, either."

"So they're here. They have access and they've come to do battle." Rafe spat the words, his fingers flexing against her shoulder.

"We don't know that."

"You know we do, Gabe. Troy and Victor were the advance warning system. We came looking for them and we exposed ourselves."

Although she understood the brothers' need to talk to each other, the mention of her former employees had Evangeline piping up. "What about Troy and Victor?"

"They were shills. And they played us. We thought their goal was to get inside the Archangel. It was really to draw us out."

"When? Where?" Her mind whirled with the possibilities. "I only fired them two days ago. I know they haven't been back on the grounds."

Rafe dropped his arms and the moment he did he took any sense of warmth and comfort with him. "Gabe and I went looking for them last night."

"You were with me last night."

"After. We went after."

She wasn't sure why—it certainly wasn't the date—but something about Rafe's answer stuck in her belly with all the finesse of razor blades. "You were so convinced I was hiding something you went after what you believed to be my connection."

Rafe remained silent, his dark eyes pleading with hers. Gabe wasn't so delicate. "Yes, we did. And we'd do it again. We need to protect ourselves."

"And in protecting yourselves, you made yourself more vulnerable to attack. Hell, you've brought the enemy to your door."

Evangeline's parting shot still rang in his ears an hour later as he paced Gabe's office. Images of the burning Hunter filled his thoughts, a strange, flaming complement to Evangeline's words. Gabe had remained strangely silent, pouring them each a whiskey and then settling into the large couch that dominated one wall of his office.

"The bastard was right there. Waiting for us. Stalking us, really." Rafe had long emptied the glass and continued to pace with the heavy crystal in his hand, torn between throwing it and hitting himself in the head in frustration.

"He got on the grounds without incident," Gabe agreed. "Strolled right on through the promenade entrance."

"He wasn't in the database of suspicious persons?"

"Nothing. Walked in pleased as punch. Tossed a few dollars in the slots and then headed on out to the grounds."

Rafe stared into the bottom of his glass, the slightest remnants of amber liquid coating the bottom. To hell and back, they had a freaking problem.

"Walk me through the wind again. Nothing showed on the cameras? You couldn't see me or Evangeline? Couldn't see us fighting against all that demonic force?"

"Not a thing. Evangeline happens across the statues and attempts to flag down security. Moments later she vanishes out of vision of the screen and the hallway looks calm and even."

"So we're dealing with an alternate dimension."

"Alternate. Parallel." Gabe drained his own drink. "It's the same reason your rotisserie act the other night on the grounds didn't show on the cameras. Our power isn't human, yet it's not divine. It simply exists in its own place."

Rafe wasn't sure he bought the whole parallel universe thing—he was who he was—but something in Gabe's tone had his temper flaring. He considered his brother his closest ally, but the past few days had found them at odds more often than not.

"If you have something to say to me, get it the hell out."

"I don't have anything to say."

"You sure? Because you've been a stubborn pain in my ass ever since the other night, poking at me about my Rejuvenation. You think I asked for this?"

"Hell no."

"Then what do you have to say to me?"

Gabe marched to the sideboard and poured another few fingers of whiskey. He downed both of them in one long swallow, his subtle wince proof he wasn't quite as stoic as he pretended to be. "I think you were careless. Which, I've already told you."

"Careless how? We run a business."

"Your regeneration was upon you and you couldn't make it back to the penthouse."

"I was entertaining clients and doing my job."

"No, you pulled the usual Rafael Stavros bullshit, which is that no one else can do your job. You're too gods-awful important that no one can replace you. Or help you. Or offer you any support."

Each word seemed to be ripped from his brother's throat by some otherworldly force and Rafe couldn't do much but stand there and take it. And wonder at the vitriol that sat beneath Gabe's litany of sins.

"You think that's what this is about? Some dumb streak of pride?"

"You tell me."

He'd come back to his brother's office expecting support. A caring moment or two as he worked through the reality of what he'd done to kill Chaos's minion. He hadn't expected a drubbing that hit far too close to home. "How long have you felt like this?"

"A while. It's been building. You're the face of the Archangel and you do it well. But hell—" Gabe broke off and rubbed at his shoulder where it met his neck. "Hell, Rafe. You put yourself in the line of fire. You're a public figure and you cut a swath across the property each and every damn day. It's like you've been doing everything in your power to draw their notice. Their attention."

"And now I did."

The realization sat heavy on him, whispering through his mind as part accusation, part truth. He had been out and about as the public face of the Archangel. And while they'd managed to stay off the Hunters' radar, Rafe well knew the threat was out there. All the Hunters needed was one break—one clue that there were Helios living in Las Vegas—and they'd make their move.

Only this was no longer about him and his people. Now it was about Evangeline, too. Because they might not know how to fight him, but a human female would be an easy mark.

Chapter 8

Evangeline plucked at her uniform—cargo pants and a tank—and tried not to feel like an interloper in the refined, rarified office environment of the Archangel. She'd not felt like going back to work, even after Rafe and Gabe deposited her in the lobby with her crew, so she'd wandered the property instead.

Through the casino, intrigued by the patrons, some of whom screamed in triumph while others groaned at another loss. She smiled at the couple obviously on their honeymoon, kissing lavishly each time they had a successful spin on the roulette wheel. She'd even watched in fascination as an older woman managed three slot machines, her cane and her purse as effective a deterrent to anyone wanting the machines as the evil eye she shot anyone who got too close.

From there she'd headed toward the restaurants, forcing herself back down the entertainment corridor. The statues were positioned where they'd started, either replaced by some supernatural force or put back by the ever-grumpy Arturo and his team. Either way, everything was where it belonged.

Her gaze drifted next over the holiday installations, pleased with the even distribution up and down the hallway. She'd not thought of them in the midst of their escape from the wind tunnel, but now that she looked, she was happy to see they were unharmed. Large trees—a mix of pine and fir—all complemented by more of her poinsettias, along with acres of tulle and ribbon.

It was almost Christmas.

And how had that happened?

Aside from its impact on her installations, she'd barely registered that the holidays were upon them. But once she did think about it, the change was more than obvious. Music blared through the casino, a mix of what usually played, along with odes to Santa Claus, being good and filling one's stocking. Outfits had changed, too. Women wore a few more sparkles and there were more pops of red and green in people's clothing.

Even the entertainment had changed. The hotel's choir had begun making stops around the casino and shops, taking requests for any number of holiday tunes while storekeepers had all decorated their storefronts with a mix of fake snow, glittering snowflakes, and more subtle hints of red and green.

"Evangeline."

His voice was quiet when he spoke her name, but she didn't miss the question underneath. "Yes?"

"I'm surprised you're here."

She turned to Rafe, bracing herself for the sensual assault that always managed a one-two punch each time she was in his presence. It was odd to realize something had changed this time. The attraction was still there—an entire army of butterflies, bats and a few hammerhead sharks had taken up residence in her stomach, but they were matched by something else.

Empathy.

Dark circles rimmed his eyes and it was hard to ignore the bleak, winter-cold look that had settled deep in his eyes. That liquid silver, so tempting and alluring, seemed to have frozen over, replaced with a cautious, wary light she'd never seen before.

And in protecting yourselves...you've brought the enemy to your door.

Her own words echoed in her mind. They'd kept her company over and over as she'd walked the grounds, a harsh reminder of how she'd behaved. She'd lacked compassion. Worse, she'd attacked his pride at a moment of deep vulnerability.

Rafe might be many things, but he wasn't a malicious killer. The sheer agony that had painted his features after he'd killed the intruder was solid proof of that fact. Yet she'd pushed him anyway, poking into a wound that had run raw.

"You shouldn't be here. Go home for a few days until things settle."

"Settle?"

"Gabe and I are working on a plan. We'll have this handled in a few days."

"Rafe, there's nothing to handle." Although she kept her voice low she was well aware of Rafe's coordinator sitting across the lobby. She gestured to his office, then walked on as if that were point enough. Since he followed, she waited until the door closed before she picked up where she'd left off. "Chaos knows where you are. His minions know where you are. The battle's begun."

"It's not that simple."

"You sure?"

"For starters, Chaos can't be everywhere. Hence needing the minions in the first place. Second, his choice in soldiers leaves a lot to be desired. When word gets around about Bruce—" He broke off, his eyes clouding once more. "Bruce was the man from earlier. Once word gets around to his friends how swiftly we dealt with him, there isn't going to be a group lining up to be next. Chaos's minions are going to go into retreat."

"You don't know that."

"No, but I have some mighty favorable odds." When she said nothing, he simply shifted gears. "You were spotted walking the grounds before. You shouldn't have done that."

"Of course I should have." Whatever trepidation she might have had entering the main concourse once more had faded at the throngs of people milling around her. None had paid her any mind, yet they'd been there. Fully present. "It wasn't like before."

"How?"

"The people vanished before. A nifty trick, to be sure, but also a tip-off to what I should expect if it happens again."

"You're sure about that?"

"Aren't you?"

Their questions were stilted and more than a little awkward and she struggled to find the right words. She'd been harsh earlier and while she'd never worried much about speaking her mind, it also weighed on her that Rafe was coming off the adrenaline rush of a kill shot.

She hadn't missed the layers of remorse and sadness and shock that had painted his features ghostly pale as soon as he'd ended Bruce's life. Whatever Rafe was—and she was still struggling to fully process that—he wasn't a killer. And even acting in self-defense, the act of taking a life weighed on him.

It weighed on her, as well.

She wanted to feel sorry for what happened, yet all she

could muster was a vague sense of distaste for the wasted life that had stood before her, trying to kill her and Rafe. What did that make her? A monster like her father?

The tears spilled up and over—hot and immediate—before she could stop them. Without questioning the urge, she raced into Rafe's arms, letting out a hard rush of air as their bodies met.

"Shh, now. It's okay."

"No, it's not. That thing was not okay. Nothing about this morning was okay. But we're okay." She leaned back, searching his gaze for some understanding. "*We're* okay."

His arms came around her as he buried his face in her neck. Hot, whispered words floated over her neck, his lips a brand against her collarbone. "We're okay."

Comfort, warm and secure, filled her as she stood in the circle of his arms. He'd shed his coat from earlier, left in nothing but his shirt and slacks, and she reveled in the warmth of his body and the solid strength of him pressed against her.

Had she ever felt this safe? This protected?

He'd stood for her today. When her life was threatened, he'd been the one to protect her. He'd killed for her to keep her safe.

"Evangeline." He murmured her name over and over again, his lips playing across the sensitive skin of her throat and neck. What had started as an act of sharing comfort rapidly changed, the sensuality of the moment not lost on either of them. She wanted him.

And in that moment, she could think of nothing she wanted more than to have Rafe inside of her. Moving within her. Filling her with his life essence, creating something new and fresh and life-affirming.

That was the harshest reality of Bruce, of her father, of all the others Chaos had tricked into service. They all lived half lives, devoted to a master who neither cared for them nor ultimately fulfilled them.

She'd spent her life avoiding that path, knowing full well what the possible consequences were. Yet she'd had no idea that she'd also closed herself off to feeling anything. By avoiding strong emotions and any possibility of loss of control, she'd also missed out on affection. On desire.

And on love.

That thought shimmered to life as she kissed Rafe, her hands cradling his cheeks as he made love to her with his mouth.

She'd missed out on this. The life-affirming joy of falling in love. And she couldn't think of a better time to start making up for it.

"Love me, Rafe. Here. Now."

Rafe heard her, yet wasn't quite sure he could believe it. Lifting his lips from hers, he searched her gaze for any hint that she wasn't ready for what flared between them. "Are you sure? Here?"

"Yes and yes." A bright, gorgeous smile lit her lips. "If you don't mind a striptease that includes cargos and a tank top."

"I can't think of anything sexier."

"Well, then. How can I resist?"

You can't. Because we're meant for each other.

It was irrational and unexpected and in complete odds with his life and his personal code, but as primal need rose up in his chest, Rafe found he wasn't in the mood to analyze it. It just was.

He wanted Evangeline.

And for some glorious reason she wanted him back. After all they'd shared, all he'd revealed and, hardest of all, what he'd done, she still wanted him.

Wanted what was between them.

He kissed her again, his lips finding hers, his tongue sweeping into her mouth before the sensual contact abruptly ended. The long, lithe body that filled his hands vanished as well as Evangeline danced out of his reach. "I promised you that striptease."

"I'd rather strip you myself."

"That's just too bad." She pointed toward the leather couch in the corner of his office. "Settle in and enjoy the show."

Rafe did as he was ordered, the carefree smile on her face as much of an enticement as her slender stomach, revealed as her tank rose up at her waist. Her hands drifted briefly over her skin, lightly caressing that visible expanse before drifting toward the closure of her pants. Her fingers hovered over the button that centered just below her navel and he itched to leap forward and undo it himself.

Heat suffused him, of a far different nature than the fire that lived beneath his skin. Where one inside provided a renewal of flesh and bone, muscle and sinew, this was a fire that stoked the spirit. Higher and higher, his fever rose as he watched Evangeline dance, her moves as old as time yet agelessly fresh.

Endlessly enticing.

Moment after moment spun out, as sleek as silk and stronger than steel, as each article of clothing fell to the side. What she missed in expertise, she more than made up for in eagerness and Rafe was captivated. Captured in her spell and unwilling to look away, even for a moment.

"You've grown quiet." Evangeline danced closer, now clad in nothing but bra and panties. The material that covered her was barely scraps, surprisingly sexy underwear for a woman who dug in the dirt around his hotel all day.

"Looks like you've kept a few secrets hidden under your wardrobe, Ms. Kennedy."

"A girl's got to have a few secrets."

Unwilling to wait a moment longer to touch her, Rafe came off the couch in one swift move, dragging her into his arms. "I couldn't be happier you're willing to share them with me."

"You're the only one I want to share them with."

The restraint he had to exhibit outside on the lawn vanished as he was finally able to pull her fully into his arms. He was desperate for her, the feel of her skin under the pads of his fingers driving that temperature ever higher.

How had he lived without this? Hell, it wasn't so much about living without it; he'd not even known it existed. Every moment up until now had been an illusion—a half life—now that he had Evangeline in his arms.

And Rafe refused to waste any more time.

He used his position near the couch to walk them both backward, pulling her into his arms and dragging them down onto the well-padded leather. He used the drop to pull her on top of his lap, positioning her legs on either side of his thighs. Unwilling to give her a moment to catch her breath, he used her position to set the pace, his fingers slipping beneath the edge of her panties to the hot, wet heat of her core.

He devoured her high-pitched scream with a kiss, well aware his office was private but not soundproof. Her muffled moan was the sweetest music as he played her flesh, slipping first one, then a second finger into her tight warmth. That luscious heat captured him, utterly responsive to his touch as he pushed her higher and higher toward her climax.

He felt the quivers begin from the inside and used the telltale signs of her body to push her over to completion. With one hand firmly anchoring her back, he lifted his gaze to watch her, utterly captivated as her head fell back, her body suffused in pleasure.

An answering response began from somewhere deep

inside of him. It came from his very center, beyond who he was—even beyond who he knew himself to be—as he watched Evangeline in the throes of her orgasm.

She was a gift beyond measure and he marveled at the deep pleasure he drew from simply watching her.

The moments drifted by, the urgent demands of his still-unsated body fading as they hung, suspended in the moment. Slowly, she came back to herself, a lopsided grin filling her face when she finally opened her eyes and glanced down at their bodies. "I think we forgot something."

"You think so?"

"Since you're still fully clothed, I'd say yes."

"I prefer to think of the last little while as our first course."

"We're not having dinner."

He leaned forward to nip a kiss just below her ear. "No, but we are feasting."

A soft sigh slipped from her lips, whispering across his ear. He thought it was the sweetest sound he'd ever heard.

"You're an awfully patient man."

Her words stilled his motions as he kissed a path along her neck. He'd never have described himself in that way. In fact, he'd often thought his impatience was one of his less favorable traits. "You think so? I never considered myself particularly good at patience."

"Then you don't see what I see."

Even though it was an odd conversation to have partway through making love, Rafe was curious enough to hear her out. "I'm hardly a patient man, Evangeline."

"Don't confuse knowing what you want with impatience. One suggests an ability to leap on opportunity when it's presented or to make one when none exists. Impatience, on the other hand, is plowing ahead without any sense of why you're pushing or where you're going."

It was an interesting observation and one he'd never heard before.

"There are many who say Las Vegas was founded on impatience."

"For the gambler, yes. For those who chose to make the arid desert their home, I'd say it's opportunity."

Since her observation closely hit on all the reasons his grandfather and extended family had settled in Las Vegas so many decades prior, he could only stop and stare.

"People confuse quick decisions with an inability to be patient and the two aren't related." It was her turn to lean forward and press her lips to his. "While I'd like to point to our current situation as a textbook example of same, I find I'm too impatient to see what comes next to fully make my point."

"This isn't about opportunity?"

"You and me, perhaps." She reached for the buttons on his shirt. "These clothes. Now these are all about impatience." When she leaned in and pressed her lips to his throat, Rafe suddenly realized the question of opportunity or impatience was rather moot.

Evangeline was in his arms and that was all that mattered.

The clothing that had provided such a barrier between their skin vanished in moments. Rafe quickly obliged her by standing and shucking the rest of it off, rather than try to disrobe from beneath her, and in moments had her flat beneath him on his office couch. She heard the discreet crinkle of a condom and knew where he'd stashed it on the floor in close reach, touched at his level of concern for her.

Her bra and panties quickly followed at the lightest touch of his fingers before he covered her fully with his body.

"You're sure you want this?"

The question was so unexpected—especially after what

they'd already shared—that she stopped her exploration of the firm lines of his chest, her gaze lifting to meet his. "How can you ask me that?"

"It's just that. Today. After today. Earlier, outside. There's no going back from here."

She lifted her head to press a soft, gentle kiss to his lips, his brief moment of hesitance melting her insides to a warm, gooey caramel consistency. His question was so at odds with the firm erection that pressed against her thigh and the erotic moments they'd already shared, she couldn't imagine he was nearing the point of pain with his need for release.

Yet he'd again show his care and his concern.

"I've never been more sure about anything. Ever. You protected me. You took care of me. And while I wouldn't call this gratitude sex, I don't want to go back. I want to go forward." She pressed one more kiss against his lips, the chaste press of flesh a subtle—yet perfect—complement to their nakedness. "I want to go forward with you."

Whether they were words he was waiting to hear or the deeper acceptance of who he was, Evangeline wasn't sure. But when he quickly pulled on the condom, then positioned himself at the opening of her body, she suddenly found she didn't care.

The hard thrusts of his body took hers back to the edge of reason and she opened herself up to the magic that lived between them.

His long, sure strokes set the rhythm and she tapped into that primal beat, matching him as he moved. Thrust for thrust, she met him at every moment, straining for what she knew he offered. Tremors rocked through her body, every inch of her flesh sensitized to the feel of him. With her lips, she traced a path across the rounded strength of his shoulder, the slightly tangy taste a heady mix of salt and sweat that only added another dimension to the moment.

He was hers.

All that strength and power and heat was for her.

Strained for her. Reached for her. And, when the moment was absolutely perfect, released for her. Evangeline knew the moment his control neared its breaking point and allowed her body to follow along, falling with him into the spiraling abyss of passion and all-consuming need.

But it was the very last moment, just before her world shattered, that she knew she'd treasure forever.

In the quietest tones, with a whisper of reverence, he uttered her name. "Evangeline."

And she knew she'd never be the same.

Joy suffused her limbs as she lay in the circle of Rafe's arms, her body still quivering from the crazy-amazing moments they'd shared.

"You okay?"

"Hmm?" Evangeline turned to Rafe with a sleepy smile, the thick plushness of the carpet beneath her back like a bed of roses.

"Did I hurt you?"

Shock painted his gaze when she didn't answer immediately and she couldn't hold back the giggle at the panic that tightened his frame and drew his mouth into a dark frown. Lifting up, she pressed a hard, smacking kiss to those down-turned lips before settling back against his side. "Rafe Stavros. I feel so good I'm surprised a unicorn hasn't walked through that door, ready to deliver Christmas presents."

The rumble started low in his chest before gathering steam. It felt good to make him laugh, but it felt even better to do it together. Long moments later, as they both wiped away tears, he struggled to sit up. "Unicorns?"

"With Christmas presents. Don't forget that part." She glanced around. "Speaking of which, where's your tree?"

"What tree?"

"Your Christmas tree?"

"Don't you think we have enough in the lobby? I think you bought out a forest with the budget for the front entrance."

"But you need one in here."

At his lack of comprehension she jumped to her feet, uncaring of her nakedness. "You really have nothing? No decorations or greens or even a few desk ornaments? It's so sterile and imperious in here."

"Imperious?"

"You know you love it." He took a moment but when he finally nodded—*imperiously*—she pressed on. "You need a Christmas tree and decorations. I've got some fresh greens I can bring up and a tree."

"I don't need those things."

"Why not? It's Christmas."

"I never bother. The hotel's filled with festive cheer. I don't need a forest in my office or my home."

She stilled, well aware her mouth had dropped. "You don't have a tree in your home?"

"No."

"Why not?"

"What if I catch it on fire?"

"You make it a habit to just burst into flame?" Before he could answer, she added, "When you're not running yourself ragged and entertaining high rollers too late into the night."

"No, of course I don't."

With a soft shake of her head, she was already six steps ahead, gathering what she needed in her mind. "You're such a holiday downer. You do realize you're on the verge of killing my unicorn?"

"I what?"

"But don't worry. I have just the thing to bring her back to life."

Chapter 9

Evangeline fussed over the tree skirt, fluffing and re-fluffing the tartan plaid material. Although she'd been impressed with the ruthless efficiency of the "supply closet," as the hotel's prop room was called, she'd had little use up until now for things that had been used in the past. Each of her installations had to be newer and better than what had come before.

But as a shopping exercise—oh, man, had she hit the mother lode.

Betsy, the closet's owner and resident drill sergeant, had stoically stared at her for the first ten minutes but had reluctantly—then happily—gotten into the act. The two of them had ripped open boxes full of decorations, raided bins of ornaments and found themselves tangled in about one thousand yards of garland before they realized each had been digging through opposite ends.

By the time they finished, Evangeline had found just what she'd come for. She'd tackled Rafe's office first, his admin ushering her in in secret once Rafe left to glad-hand the high rollers. They'd put up the tree and efficiently decorated it in muted golds and powerful reds, scurrying back out of his office like little elves nearly an hour later.

Satisfied the office was no longer a dismal, commanding wasteland of power and ruthless efficiency, she moved on to the coup de grâce. His apartment.

Rafe had given her the keys earlier, inviting her to make herself comfortable before he joined her for dinner. She'd used the time to her advantage, setting up the tree on its stand and laying down the tartan as a tree skirt.

The decorating, they'd do together.

Standing back, she assessed the towering tree and the boxes of ornaments she'd lugged up earlier. Reds and greens, golds and silvers reflected light back into the room, a vivid display of holiday cheer.

Would Rafe enjoy it? Did he even realize what he was missing?

Perhaps a better question, Evangeline realized, was if she understood what she'd been missing.

She'd always loved her work but something washed over her—warm and happy—way down deep inside as she thought about sharing her work with Rafe. Not as a member of his staff, but as an equal. As a lover. And even more wonderfully surprising, as a friend.

She had someone to share her talents with. Not nameless, faceless patrons or competitors from hotels down the Strip, or even the cool brass who owned the place where she worked.

But someone who—just maybe—cared for her as she cared for him.

Chaos floated through the secondary plane, watching over the streets and surrounding areas of Las Vegas. The gods may have locked him up, but all their power couldn't fully contain his essence.

Even if their damn chains did ensure he had to channel his precious energy into bumbling, inept minions who had the freedom to do his bidding.

And what had it gotten him?

Frost had promised him his next attacker would make good on their goals and get into the Archangel undetected, but the zoned-out moron sent in for the job was now a dead French fry. Worse, though Frost hid it well, Chaos was well aware he was at his wit's end to find another subject to do his bidding. Fear had spread quickly among the addictive set and they'd all scurried to their burrows like frightened rats. Even promises of a fresh score for a job well done hadn't paid dividends like they'd expected.

Which meant he needed another approach. Humans only went so far and his powers were limited on this plane. Unlike the Helios, he wasn't mortal and there were the damned rules.

Always rules.

Frigging Titans and their odd sense of supreme order. What the hell good was being a god if you couldn't rig the game to your benefit?

So he hovered, swirling through the atmosphere like a wraith as he considered his plans. In the blink of an eye he moved to another casino, his focus on the craps table as he hovered low. Some woman was throwing dice like a champ, the entire table screaming and cheering when she tossed a ten—the point she'd been aiming for.

Chaos watched, bored yet intrigued at the avarice that painted the human faces around the table as they, one by one, reached for their winnings. When the money had been paid out and the game begun again, he watched as the roller threw a seven amid many cheers. Then another one. And then a six.

He knew the game—that knowledge was something that simply existed in his conscious fully formed—and he began whispering around the table to increase bets. When the amounts weren't enough, he then encouraged play on the sucker bets in the middle of the felt table. Once all was laid out as he'd intended, he leaned over as the woman tossed the dice—she nearly had her six—and then he flipped a single die one more digit.

Groans lit up the table, and the loss of the point—and all the money wagered on its arrival—filled the air. Several gamblers gave her grudging thanks and good wishes, but as the woman's face fell in disappointment, he knew he had his answer.

And wondered how he hadn't thought of it sooner.

He needed others to do his bidding, but he was hardly limited to using Hunters. How had he been so shortsighted?

Rafe rubbed the back of his neck, willing away the strange sense of premonition that tingled there at the base. He wasn't prone to the fanciful—he kept an army of well-trained security experts for that—but he also knew the stakes had changed. Their world was threatened, and no amount of planning or watchfulness could change that.

And then there was Evangeline.

The woman hadn't been far from his thoughts for the past six hours. She filled his mind—images of her, the scent of her and the warm, willing imprint of her body wrapped around his. He'd nearly abandoned his afternoon commitments, but had persevered, pushing through mind-numbing discussions of the stock market with his high rollers and an endless meeting with the gaming commission that nearly made his ears bleed.

But now he was home.

He could already sense her as he pushed through the

door, muted lighting and soft music spilling through the entrance in welcome.

When he came face-to-face with a ten-foot tree he nearly lost his footing. "What is this?"

"Your unicorn."

Rafe shook his head, the silliness of their earlier conversation taking root. He'd sensed the tree was important to her, but hadn't realized quite how much. "Looks like a tree to me."

"Oh, it is that, yet it's so much more." She drifted over to him and pressed a kiss to his cheek. Her daily uniform of cargos and a tank, with a long-sleeved shirt wrapped around her waist for good measure, had vanished, replaced by another frothy concoction he believed he'd seen down in one of the boutiques.

"You'll have to enlighten me. I'm not that good with trees. Or holidays, for that matter."

"You don't celebrate?"

"We congregate. My family is large and my father has always insisted on throwing something lavish. It's not so much a holiday as a day of feasting, drinking and platooning back and forth to the security center to keep an eye on things at the hotel."

"The casino business never rests."

"Never."

She patted his chest. "Poor rich hotel magnate. Looks like we'll have to bring the holiday spirit to you, then."

He watched in fascination as his holiday sprite did her level best to do just that. In a matter of moments, she had his coat off, a drink in his hand and was gesturing him across the room to the feast she'd laid out on his dining room table. "First we eat. Then we decorate."

"I have to work for my holiday?"

"Absolutely."

"Seems like a vicious plot."

"Or part of the fun."

While there was a large part of him that would be perfectly content with dinner, followed by endless hours of lovemaking through all the rooms of his apartment, Rafe had to admit there was a simple sort of joy in watching her. She was happy. Lighter, somehow. And for the first time, he realized more had changed in her than the sensual moments they'd shared.

The woman who powered around his property like a whirling dervish, never sitting or settling, had used that endless motion as a way to hide.

"What are you looking at?" Evangeline looked up from where she twirled angel-hair pasta around her fork.

"You."

"You look like you have questions."

"No questions." He laid down his fork. "I've come to an understanding. Of you."

He liked that he could keep her off guard, but the hint of wariness that crept into her gaze was a clear indicator of how much in her past still haunted her.

"It's a good understanding. A happy one." When that wariness faded, replaced with the brighter shades of curiosity, he continued. "You've made an incredible contribution here at the Archangel. Your installations are the best in the business and your passion for your work is visible in everything you do."

"I sense a *but*. Am I being fired for having sex with the boss?"

At her wry smile he could only shake his head. "Cheeky woman. You're not paying attention."

"I am. And I appreciate the compliment but I do what I love. I'd say the same about you. About Gabe. About Madelina down in the spa. You and your family have created a magical oasis here in the middle of the desert and it's a professional privilege to be a part of that."

"You really don't see it, do you?" The tension he'd seen in her shoulders was still vivid in his mind. Evangeline had carried the weight of the world on her slim frame and he was beyond pleased to see that lifting.

"I guess I don't."

"You're free. I see the smile that reaches your eyes and the relaxation that fills you and it makes me happy. It's like you've become untethered, somehow, to what held you back in your past. It's wonderful to see."

"You're a big part of that. What's happened over the past few days." Her gaze stayed level on his. "What has been the outcome of something I felt from the very first moment."

That first moment they met. She speaking her mind to their poor, hapless horticulture lead who'd been drunk and sloppy on the job. Rafe had carried that image in his mind all year, clinging to it like a lightning rod every time he saw her, so he wouldn't be tempted to get too close.

That, and a dossier full of details on parents who didn't love or support her or see the beautiful gem of a person they'd created.

Of all the oddities in his life, he'd never questioned his parents' love. While they'd determinedly lived their own lives, traveling, spending time with family and seeding the Stavros hotel empire throughout the world—all while his father built his own career and reputation—they'd always been there for him. He'd always known he was loved.

"Maybe Gabe was wrong."

"About?"

"Maybe my early Rejuvenation was my body giving me a kick in the ass to make a few changes in my life." He extended a hand, taking one of hers tightly in his own. "A change that is more welcome than I could have ever described."

* * *

"The garland and tinsel go on last."

"We need both?" Rafe stared at her over a long strand of garland, currently stretched between his hands like a skein of yarn.

"It will be pretty."

"It'll be gaudier than a whorehouse."

"You spend a lot of time in those, Stavros?"

He had the decency to look contrite and Evangeline fought to keep a smile from her face. "No, but this is Vegas. I'm not totally ignorant of the other entertainment options that draw my customers out of my hotel and away from my casino."

"I never considered the competitive angle."

"I did. And let me tell you, it takes a bite."

"Poor, powerful hotel magnate."

He nodded, his gaze solemn. "Perhaps you can console me and make me feel better about it."

"Perhaps I can."

Holiday music drifted out of hidden speakers, a low, jazzy version of some well-known Christmas carols, and Evangeline used the swinging beat to dance around Rafe, sliding a large, shiny red ball into a gap on the branches.

"Thank you for this."

With his hands still wrapped in the garland, Rafe leaned over and pressed a hot kiss to the shell of her ear before following it up with a lazy drift over her neck. A wave of heat suffused her nerves, that ready desire flaring to life in a near explosion.

How did he do this? Even more amazing, how could he? She was a levelheaded woman who had never considered herself wrapped in her baser nature. Yet the moment he touched her, everything inside of her stood up and focused on him.

Only on him.

He plied her with kisses, that tantalizing journey from ear to neck to collarbone, shifting, morphing as he found her mouth. With his hands still wrapped up, all he had was his mouth and oh, wow, could the man kiss. Her knees grew weaker as he pressed his lips to hers, using teeth and tongue to further coax a response.

"Rafe." His name drifted out on a sigh.

She used his temporary capture in the garland to explore the hard planes and angles of his body. Those broad shoulders, so impressive beneath the crisp white shirt he wore. The solid expanse of muscle that architected his chest, firm as a sculpture, yet able to yield to her touch. Still, she drifted on, her fingers following a lazy path over his body.

The closure of his slacks beckoned and she slid open the material before slipping her hands beneath his briefs. She found him hard and ready for her, the warmest sort of welcome, and she plied his body with the same urgent tenderness he'd applied earlier.

A long, low moan ripped from his throat as she curved over and around the generous length of him. With each passing moment, a sensual magic seemed to wrap around them, more binding than the garland that currently wrapped his hands.

"I seem to be at a disadvantage." The words vibrated against her ear where he pressed his mouth, hard shudders racking his body as she pressed him ever onward.

"How's that?"

"Your hands are free—" He broke off as she captured the wetness at the tip and used it to further lubricate her actions up and down his shaft. "And mine are otherwise engaged."

"Maybe it's good to give up control every once in a while."

"Evange—" Her name faded on his lips as his pleasure overtook him. Heavier shudders ripped through his body with all the force of a tidal wave, made that much more luscious by the capture of his hands.

She used his disadvantage to her advantage and sank to the floor, her mouth quickly replacing her hands as she drew him through his orgasm.

The garland fell in a jumbled ball beside them, his suddenly free hands wrapping around her shoulders to pull her against him. She sensed his urgency and his rapidly fading control, but she refused to stand, linking their fingers instead.

And that's when she knew the sweetest feminine victory.

His release was magnificent, the moment a gift, just like all the moments with Rafe that had come before.

But in *that* moment—that bright, singular shining moment—Evangeline knew what it was to love. To give selflessly to another. To care deeply for their happiness and their pleasure.

To share it with them.

For in that moment, Evangeline knew she'd fallen irrevocably, irresistibly and undeniably in love.

Chapter 10

"How does it work?"

"Hmm?"

"Your fire. How does it work?"

While he appreciated the interest more than he could describe, Rafe had no idea how the woman even had the strength to speak, let alone ask questions. He pulled her tighter against his body and let one eye drift open to read the clock: two in the morning.

After the mind-bending explosion of pleasure he'd experienced in his living room, they'd worked their way through his apartment. From the long formal table he kept in his dining room to the multijetted shower in his master bathroom to—just a few minutes ago—his bed.

"Seriously. Tell me how it works." Evangeline scrambled out from beneath the weight of his arm, scooting herself back against the pillows at the head of the bed.

"How what works?"

"Your fire, Rafe Stavros. I want to understand it. When

I touch you here—" She broke off, painting a line down his spine before drifting those long, glorious fingers over his cock. Defying every bit of logic he possessed as a man, he felt himself springing to life at her tempting touch. "I feel the heat of your body, but there isn't an actual fire. You just feel like a man."

"I am a man." He intended to growl out the words but they came out on a half moan as her fingers tightened.

How was this even possible?

He'd experienced lust before and had enjoyed more than his fair share of the company of women. Yet none of them had this effect on him. He was more sated than he'd ever been in his life, yet needier than he could ever imagine. Those twin states—the urgency and the satisfaction—were inexorably linked, the strangest of bedfellows.

Sort of like them.

Evangeline continued on as if she hadn't heard him. "So if this is just normal body heat, where do the flames come from?"

Since it was evident she wasn't going to let up, Rafe decided to have a little fun. Placing his hand over hers to hold her in place, he shot a small burst of flame off of his shoulder. Her surprised shriek was what he was going for and he opened his eyes once more, anxious to see her expression.

And wow, she didn't disappoint.

Her hair drifted in tousled disarray around her shoulders and her dark eyes were wide with shock as he allowed the fire to dance from his shoulder, down over his biceps and on to his forearm before he wrapped it around their hands.

"How? I mean, why?" She stared at her own hand, wrapped in flame. "Why don't I feel it? I mean, I feel it, but it's like a warm blanket, fresh out of the dryer."

"You're here. We're touching and you're inside my aura. You're safe here."

"That's why. Before." She stopped, the memory of earlier suddenly joining them in the bed. "If I'm touching you, I'm safe."

"Exactly."

If she continued to contemplate the distance he'd needed earlier to slay his opponent, she said nothing. Instead, she focused once more on their hands, her gaze reflecting back the fire that leaped between them. "It's amazing."

"At times. At others it's a pain in the ass." The fire winked out, along with his interest in discussing it. She may have forgotten their earlier tangle with Chaos's minion but he hadn't. She'd been in danger.

And he'd killed for it.

Although he'd been threatened before, he'd never killed anyone—even a Hunter—and the knowledge sat hard on his shoulders. By silent assent, Evangeline seemed to understand his reticence to talk, asking no more questions as she snuggled into his arms. But an hour later he still hadn't fallen asleep. It had taken Evangeline quite a while to sleep as well, but he'd finally felt her body go slack. Satisfied she was fully asleep, he slipped his arm from around her, got out of bed and padded into the living room.

The tree shone brightly from its proud place in the center of his apartment. The boxes for the ornaments were stacked neatly on the coffee table where she'd placed each, once emptied, but the garland still lay in a ball at the base of the tree, abandoned once she'd so generously made love to him with her mouth.

Love.

The word echoed in his mind, a living, breathing reminder of all he'd avoided in his life. Affection. Desire. Love. All were real. Tangible. Feelings that had weight and depth and far too many emotions layered through them to give him any sense of objectivity.

Any measure of distance.

He cared for her, that he knew. And he'd kill to keep her

safe. He'd already proven that to both of them. But love? Was it possible?

Perhaps the better question was if it was possible not to love her.

She'd swooped into his life without invitation and disrupted everything he knew. With all that was happening in the battle with the Hunters, did he dare let himself be this distracted?

This unfocused?

He'd thought about her all afternoon and had spent all evening decorating a damned Christmas tree like he was eight. He couldn't afford this sort of distraction, because after only one day of making love to her, he knew she was exactly that. A woman who had the ability to wield an inordinate amount of power over his emotions.

Which made her a distraction he couldn't afford to indulge.

Hell, he'd kissed her on the grounds of the Archangel and had nearly missed the presence of a Hunter of Chaos. The battle was too close and he needed every bit of vigilance he possessed to fight it.

So it was time to back away. To back off, even if it killed him.

Chaos fed on weakness and Evangeline was a weakness as surely as he stood there, staring at the bright lights of the Strip from his window. She was life and light and every good thing in the world, and Chaos and his Hunters would be drawn to her like a magnet to true north.

So he'd let her go. Give her the world-famous Rafe Stavros brush-off and send her on her way. The faster he got her off the property, the better.

Just as soon as he figured out how to say goodbye.

Evangeline woke to a hot cup of coffee and a note on the end table. He couldn't have been gone that long since the coffee was still piping, but a quick inspection through the lavish, endless rooms of Rafe's apartment didn't turn up any sign of him.

Something about the abrupt departure nagged at the back of her mind but she firmly pushed it away. He was busy—they both were—and he had a casino to run. And she had a replanting on the south lawn that she'd ignored for too many days. Holiday madness had started already and she was down two people today who were using vacation time. Moping around Rafe's apartment wasn't going to get a half acre of plants in the ground by themselves.

Renewed by the thought, she snagged her mug of coffee and sipped it as she inspected his living room. They hadn't left much of a mess, although she would take the hopelessly tangled garland with her and drop it in the trash. Even if it was ruined, she couldn't hold back the smile at the memory of just how it had gotten so tangled.

After a firm walk around the tree, inspecting their hard work, Evangeline was satisfied Rafe had a damn fine Christmas tree to show for their evening. He hadn't turned off the lights before he left and she crossed the room to consider the eight-footer from her perch at the window. She continued to catch the rich, subtle scent of pine on the air as she enjoyed her coffee and let her mind drift over the past few days.

Was it really possible she'd started an affair with her boss? Was *affair* even the right word for what they'd shared? Especially since it felt far more like a relationship than something hidden in quiet moments, away from prying eyes.

Although it was far from her usual style, Evangeline had to admit to herself it felt right. Better than right, she felt whole.

Complete.

And head over heels on her way into love.

Which was a bit of a joke, really, since she knew damn well that she was all the way in love and hopelessly infatuated with Rafe Stavros.

Her phone pinged from where she'd left it on the counter the night before and she walked to it, flipping off the tree lights as she went. Images of love notes from Rafe filled her thoughts as she opened up her messages.

And wondered instead at the tersely worded summons to his office.

A sleepless night and far too much coffee this morning had combined to put Rafe in a foul-ass mood. The abrupt departure of one of their high rollers and a water-main leak on the fortieth floor added to the one-two punch of crappy timing. And a frigging six-foot Christmas tree cluttering his office had added the final straw to his morning.

Which was all a lie, because he could have drunk a gallon of water, slept the sleep of the dead and still had a few extra million flowing through the high-rollers' room, and he'd be in a rotten, foul-ass mood anyway.

The hard knock on the door belied the person on the other side and Evangeline didn't wait for a "come in" to march into his office. "You summoned me?"

"I'd hardly call it that."

She dragged her phone from the back of her pants but didn't even turn it on before mimicking back his text in gruff tones. "Evangeline. My office. Now."

"You were expecting a love letter?"

"I was expecting civility."

And there you had it, Rafe thought in grim satisfaction. Phase one of the Stavros ass-hat routine was well under way.

"Perhaps I was expecting the same."

His words tripped her up and Evangeline stammered for the moment before catching herself. "When wasn't I civil? I didn't even see you this morning, though I did appreciate the hot coffee you must have left at my bedside just as I was coming awake."

And check on phase two. Recipient is aware and responsive to the Stavros ass-hat routine.

"You took it upon yourself to leave a fully decorated tree in my office, spilling Christmas decorations and copious amounts of glitter all over my floor."

"It was a gift."

"One I said I didn't want."

Something dark and achy filled her gaze and Rafe tamped down hard on the remorse threatening to suffocate him. *Hit opponent where it well and truly hurts.*

And with that, phase three was well under way.

"Well then, I will see to it that it's removed immediately."

"I have appointments all morning. I expect it will be gone by lunch when I return."

"Of course."

Evangeline stood tall, anything she might have felt hidden behind a stoic mask of reserve. He'd seen that look before—she'd worn it the first night she'd arrived. He'd wondered at it then and had assumed it was a layer of cold disdain.

Oh, how wrong he'd been. Wrong and misguided. And woefully misinformed on the forces that had shaped her.

That stoic mask was her only protection against the world. Over the past year, as she'd grown more comfortable at the Archangel, it had slipped from time to time, until it had vanished over their last few days together.

But this morning, he'd been the one to put it back on her face.

How dare he?

Between the summons in his text and the jerk behavior

over the damned Christmas tree, Evangeline would have preferred a public flogging out by the greenhouse.

Naked.

She'd have felt less exposed than she did right now.

What had possibly happened between their repeated bouts of lovemaking into the wee hours of the morning and his emotional ass-kicking before the clock had hit 9:00 a.m.?

Her booted feet struck hard against the pale marble of the lobby as she marched toward the back exit onto the grounds. The prior night whirled through her mind, but no matter how many times she rewound those moments, she couldn't find anything to suggest he was upset.

They'd laughed over dinner. Had laughed even more over decorating the tree. And then they'd made love, through room after room of his home.

What had possibly happened to change his mind?

She'd already groped for the easy answers—she'd sucked in bed and she'd been in some sort of delusional fantasy over the tree—but quickly discarded both. If a man didn't enjoy sex he didn't go out of his way to belittle his partner—he just went out of his way to disappear. Far too much pride on the line with that one.

And who got that mad and irritated about a tree?

Again, far too much emotional energy for something he could just ignore and walk away from. Which only meant one thing.

Rafe Stavros was an ass. An ass who was running scared.

The thought had bubbled up during her elevator ride down to the lobby but it hadn't taken root until she'd cleared the back doors and walked into the bright morning sunshine.

He was scared. Chaos had found some way to further his power with those who did his bidding, and Rafe thought he'd keep her safe if he kept his distance. Silly man.

Didn't he understand they were stronger together?

The fact he didn't nearly had her pushing on in anger, but something stopped her. These last days with him had been transformative, showing her a new side of Rafe and a new side of herself.

She'd found love. And more important, had found herself capable of giving love. It'd be a shame to cut and run at the first sign of trouble.

Those thoughts kept her company as she turned on her heel and retraced her steps back through the casino. The normal quiet and calm that settled in during the morning hours was nowhere in evidence as she worked her way around milling guests, packed gaming tables and a persistent hum that grated on her nerves.

Maybe she did need that vacation Rafe had ranted about. Some time away. And blessed relief from the endless throngs of humanity that filled the Archangel. They were a bunch of heathens, anyway.

Gambling. Drinking. More than a few even whoring, if Rafe's story the night before was to be believed. Why was she busting her ass to make the environment nice and attractive for these people when they were so damned ungrateful?

She shoved hard through a crowd thronging between roulette tables, a woman's hard cry breaking through her anger. The large woman wobbled unsteadily on her feet from the domino-like impact of the other bodies who'd been shoved into her and Evangeline reached out immediately, steadying the woman.

"Watch where you're going. You're going to hurt someone!"

A hard retort and the urge to shove harder gripped her before Evangeline stilled.

What was she doing?

Gentling her grip, she laid a hand on the woman's back.

"I was moving too fast and not paying attention. I really am sorry."

The woman's deep frown smoothed out, even if her companions continued to look upset. Militant, even. "Thanks."

Evangeline hovered another minute, part to confirm the woman was fine and part to take stock of herself.

Why was she so angry?

Yes, Rafe had her upset. Worse, he'd hurt her—deeply. But the roiling, churning anger inside of her wasn't normal, nor was it a response to Rafe. Shoving her way through the casino, she'd wanted to hurt someone. A state that had nothing to do with Rafe and everything to do with her.

A young woman, barely old enough to gamble, screamed at a nearby table and Evangeline used the distraction to her advantage. Several patrons had gathered around to see what she'd won and Evangeline joined their number, stilling herself to take stock of her surroundings.

A light breeze whispered around them, out of character for a casino closed off from the outside elements. The wind had a slightly caustic edge, seeming to jump and swirl from person to person. As it moved on, Evangeline began to hear comments.

"She didn't deserve to win. Ball dropped into her number at the last minute."

"Did she wager early enough? Dealer wasn't watching. I think she placed that bet late."

"Where'd she get the money? She's been losing all morning, bleeding chips."

Dissention. Disenchantment. And a determined layer of anger that seemed to take purchase, like seeds taking root in fertile soil.

Chaos.

Without worry for who she might knock down, Evangeline took off at a run for the corporate offices. Rafe was in danger.

No, she amended to herself. They were *all* in danger.

Those last moments with Evangeline played over and over in his mind as Rafe entered the private elevator to the security suite. That bleak gaze and empty stare. The way she seemed to wrap herself up in a quiet cloak of self-protection. And worst of all, the dark, desperate hurt that telegraphed from her in short, choppy waves.

Others might not see it, but he knew her. Understood her. And he loved her.

The elevator stopped, and the double doors slid open with silent grace. He was nearly through them when those words whispered through his mind once more.

He loved Evangeline.

So what in the gods' names was he doing here?

He caught sight of Gabe marching his way, but waved him off. "Gotta go."

"Rafe!" His brother barked out his name, gesturing him into the security center. "I need you."

Irritation layered beneath the urgency to get to Evangeline and he was midway toward stabbing the close-door button when something in Gabe's stormy visage registered. "Gabe?"

"We have an intruder."

"Who?" Even as his answer lingered in the air, Rafe already knew.

Evangeline hovered at the elevator bank, shifting from foot to foot as the noise behind her grew louder. Her employee badge allowed her access to the executive suite of elevators but the employees-only sign and waving her badge didn't seem to deter the noise that built steadily behind her.

The crowd she'd glommed onto at the roulette tables had followed her. She'd avoided saying anything, but a few stumbled behind her when she'd left the table, their numbers growing with every yard she narrowed to the elevator bank.

Hard whispers, as blatant as those she'd heard at the roulette table, bounced off her back.

"Going to give Stavros a piece of my mind."

"Damn games are rigged."

"How'd I lose so much so fast?"

Chaos's stamp lit up each and every word, his ability to twist human frustration to his will on clear display. Could she get to Rafe in time?

And could she convince him once she did?

Again, she shook off the dark, dour thought. She *would* do this. And Rafe *would* help her. If the past days had taught her anything, it was that Rafe and his brother were more than willing to take on the hard job of protecting his people.

As people crowded in behind her at the elevators, she debated the wisdom of leading them to Rafe, even as she knew it was the only place they'd be safe.

Gabe rewound the video feed and played it once more. Evangeline marched through the casino, nearly toppling a heavyset woman who wasn't strong on her feet. He'd watched the exchange, then had Gabe rerun it, watching Evangeline's face on the second go-round.

Bright, vivid anger painted her features when she first collided with the woman. But then something morphed, her muscles relaxing as she seemed to surface from a deep depth. Her shoulders relaxed and that dark mask vanished. The women exchanged apologies, the stranger seeming to calm under Evangeline's warm smile.

"One more time."

It was that mask of anger that got him. When she'd left his office she was upset, but she was still herself. There was an otherworldly quality to her features on the video and as Gabe rolled the feed a third time, Rafe saw that look was matched on the faces of the crowd around her.

"Chaos. He's here and he's clearly not using one of his Hunters to do the job."

Gabe paused a view he had up on a different screen and moved closer. "How? He's locked up."

"I don't know how but look at them all. Those matched expressions aren't a coincidence."

Gabe pointed to his paused screen. "Looks like Evangeline's the pied piper."

As Rafe took in the swarm of people who surrounded her at the executive elevators, he knew. "Or the lamb to slaughter."

Evangeline turned, the throng becoming increasingly angry behind her. She positioned herself against the elevator call buttons and focused on the people in front of her.

"Hey, lady, get out of the way!"

She held her composure and forced a bright smile onto her face while she kept her voice calm. Level. "This is the employee wing. No guests are allowed."

"Casino should have thought about that before it started taking our money."

She avoided mentioning that was exactly how the casino made money and kept up the continued distraction. If she could only calm them down, she could find Rafe and get his help. "Gambling's about lucky days and not-so-lucky days. You had fun. And you're here, in this beautiful hotel. Get out on the Strip for a bit, take in the sights."

"Corporate shill. Here to spout the party line."

"Oh, I'm just a worker bee." She forced more sunshine

into her smile, more honey into her tone and pointed at her chest. "I've even got a name badge to prove it."

A man in the back shouted, "Then they're using you, too!"

Mind whirling with Rafe's explanations, Evangeline knew Chaos wasn't physically here. He was channeling emotions, but he couldn't do more than that, so she'd channel them right back. "It's too pretty a morning to be stuck in here. Get out on the sidewalk and get some air. People watch. Take in the new holiday plants over by the infinity pool."

She had the vaguest notion that sending them out into the world might cause more problems, but leaving them in a clustered mob wasn't doing much good, either.

"Since when do we give tours?"

That warm voice, deep, husky and so totally Rafe, washed over her. She took in the sight of him—so sure, so strong—and smiled. "I thought our fine guests might enjoy a walk around the property."

Rafe laid a hand over hers, his fingers squeezing tight before he turned to the crowd. "I'm Rafe Stavros and my family owns this casino. I'd like to invite you to drinks and breakfast at the infinity pool."

Gabe and a few guys she recognized from the security center began shuffling the crowd away and she heard a few bright comments amidst the grumbles. "Drinks aren't so bad. Maybe some food."

Once the crowd was managed, the last few men fading out of view, Gabe moved in beside them, his gaze on his brother. Evangeline caught the silent communication, even if Gabe's words were at odds with the look. "Like lemmings to the edge of a cliff. Some free food. A few watered-down drinks. Disaster averted."

When Rafe squeezed once more, Evangeline knew she needed to play along. "Seriously? That's your plan? Stuff them with bacon and send them on their way? What kind of business are you two running?"

Approval lit Rafe's gaze, but his tone remained as mocking as Gabe's. "It worked, didn't it? Besides, we already won all their money."

"What little the slobs brought with them."

"I don't believe you two!" Evangeline added a hand to her hip for good measure. "You manipulated them."

"Yes," Gabe nodded, his grin wicked. "We did."

That cruel, taunting breeze slithered in, wrapping around their legs before whispering along her nerve endings. She practically heard the purr, urging her to anger. To melancholy. To misery.

And it was that greedy push for just a bit more that made Chaos vulnerable. On some level, she didn't understand, yet simply *knew*, he'd placed himself in danger.

With the slightest shake of her head to let them know she was ready, she gripped Rafe's and Gabe's hands. The moment they were connected, life-giving warmth wrapped around her, battling the anger of the wind.

The cool fingers that had tried to slide around her went to work once more, their firm hold tighter, the grip more desperate as it scrabbled for purchase. A hard, heavy manacle sheathed her wrist, determinedly pulling her from Gabe.

"Don't let go!"

"I can't...help it!" Evangeline fought to keep her hold on Gabe but the pressure on her wrist was too strong. The bite of those icy fingers was too deep—too desperate.

The moment her grip released from Gabe, the cold changed tactics. Rafe's hand tightened on hers, even as the cold crept up her arm, latching itself around her neck.

"Hold on, Evangeline!"

"Rafe—" His name died on a strangled breath as those fingers closed around her. The world around her began to fade and all she could do was think about Rafe. About the warm hand that enveloped her.

And the slow, welcoming arms of the cold.

A vicious, primal scream echoed in his head as Rafe felt Evangeline's body go slack. Gabe shouted orders from beside him but Rafe was beyond hearing.

This was his battle. His fight. His woman.

Without breaking contact, Rafe banked his fire and positioned himself to hold Evangeline's fading form. Wrapping his free hand around her, he cradled her against his body, willing as much heat into her as he could.

That cold air slithered along his arms, the chill bone-deep as it continued to work on Evangeline.

And that gave Rafe an idea.

Fighting the urge to throw his body over her, Rafe stilled, allowing the cold to fill in the gaps. Blue tinged the edges of Evangeline's features and he struggled with allowing Chaos even one more moment to touch Evangeline and harm her.

"Rafe?"

Gabe's question faded, his brother's understanding telegraphing over the top of Evangeline's head. It was a move they'd played as children, tormenting their cousins with the play of their fire.

What had been a youthful prank suddenly took root as the answer to saving Evangeline.

To saving all of them.

Even though it killed him, Rafe stared down at her, allowing the cold to continue to spread. Blue lips extended into pale skin; her tan vanished under Chaos's relentless work.

Rafe would give him his moment, for the extra effort would cost him.

It was only when Evangeline's head fell to the side,

her breath exhaling in one hard puff of air, that Rafe's gaze met his brother's. On Gabe's whispered "now" Rafe pushed into him, his brother's arms circling his neck in a scrum circle.

In unison, they drew on the fire that lived in the deepest part of each of them. It was their bond. Their past. And their legacy.

And in the tight circle they made around Evangeline, it was the life force that smothered whatever ground Chaos had managed to steal. Heat flooded his body, pounding through him like hoofbeats of the wildest mustangs, like flapping wings of the largest eagles. Relentless, he and Gabe pushed on and on, using what was inside of them to beat back the dark.

He knew the moment they won, the air around—and between them—changing. The cold vanished and Evangeline struggled in his arms. Still, Rafe held on, waiting for that lone moment when he heard Chaos's subtle control snap.

And a great, gulping scream lit up the secondary plane in agony.

Gabe broke contact first, his hands falling to his sides and his head dropping to his chest. Rafe staggered back, Evangeline's weight suddenly heavy against the adrenaline rapidly burning off in his system. He staggered against the wall, using the support to steady himself as he held her close.

"Rafe?" His name on her lips had him smiling as she slowly came back to herself. "What happened?"

"I'd say Chaos thought his prison bars allowed more freedom than they do. We pushed him back and likely did quite a bit of damage in the process."

"Is it over?"

He stared down at her, the reality of her question not lost on him. "For now."

But it wasn't over. The battle he'd spent a life preparing for had begun and he didn't know what was to come.

"I can stand." The moment he had her steady, she pulled him against her, her arms tight bands around his waist. "You, too, Gabe." She waved his brother over and pulled him close as well, the three of them leaning against each other for solace and support.

"You think this one's going to make the news?" she asked, concerned about who saw their battle.

Gabe's laugh was extra harsh. "No one saw us."

She lifted her head at that. "No one? What good is having a hotel full of cameras if they don't capture anything?"

"They capture what's important." Gabe leaned in and pressed a kiss to her forehead before turning on his heel. "Now I need to go see about buying breakfast for fifty."

Gabe added one more hard hug for good measure before he headed for the casino at a swift clip.

Evangeline pulled Rafe close once more. "You're okay?"

"I'm fine. You're the one who spent some time in Chaos's proverbial freezer."

"I knew I wouldn't stay there." Warmth filled the cheeks that had so recently been pale and lifeless and he'd have given anything to stay there and stare at her forever.

"Oh, no?"

"You had me. I knew you'd keep me safe."

"But I didn't. Not this morning." He dropped his hands from where they caressed a path over her spine. "I hurt you this morning."

"Yes, you did."

"Aren't you mad?"

"I was." She pressed a kiss against his chin. "And then I realized I'd better get used to it. If you think a relationship between us isn't going to be volatile and downright unpleasant at times, I figure we should both cut and run now."

Rafe gazed down into the fathomless depths of her eyes. "You want to cut and run?"

"Nope."

"Neither do I."

Her smile shined up at him, a bright, warm benediction over their relationship. "I love you, Rafe."

"I love you, too."

He'd nearly had his lips on hers when her words stopped him. "Then come with me."

"Where are we going?"

"We have a tree to deal with."

Rafe reached behind and hit the elevator button. "I don't want to take it down."

The doors slid open and Evangeline pulled him through them, her hands insistent and urgent as they played against his hips. "We're not taking it down."

"Then what are we doing with it?"

That warm, vibrant smile shifted, growing sexy as her eyes filled with all the secrets of the universe. "We're going to have sex underneath it and get wrapped up in all that glitter you seem so determined to hate."

Rafe pulled her against him, his lips pressed to hers. "I can't think of a better way to spend the day."

* * * * *

Dear Reader,

The lights and sounds of Vegas are familiar to me. It's one of my favorite places to go for a long weekend. Being there, I can be someone I'm normally not. I stay up late and gamble my hard-earned money (okay, quarter slot machines are as high as I go, but still...). Over the years my husband and I have seen many shows there, eaten some fabulous, romantic dinners and come back with a lot less cash than we had when we left. Writing a story set in Las Vegas was a blast. Add in Christmas, my favorite time of the year, and I was in heaven, especially since we usually go in late November or early December.

The mythology of the Helios was new to me. Addison Fox and I exchanged a flurry of emails to decide what they were and did, and that was so much fun, as well. Greek men—tall, dark, handsome and mysterious—another yay! Plus I've always wanted to write a musical superstar, and the fact that she's my hero's opposite—okay, sworn enemy—made me laugh out loud. I loved writing this story and I'm grateful to the editor who challenged my own ideas and made them better—that's Carly Silver.

I hope you enjoy the sizzling *Heat of the Helios*. And if you haven't, visit Vegas. Just for the fun!

Karen Whiddon

HEAT OF A HELIOS

KAREN WHIDDON

Dedicated to Lonnie, my hubby and Las Vegas cohort. We've had a lot of fun there over the years, haven't we?

Chapter 1

Meghan Frost. She'd been promised her name, surrounded by lights on one of the huge billboards on the Vegas Strip, her image flashing brightly so the throngs of tourists could stare. Though she'd reached the pinnacle of fame some time ago, this small thing had been something she'd always dreamed of and longed for. She couldn't wait to see it, though right now all she wanted to do was pull her baseball cap a little lower over her eyes and pray no one recognized her once she landed.

Her new show, slated to start in a little over two weeks, would be thrilling. Every song, every move, had been perfected, practiced endlessly in a special studio in downtown Los Angeles. Now, she and her crew had time off for the holidays before rehearsal began again, this time on the actual stage at the Archangel.

The Archangel. The name made her shiver. If ever a place suited her image, the newest and edgiest casino and hotel on the Strip did. She'd been flattered when they'd offered her their first musical residency, and even more stunned when they hadn't balked at her enormous fee.

Still, she hadn't been entirely sure she wanted to do it. The mystery behind her enigmatic pop star image might peel away under the bright lights of Vegas.

Not so, her publicity people had argued. Even her agent, whom she trusted more than her own family, had advised her to take the three-month stint.

Now, contract signed, advance cashed and in the bank, she was flying in early to check out the hotel. The only one other than her own people who knew about her arrival was Gabriel Stavros, one of the two brothers who owned the Archangel.

He'd promised discretion. He'd also assured her that everything would be exactly as she'd stipulated. She'd thanked him, even though she had no idea what kind of ridiculous clauses her team might have put in her contract. Her two necessities, of course—a variety of tea bags and a teapot as well as a blender so she could make her protein shakes—and then whatever else Team Meghan thought appropriate for a musical superstar of her standing.

Whatever. In reality, she was the least diva-like of her peers. Of course her PR people might have asked for the moon made out of cream cheese, for all she knew.

Checking her watch, she glanced out the window of the private jet—sent by the Stavros brothers—and waited for her first sight of the lights of Sin City. While the loud flashiness of Vegas clashed with her innate quietness, she still found something magical in the way the Strip lit up at night. Performing was like that for her, too—the music and the energy of the audience lit her up from within.

There. Neon red and yellow, orange and blue, all competing with each other for attention. The Pyramid, one of the less brightly lit places, guarded one area, while the MGM Grand warred with the Bellagio, the Venetian and the Paris. A place for mindless fun, good to stay in for a few days, gambling and walking, eating and drinking, before heading back home to reality.

Smiling to herself, she watched as the jet approached the airport, her gaze fixed on the well-lit runway as they landed. Now on to the Archangel. Time to meet the Stavros brothers and check out her new, temporary home. She'd asked for a small Christmas tree, too, even though no one would see it but her.

Once more, the thought of being alone—again—at Christmas stung. Her family not only wasn't big on human holidays, but even more important, there were certain times of the year when all they wanted to do was focus on the hunt.

December 21, the winter solstice, happened to be one of those times. Before Meghan had become famous, she'd let them drag her along, willing to participate in something she no longer believed in just to keep from being alone.

Now she used her career as an excuse, unable to keep from wishing, just once, that her family would choose being with her over the thrill of the ever-elusive hunt.

Not likely. Why should anything change now?

Stretching, she focused on preparing for the upcoming meeting. No sense in allowing herself a pity party, not when everything in her life had begun to come up roses.

This would be her first time meeting the Stavros brothers. All the details of her residency had been handled by her people and theirs. While she didn't expect this to be much more than a few pleasantries and a handshake, since this entire thing was already a done deal, she still wanted to make a good impression.

So she'd chosen to wear something completely outside of her public and professional wheelhouse. No leather or lace; instead she wore a smoky-gray cowl-necked sweater and black leggings. She could only imagine the horrified reaction from her stylist if she were to find out. Luckily she wouldn't. Meghan had given the other woman time off until after Christmas.

Finally disembarking the sleek jet, Meghan noted with relief the lack of a crowd. She'd asked that no press be made aware of her minivacation, even though she'd half expected her new employer to disregard that. The lack of flashbulbs going off in her face coaxed a second genuine smile. She'd try to remember to thank the Stavros brothers for this small blessing.

It wasn't that she abhorred publicity—she'd been around long enough to understand the necessity and the love/hate relationship most stars had with the press. But she'd been performing nonstop on a tour to promote her new album that had seemed endless, though it had only been three months. Right after the tour had ended, she'd plunged into rehearsals for this Vegas show, and she was thankful for the hard work of her team, especially the choreographers who'd put together an event worthy of all the hype.

Everyone had been sent home, told to enjoy the holidays and come back refreshed. Including Meghan. She'd need this time off to refill her creative well, to rebuild her energy so she could knock it out of the park on opening night.

And somehow during this time she had to figure out a way to keep from letting loneliness destroy her.

"Is everything ready?" Impatience riding him like banked embers about to burst into flame, Gabe Stavros made one last circuit to check the penthouse suite. He and his brother, Rafe, had been thrilled to offer the pop megastar Meghan Frost the first residency at the Archangel. She would be arriving that night, two weeks ahead of her show opening and just before the holidays. "Her people sent a list of her demands and I want to make sure we not only met them, but exceeded them."

"Everything is in place," Miguel Vargas, head of housekeeping, assured him. "Fresh flowers to be replenished daily. Her refrigerator is stocked, and we've made sure she has the requested blender and every variety of tea."

Gabe nodded. He understood why Rafe had left the chore of greeting Meghan Frost to him. Of the two men, Rafe had less tolerance for spoiled, narcissistic women. Which, even though they'd never met her before, both men assumed Meghan Frost would be. She was a superstar, after all.

He checked his watch again, reining in his impatience. By now the private jet should have landed and Ms. Frost should be in the limousine on the way there.

Pacing, he strode to the balcony and slid open the doors. He just needed to exercise a little patience. Never one of his strong suits.

His phone chimed. He'd asked the driver to alert him once they'd arrived on the premises. They were here. Ms. Frost would be escorted up to her suite as quietly as possible, per her request.

Stepping inside and closing the patio door behind him, he did one final sweep of the rooms, just to be certain. His people had, as usual, done a wonderful job. Of course, they'd had plenty of practice, since the Archangel had quickly become a favorite of celebrities and athletes alike. Though none were of this caliber. Nothing but the best for the Archangel's first artist in residence. Her first month of shows were already sold out. If this kept up, they'd set a Vegas record.

Stepping into the hall, he crossed to the private elevator to wait, glad of the comfortable fit of his custom-made suit and Western boots.

With a discreet chime, the elevator doors slid open. Professional smile in place, Gabe took a deep breath, and prepared to welcome one of the most beautiful women he'd ever seen to the Archangel.

Exhausted and trying very hard not to give in to crankiness, Meghan steeled herself as the elevator glided to the penthouse floor. She fervently hoped this would be a small, private greeting, that the Stavros brothers hadn't arranged some kind of welcoming reception. All she wanted to do was shake their hands, bid them a nice evening and crawl between Egyptian cotton sheets to sleep.

She'd done a little research on them. They were both tall, dark and handsome, in that mysterious Greek way. Rich, too, which meant all that money had given them power. In her experience, men who'd gotten a taste of such power were hard to deal with. She hoped these two would be the exception.

Finally, the elevator came to a stop and the doors opened. A tall, broad-shouldered man in a well-cut suit waited, his dark head bent as he studied his phone.

Security? But no, she gave him a second glance and realized this was one of the Stavroses. Influence and authority radiated from him, as well as the kind of masculine confidence only a man as good-looking and wealthy as him could pull off.

To her surprise, she felt a twinge of sexual attraction.

"Ms. Frost, welcome to our hotel." Taking her hand, he inclined his head in greeting. His longish raven hair and caramel eyes would have looked more at home on a musician, but oddly enough, they suited him, in fact enhancing his craggy features.

Another sharp tug of attraction hit her, stronger this time, making her breath catch. "Thank you," she managed. "I'm really looking forward to my stay."

With the basic pleasantries exchanged, now would be his cue to give her the room key and leave. Right?

"Let me show you to your suite," he said, stepping aside and gesturing for her to precede him. The intensity in his gaze brought an answering simmer to life inside her. Her exhaustion appeared to have disappeared, too. Interesting.

And dangerous. There were a thousand rational arguments why she shouldn't get involved with one of the men paying her salary. Her PR people worked hard to make it appear as if Meghan Frost flouted the rules, but in reality, she much preferred coloring inside the lines in everything but her music.

She sniffed, taking in the scent of spearmint and a tasteful hint of expensive men's cologne. As she moved past him, fighting the urge to brush up against him like a cat, she reminded herself this could all be one-sided, too. Her fame and the bad-girl persona her team liked to cultivate wasn't for everyone. Particularly rich hotel owners who dressed in four-thousand-dollar custom-made suits.

"Here we are," he said, using the room card to open a pair of ornately carved, mahogany doors. He made a half bow and flashed a wicked smile. "Your suite. Please, look around and let me know if there's anything not to your liking."

Moving past him, she stopped, stunned. Walls of floor-to-ceiling windows showcased the illuminated Strip and she could see the bright balloon of the Paris in the distance. Dark hardwood floors polished to a high shine, comfortable, yet elegant furniture, decorated with a flair of color which instantly made her feel at home.

"Very nice," she managed, even though the penthouse was so much more than that. *Spectacular* was one word that sprang to mind.

Like him. Her toes curled in her knee-high leather boots.

"Is there anything else you need?"

Even his voice, low and husky, turned her on. Wow. She

couldn't even remember the last time someone had affected her like this. To hide her reaction, she prowled around the suite, noting the expensive blender and teakettle, the fragrant floral arrangement and the well-stocked refrigerator. Everything she'd asked for.

"Let me know if there's anything else you like us to get for you," he said, reminding her she hadn't yet answered.

You. I'd like you. She bit back the words, which were completely out of character for her, despite the nonsense the tabloids printed. "I don't think so," she said instead, spinning around to realize he'd moved closer. Heat flooded her. She couldn't help but check his left hand. No ring. Even more interesting.

He inclined his head, the heat in his gaze warring with his impersonal, professional expression. "Then I'll leave you to get some rest. Please don't hesitate to call me if you need anything. Anything at all."

Then, while she struggled to formulate a response, he backed away, moving out the door with a sensual grace that made her wonder if he danced. The door closed behind him and just like that, he was gone. The room felt empty without his vibrant energy.

Holy moley. Staring at the closed door, Meghan shook her head. "Wow," she said out loud. "Just wow." In her business, there were a lot of good-looking men. She hardly even noticed them anymore. But something about Gabriel Stavros made her insides hum and her body come alive in a way that only music had before.

Chapter 2

"Well?" Rafe demanded, grinning as he waited to hear what Gabe had to say.

"She's beautiful," Gabe said slowly, struggling to find the right words that would be truthful, yet not give his tangled emotions away. "Even more than she is on TV or in magazines."

"Sexy, too, I bet."

The instant flash of jealousy that slammed into him surprised Gabe. "That, too," he managed. "I didn't spend a whole lot of time with her, but she seemed quiet. Probably tired."

"Most likely." Rafe moved around the room, his long-legged stride eating up the space. "Sorry to change the subject, but you know next week is the winter solstice, of course. We got to nail down some plans."

"I agree. My internal alarm has been sounding, loud and clear. It's getting more and more difficult to fight the urge to Rejuvenate."

Both men grimaced. Unfortunately, their kind had no choice. Four times a year, they had to Rejuvenate—the vernal equinox in March, summer solstice in June, autumn equinox in September, and the winter solstice, which this year fell on December 21. When they Rejuvenated, they'd burst into flames, which seemed pretty crazy on the surface, especially if one were merely human. Luckily, they were so much more. Human, yes. And special, as well. As Helios, the fire cleansed all impurities from their earthly bodies, leaving them clean and strong. Rejuvenated, their powers refilled.

Helios considered this both a blessing and a curse. They must manage their Rejuvenation carefully, making sure no one saw. Especially the Hunters. He shuddered at the idea of their legendary nemeses actually locating them.

Rafe cursed, making Gabe wonder if he'd actually spoken the dreaded name of their adversaries rather than thinking it. "Damn Hunters will be showing up all over the world. You just know they'll be out in force around here."

"They always are." Making his voice deliberately cheerful, Gabe's thoughts returned to Meghan Frost with her dusky skin and long-lashed green eyes. Her effect on him both startled and worried him. Intrigued him, as well. He couldn't recall the last time he'd met a woman who made him feel as if he'd already burst into flames. Not good. This time of the year could be dangerous for his kind. The last thing he needed was a distraction. Any distraction, no matter how tempting.

"Remember the plan," Rafe said. "If we positively ID a Hunter, lure him outside. We can't endanger any of our other patrons, human or otherwise. Not to mention the bad publicity such a thing would generate."

"Of course." Every season, every year since opening the Archangel, they'd had a variation of this same conversation. While they were forbidden from outright attacking a Hunter, they could definitely defend themselves. "Nothing bad is going to happen. It never does. At least to us," he amended.

"I know." Rafe's rueful grin had Gabe grinning back. "You just make sure and keep that pop star happy. She might be the key to taking things to the next level."

And that in a nutshell was everything his brother wanted. Him, too. The entire family, actually—though the Archangel becoming the best-known, most successful hotel and casino in Vegas had long been his brother's dream. Gabe would do everything in his power to make that happen, including wining and dining a spoiled diva named Meghan Frost. And somehow remaining immune to her considerable charms.

Meghan should have known better. No matter how fast she ran, or where she went, she couldn't outrun herself or the bone-crushing, soul-sucking loneliness that continually dogged her. It didn't matter if she surrounded herself with people, since she knew if her talent and fame were to totally vanish, so would they. At least alone, she could think. Except ever since arriving at the Archangel, all she could think about was one of the handsome casino owners Gabriel Stavros.

Maybe a distraction was exactly what she needed. Something to stave off the loneliness. She'd seen the flare of interest in his caramel-colored eyes when he looked at her. The undeniable attraction sizzling between them had to be mutual. The question was, should she act on it?

Clicking on the radio, the cheerful carol made her wince. When she'd been small, like children everywhere, she'd loved Christmas. Gifts and candy and a visit from a fat man in a red suit. But as she and her brother Damon had grown older, the family had focused more on the hunt, the quarterly search for the mythical beings known as

Helios. Legend had it that the Helios guarded the gate to the world of the Ancients. The Hunters, who supposedly could boast a lineage all the way back to the ancient god Chaos, covered this world and the knowledge contained therein. After all, the best way to bring Chaos to the modern world would be to make humans aware of the ancient gods' existence and give them access to their world.

Personally, Meghan didn't buy any of it. Not her family's supposed history or their mission. As far as she could tell, the modern world was doing a pretty good job of descending into chaos all on its own. She'd grown up believing, but after years of watching her people put the hunt before everything else, including family, she'd made a conscious choice to reject their beliefs. Even if they were doing what they felt was right, she no longer wanted any part of it.

Whatever the truth, her family not only believed all of the hype, but four times a year, their dogged determination became a frenzy that bordered on madness. Unfortunately, Christmas always occurred right after the solstice. Which mean if Meghan didn't go on the hunt with them, she was doomed to spend the holiday alone.

Her choice, they said, refusing to feel any guilt. They weren't the ones that had changed. She had. Small wonder she'd gotten out of there as quickly as she could.

Meghan sighed. At least she hoped to be able to walk around the bustling Las Vegas Strip without attracting any attention. The paparazzi hadn't gotten wind of her new haircut—even her own people weren't aware she'd shorn her long hair to a spiky, short do. And the color—where she'd recently dyed it a candy-apple red, she'd gone back to her true shade, a nice deep mahogany. With a baseball cap, some baggy clothes and sunglasses, she hoped no one would recognize her.

Right now, though, she needed to sleep. Tomorrow would be a new day. She planned to face it with a smile.

* * *

Though the Archangel hummed along like a well-oiled machine, both Gabe and Rafe preferred to remain as hands-on as possible. With the Christmas season full upon them, the decorations, festive music and the throngs of holiday visitors kept the casino hopping and the hotel and restaurants full. It was, Gabe thought, his favorite time of the year. The rest of the Stavros family lived in a sprawling estate out in the desert and Gabe and his brother always went home for Christmas Day dinner. His parents' huge tree rivaled the one in the Archangel lobby but with one exception. His mother started her holiday shopping in August and the mound of brightly wrapped gifts seemed to grow larger every year.

Gabe winced, aware he needed to get started on his own gift-buying expedition. Even Rafe, a notable procrastinator, had begun ribbing him about his lack of preparation this year. Shopping. The chore made him shudder. But he hadn't made time to do any online gift-buying, so he'd have to get out there in person. Maybe if he was lucky, he could knock it all out in one day.

Tomorrow, he vowed. He'd get started tomorrow. Stifling a yawn, he headed out to the casino floor to make his rounds before heading up to his suite. Often, the buzz of energy from the slots and the poker players gave him an extra shot of vitality, enabling him to last a few more hours. Not tonight. He circled the floor, noting with approval the crowded machines and full poker games. Waving a greeting at several of his dealers, he strode to the elevator to go to bed.

The next morning, he woke before his alarm, exactly as he always did. He'd slept well, he thought, though his sleep had been punctuated with erotic dreams. Not surprising, since he couldn't stop thinking about the lovely Meghan Frost.

He knew everything about her. Professionally, that is. Before approaching her people, he'd done his research. Not just sales figures and stats, but her image and reputation. The world widely regarded her as edgy and smoky, a bit wild, but he'd learned she was in fact a very dedicated worker and a perfectionist, which he could definitely appreciate since he was a bit of one himself.

The contradiction of her two sides had fascinated him before he'd even met her. Now that he had, he knew he'd enjoy peeling off the layers to discover the true Meghan Frost.

If it were any other time of the year, that is.

Heading toward the gym for his daily workout, he stepped inside and froze. Usually at this hour of the morning, he had the place to himself, though occasionally his brother joined him. Today one other person ran on the treadmill, earbuds in place.

Meghan Frost.

Gorgeous, with perspiration creating a sheen on her smooth skin, making it glow.

He'd never seen a woman with a body like hers. Not one ounce of fat: all lean, toned muscle. Powerful and strong, yet also feminine. Sexy.

While he stared, hopefully without his mouth open, she noticed him and gave a little jerk of surprise. This momentarily broke the rhythm of her stride, though she regained it immediately after that one little stutter.

"Hey," she said, slightly out of breath as she removed one earbud. "You like to work out in the morning, too?"

Not entirely trusting himself to speak, he nodded and crossed to one of the other treadmills. Today was cardio day; he only did weight training three times a week.

Once he'd started his machine, he glanced over at her

only to see she'd gone back into the zone, earbuds back in place. Still running.

Slightly unsettled and a bit aroused, he threw himself into his workout, trying desperately not to notice how well she filled out her workout clothes. Damn. If he kept staring, she'd think he was some sort of creep, but how could he look away from female perfection? He wished he'd brought his earbuds, but more often than not he used this exercise time to think and plan the day ahead.

She punched the stop button to shut off her treadmill.

"Done," she said, her smile triumphant. "I'm just doing cardio this morning. What about you? I can tell you lift."

Trying not to grin at the compliment, he nodded. "Cardio today for me, too. I only work out with weights three times a week. I'm guessing you do the same?"

The flash of approval in her green eyes made his heart stutter. "You got it. Of course, when I'm working on my show, that's more than enough of a workout, believe me. You'll have to come by and check it out once we resume rehearsals after Christmas."

"I'd like that," he managed.

"Good." Still smiling, she stepped off the treadmill, lightly dabbing at her overheated body with a white hand towel. Eyeing her, he desperately wanted to be that towel. Would the slightly salty tang of her skin taste as good as he thought?

Clenching his jaw, he looked away. He had to stop this nonsense. Maybe his heightened awareness of her had something to do with his need to Rejuvenate. He could only hope so, or this was going to be an interesting three months.

"Um, I was wondering," she began, glancing at him with another smile, clearly unaware of his erotic thoughts. "Would you be available anytime later today to show me around?"

He winced, unable to keep from thinking of all the work that would entail. They'd need to assemble a security detail, call ahead and make sure certain venues were prepared to whisk her inside quickly, away from gawking onlookers.

"That's okay." The hurt flashing across her face along with the tightness in her voice told him she'd misinterpreted his reaction. "Never mind. I'll figure out something by myself."

Punching the pause button, he hopped off and crossed to stand closer to her. "My apologies. I was thinking I'd need a bit more time to put together security. Unless, of course, you have your own people."

"Very diplomatic, aren't you?" She narrowed her eyes. "But I don't want to go out as Meghan Frost the pop star. No one knows about this new haircut and color. I figure if I dress down, maybe wear a baseball cap and sunglasses, no one will even recognize me."

Was she kidding? Not sure how to react, he finally nodded. "We can try." Then, as she began to smile, he held up his hand. "On one condition. If you're recognized, you let me get you back up to your room. We can't risk you getting hurt or mobbed by some overzealous fans."

"Agreed," she said happily, now towel-drying her hair. The short, spiky cut complemented her heart-shaped face and impossibly long neck. "When?"

He realized she'd asked him a question, though he had no idea what it was. Resigned, he asked her to repeat it. Once she had, he considered how to answer.

In actuality, he had very little scheduled today. "Do you like to shop?" he asked, figuring he'd be safe with that since he'd never met a woman who didn't.

"Sometimes." She delivered her response with a notable lack of enthusiasm. "I haven't in a long time. I actually pay someone to do that for me."

"For Christmas gifts?" Astounded, he shook his head. "Or have you already done your holiday shopping for your family?"

Just like that, her expression went blank. "I haven't. But my family isn't really big on celebrating."

"I get it." He'd met people like that. "Do you even exchange gifts?"

She lifted her chin, her shoulders tense as if she expected him to criticize her. "No."

Though he felt like he was peppering her with questions, he desperately didn't want her to go. Not yet.

"Are they flying out here to spend Christmas with you or are you traveling to them?"

"Neither." Her shrug appeared carefully casual. "They have other plans for the holiday."

She didn't sound upset. Most people he knew would be depressed at the very least or angry. He'd known a few for whom the family dynamics made group get-togethers impossible, and without exception, this had made them furious. He himself couldn't even imagine such a thing. He loved his family and would be devastated if he couldn't see them.

Not Meghan Frost. She truly seemed unbothered.

"Okay," he commented, forcing himself to focus on the topic at hand. "Here's the thing. I have to get started on my Christmas shopping today. You're welcome to join me, at least until someone recognizes you. Or, if shopping truly isn't your thing, we can meet up later, and grab a bite to eat and go listen to music or something."

Fully expecting her to answer she'd take the second choice, he waited.

"I think I'd like to go shopping with you." Her shy smile made his chest tighten. "That way, I can accomplish two things. Learn my way around the shops in your hotel and see what normal people buy each other for Christmas."

She didn't seem to realize the pathos in her statement.

Chapter 3

"Sounds like a plan." Gabe had to swallow hard and force the words out past the lump in his throat. "How about I meet you up at your suite around ten?"

She nodded. "That's perfect. See you then."

He watched her leave, mentally chastising himself for how much he looked forward to seeing her again. Now they had a date that wasn't a date. This close to the solstice, he had to be careful and keep his distance. Still, tell that to the thrum of excitement running like an electrical current through his body. Again, he felt the flickering heat of banked embers, as if he might burst into flames at any second.

Ruthlessly, he got this under control. As the time for Rejuvenation drew closer, he frequently experienced such impulses, though never with so much intensity. Since Rafe had just had a major problem, accidently Rejuvenating before the solstice, he knew he needed to be extra careful.

Pushing the thought away, he hit Resume on the treadmill and started to run, refusing to turn and watch as Meghan left.

When he got back to his room, looking forward to a quick shower and then breakfast, he nearly groaned out loud to see Rafe waiting for him.

"What are you doing up so early?" Gabe teased. "Don't tell me you want to start working out with me."

Rafe didn't even crack a smile. "This is serious. I've gotten word that several Hunters are here."

"Already?" Gabe raised a brow. "They don't usually show up a full week before the solstice. I wonder what's up."

"Me, too." Rafe began to pace, his lithe movements resembling an elegant panther in his tailored suit. "This can't be good."

"Definitely not, but we've dealt with them before. As long as we're careful, you know we'll be fine."

Rafe nodded. "Maybe we should go out to Mom and Dad's for you to Rejuvenate. Less chance of one of them spotting you."

"Maybe." Gabe frowned. "This time the urge has been unusually strong. I've been fighting the impulse to burst into flames at the most inappropriate times."

"Me, too." Rafe's glum voice matched his dark expression. "I hate it. Especially since I've already lost control. That was awful. Now my solstice is messed up since I Rejuvenated early."

"I don't know. It got you together with Evangeline," Gabe teased. "I've never seen you so happy."

As usual, just the mere mention of his brother's girlfriend lifted Rafe's mood. "True." He flashed a grin. "Are you ready to go to breakfast?"

Even though they could have the hotel chef bring them whatever they wanted, the brothers made a practice of eating in the restaurant or buffet several times a month. Quality control, they called it.

Gabe shook his head. "No. Give me a few minutes to take a quick shower and dress. Do you want me to meet you there?"

"No, I'll wait." Rafe walked over to the balcony and drew back the drapes. "The sunrise is spectacular. I'll be out here waiting for you."

A short while later, having showered and shaved before donning another of his own custom suits, Gabe fetched his brother.

Rafe's black mood had completely vanished and he hummed under his breath as they walked to the elevator.

"What's on the agenda for you today?" he asked.

Refusing to feel awkward, Gabe outlined his plans.

"About time you got started on your Christmas shopping." Rafe shook his head. "Though I'm not sure of the wisdom in bringing a pop diva along."

"So far she seems pretty normal." Gabe shrugged. "No big deal. She claims no one will recognize her with her new haircut and color. Plus, I think she mentioned some sort of mild disguise. It'll be fine."

"Will it?" Rafe pressed the elevator button. Instantly, the doors slid open. One of the perks of having a private elevator reserved just for the suites meant they never had to wait in line to go anywhere.

"You're always overly optimistic," Rafe continued once the doors slid closed.

"And you're always overly worried," Gabe countered. "We'll be fine. We always are. The Hunters come, they hunt, and they rarely ever find us. They can be dangerous, but only once they find their quarry, you know that."

"I do. I also hate that they seem to hunt in groups." With a quiet ping, the doors slid open. Rafe always stressed. He hated being hunted, claiming he felt like all he did was look over his shoulder. His fears increased the closer they got to the solstice or equinox, depending on the season.

As for himself, Gabe figured, why worry? He felt confident in their ability to handle whatever threats came their way. Of course, he'd always been the more adventurous of the two.

Once on the lobby level, the constant tinkling and music of slot machines and just the faintest hint of cigarette smoke made Gabe smile. "Last time I checked, the numbers were looking really good for last night."

"That's what I heard." Rafe picked up the pace. "I'm starving," he commented. "Maybe they'll have the numbers ready if we stop by after we eat."

Though that would be pushing it, Gabe figured it wouldn't hurt to check. Though they weren't demanding employers, it didn't hurt to keep everyone on their toes. A sort of benign quality control.

The instant the hostess saw them, she led them to a prime table near the waterfall. "Here you go, gentlemen," she said, handing them both a menu. "Enjoy your breakfast."

Gabe met Rafe's gaze and gave a slight nod. He glanced around the room, pleased that so many tables were occupied already. This didn't always happen, as so much of the action went on late into the night and early into the morning. A lot of people slept in. This was one of the reasons Gabe had insisted breakfast be served 24/7.

By the alcove overlooking the casino, he spotted a woman eating alone. She had a paperback book propped up in front of her, reading as she sipped coffee and waited for her food. Her high cheekbones, delicate features and full mouth caused him to give her a second look.

A heartbeat later, he realized it was Meghan Frost. With her baseball cap, lack of makeup and her oversize sweatshirt, no one gave her any unusual glances, at least not any more than they would any beautiful woman.

"Why do you keep staring at that woman?" Rafe asked, ever perceptive.

"It's her." Gabe lowered his voice, though he still didn't want to take the chance of uttering her name. "You know who. My shopping companion for later today."

"Seriously?" Luckily, Rafe picked up on who Gabe meant immediately. "Wow. She was right. If you hadn't pointed her out, I never would have guessed. Good disguise."

Just then the waitress arrived to take their orders. Clearly overwhelmed at the prospect of waiting on the two owners, she stammered as she asked them what they'd like to drink.

"It's okay." Reading her name on her tag, Gabe smiled to put her at ease. "Beth, you can relax. Are you new?"

"Yes, sir." She attempted a nervous smile and failed. "It's my second day."

"You'll be fine," Gabe reassured her. "I'd like a coffee and a large orange juice."

"The same for me, except make my juice tomato," Rafe put in, also flashing her a smile. To both men's amusement, she blushed before nodding and rushing off to get their drinks.

"I hope she hurries with the coffee." Stifling a yawn, Rafe drummed his fingers on the tablecloth. Gabe nodded absently, aware he could also use a nice jolt of caffeine.

"Do you want to invite her over?" Rafe asked, making Gabe realize he'd gone back to watching Meghan, who so far appeared completely unaware of his scrutiny.

"No," Gabe answered quickly, maybe too quickly, judging by his brother's raised brows. "I'll be spending all day with her. She probably needs a little peace and quiet."

"Like we all do," Rafe murmured. "After the New Year celebration, Evangeline and I plan to go off somewhere alone together."

Surprised, Gabe nodded. "Good for you."

Beth arrived with their drinks and both men ordered.

Nothing fancy, just one of the ordinary breakfasts right off the menu. "Oh, and do me a favor, Beth," Rafe asked. "Don't tell the cook who it's for. We want to sample the same thing our customers are served."

Color still high, she nodded before bustling off to the kitchen.

"Think she will?" Rafe asked, watching her go.

Gabe dragged his gaze off Meghan long enough to shrug. "Who knows? Fifty-fifty chance. Depends if she likes the cook or not."

Meghan twirled one short strand of hair around her finger as she read. Adorable and, even in her disguise, sexy as hell.

Rafe cleared his throat. "Look, bro, if you keep staring at her like that, she's going to notice. Hell, other people are going to notice. Just go and invite her to join us."

Gabe wanted to. Really wanted to. But he also knew women who looked like her were used to men fawning all over them. He definitely didn't want to join the ranks.

So instead, he focused on his coffee and made a determined effort to keep his gaze focused on anything beside her.

Finally Meghan had begun to relax. She'd been a little—okay, a lot—worried, but once she'd ventured out in her halfhearted disguise and no one mobbed her, she could feel the tension leave her body.

Fame and attention were givens, considering what she did for a living. But every now and then she yearned to be a regular person living a normal life. Like right now, she could have coffee and read the latest romance novel she'd picked up before leaving home. The cheerful sound of multiple slot machines made a pleasant background noise. No one paid the slightest bit of attention to her. Mornings didn't get much better than this, at least lately. Maybe this Vegas residency had been a good idea.

Anything to shake up the endless touring and pretending to be someone she wasn't. Even her dates had all been arranged with an eye on publicity.

Even the prospect of shopping sounded appealing. Just like in the old days, before paparazzi with their endless cameras and questions. She could help the handsome casino owner get his Christmas shopping done. She felt a pang at the thought. She hadn't bought Christmas presents for anyone in a long, long time. Her family simply didn't celebrate anymore.

Which was the absolute last thing she wanted to focus on, especially surrounded by Christmas decorations and holiday music. At least today, she could have a normal afternoon, as long as her disguise held up. No one but the Stavros brothers even knew she'd arrived in Vegas so early.

Trying to focus on her book, she found herself thinking about Gabe Stavros instead. She'd never seen a man fill out a suit jacket so well. With his longish dark hair and caramel-colored eyes, she wondered how he dressed when he wasn't working. Or...how he'd look without any clothes on at all. All hard muscle, she'd bet. For the first time in a long time, she found herself fantasizing about exactly that.

A shiver skittered up her spine, just like it always did when someone was watching her. Equal parts dread and curiosity had her slowly lifting her head to see why, even as she prayed she hadn't been recognized. Of course, 90 percent of people would be unsure, and if she laughingly denied being herself, they'd leave her alone. Or so her manager claimed. Personally, Meghan hadn't had a chance to actually try this theory out. If she had a choice, she'd opt for not being recognized at all to begin with.

All around her in the crowded restaurant, diners ate or drank their coffee and read the paper. Families in large groups and small, some talking and passing around a platter of perfectly toasted bread, others chowing down on their food and checking their phones. No one appeared to be paying attention, staring at her, or whispering and pointing while trying not to stare. So far, so good.

And then she swiveled her head to the left and met Gabe Stavros's gorgeous whiskey eyes. Inside, a flame sparked to life, suffusing her with heat. Despite this, she managed to keep her cool. Inclining her head in a tiny nod of recognition, she pretended to go back to reading her book.

Luckily for her, the waitress arrived with her breakfast. This morning, Meghan had splurged and ordered eggs Benedict with salmon along with a side of fruit.

And it looked every bit as wonderful as she'd pictured. She rarely allowed herself to indulge like this, but since today was the start of her vacation, why not?

While she ate, she could tell every time Gabe glanced her way. She felt the intensity of his gaze as strongly as if he'd touched her.

Interesting. Finishing, she blotted the corners of her mouth with her napkin and looked his way. His gaze darkened as their eyes met again.

Her breath caught. Him. For the first time in too many years to count, she wanted to skim her hands down a broad and no doubt muscular chest, over the washboard abs of his stomach, hesitating only when she reached the top of his leather belt.

Thoroughly aroused, she realized if he could make her entire body tingle with just a look, his touch would send her up in flames.

The next few weeks suddenly seemed to hold a lot more promise. This could definitely get interesting.

Once she'd charged her breakfast to her room, she went over to Gabe's table. His companion looked enough like him that she figured he had to be his brother.

"Good morning." Her confident smile was part of her onstage persona, though they had no way of knowing that. In fact, judging from the slightly dazed look on the other Stavros brother's face, it had the desired effect.

Gabe smoothly performed the introductions. She shook Rafe's hand, admiring the firm grip while noting his touch didn't affect her the same way Gabe's did.

"I'm going to go upstairs and change," she told Gabe. "I'll be ready shortly."

Though he nodded, he let his gaze rake boldly over her. Again, she felt the trail of his eyes like heat skittering across her skin. "Define 'shortly,'" he drawled, smiling faintly. "Do you mean a few minutes or a few hours?"

Just like that, her charmed bubble burst. He didn't know her and like so many others, assumed she was some sort of diva like many other female performers.

Keeping her smile firmly in place, she straightened her shoulders. "I'll be ready on time. I don't believe in keeping people waiting." Turning, she sailed out the door, smiling all the way to the elevator. Only once she'd gotten inside did she relax.

Deep breaths. Those two men were her new bosses and if their experience was anything like hers, words didn't matter half as much as actions. Unlike other superstars, she would never even consider making an audience wait, nor did she expect other people to constantly adjust their schedules to accommodate hers.

They'd see. She'd gotten ahead by dint of hard work and a sprinkling of talent. She had no reason to change what, until now, had always been a winning formula.

"Wow," Rafe commented the second Meghan sailed out of the restaurant. "I'm guessing she didn't like you teasing her about being on time. She went from warm and friendly to frozen statue in seconds."

Gabe nodded. "She doesn't know me well enough to get my bantering. It's okay. Give her time."

"Defending her?" Openly amused, Rafe leaned back in his chair. "Of course, I can't say I blame you. She is one fine-looking woman."

The second instant flash of jealousy at his brother's joking words both amazed and worried Gabe. How could he be feeling so possessive toward a woman he'd just met the day before?

"Though not my type," Rafe said, redeeming himself.

"Of course not. You've got the beautiful Evangeline."

"That I do." Rafe grinned. Glancing at his watch, he stood. "Sorry to run, but I've got a meeting with the housekeeping department. I can't wait to hear how your little shopping trip goes."

Gabe grimaced. He'd already begun to regret impulsively inviting Meghan Frost to join him. Christmas shopping was hard enough without having to deal with her. Never mind the simmering attraction between them. He knew with the right provocation, it would burst into flames as swiftly as he would when he Rejuvenated.

Chapter 4

At exactly ten o'clock, Gabe found himself outside her door, fist poised to knock. His heart sped up in anticipation as he found himself wondering what she'd be wearing. Then he shook his head. Asking himself what he was doing, he rapped sharply on the wood, three times.

Immediately, the door swung open. She wore a baggy T-shirt, faded jeans and brightly colored sneakers. The loose-fitting clothes made it impossible to spy the lush curves he knew they concealed. "Hi there," she said, her mouth curving slightly at his staring. "Let me grab my purse and I'll be ready to go."

Since she didn't invite him in, he nodded, waiting in the hallway. She seemed different, less at ease. Almost…shy. Which would be ridiculous. He reminded himself what she was. Above all else, a performer.

"I made sure to get cash from one of the ATMs," she said. "I don't want to use my credit cards since my name is on them."

"Wise choice." Taking her arm, he pretended not to notice her slight start. "I'm counting on you to help me, you know." He dug in his pocket and produced his list. "I've got quite a few people to buy gifts for."

"Let me see."

He handed her the piece of paper, waiting while she read over it. "That's not too bad," she said, handing it back to him. "This is going to be fun. Let's get started."

He couldn't tell if the enthusiasm in her voice was real or not, but decided he didn't really care. With her, it'd be easier to simply take her at face value. Much less complicated when one didn't go around looking for hidden meanings behind everything. Long ago, he'd tried to rid himself of this bad habit, since it got in the way of living. Most times, he thought he'd succeeded.

As they walked to the elevator, her arm in his, he realized she might be right. Though he disliked shopping, this actually had the potential of becoming enjoyable.

"Let's start with the most challenging name on your list. Your mother." They stepped into the elevator and he pushed the button that would take them to the casino floor. As with all hotels on the Vegas Strip, guests had to walk through the bustling casino to get to the rooms, shops or restaurants. Lots of revenue was generated that way.

"I have no idea what to get her," Gabe confessed. Among their kind, his mother was known as a wisewoman and healer. She had a huge indoor herb garden and enjoyed concocting homeopathic remedies for friends and family. He relayed this information on to Meghan. "Unfortunately, she already has tons of gardening books and every tool known to mankind." Which wasn't far from the truth.

"What about seeds?" Meghan asked. "I know it's not something you can buy here in the hotel, but I'm betting you could go online and find some amazing packages."

"While that's a great idea, not only would I have no idea

what kind of seeds to get her, with only a week left until Christmas, there's no way I could get them here on time."

"Maybe not." She conceded the point with a shrug and a smile. "What about clothes or jewelry? What does she like to wear?"

He sighed. "She has quite an extensive scarf collection. For years, that's all Rafe and I got her. She finally told us she had enough and to stop."

The elevator doors opened. The boisterous casino sounds, along with the ever-present odor of smoke, announced they'd arrived. As always, the noise made him smile.

"Do you gamble?" he asked, steering her through the crowded casino, dodging the occasional meandering tourists who never appeared to notice when someone was behind them.

"I have a few times." She stayed close to him, nearly melded to his side. "Quarter slot machines only. But I'm not a big fan. I work really hard to earn my money. I don't like to watch it disappear just like that."

He stayed silent while they navigated around groups of people, some already with drinks in their hands. Once they made it to the perimeter, there'd be one long hallway, and then the entrance to the opulent shopping mall would be right ahead of them.

"Come on." Impulsively he took her hand, dragging her along through the crowds. She didn't protest. In fact, a glance back at her revealed a mischievous grin. Surprised, he grinned back, his mood surprisingly light.

Once in the crowded mall, he stopped outside a huge Christmas tree made up entirely of poinsettia plants. Deep red flowers were interspersed with white and the occasional pink. Gold glitter had been sprinkled over the entire thing, and twinkling white lights gave it a true holiday feel.

"That's amazing," Meghan said, stopping to stare. "It

must be at least thirty feet tall. I can't imagine how much work went into making that."

"I watched them build it. Underneath are levels of wooden platforms, which is what they place the flower pots on. To keep it looking fresh, the gardeners come by every couple of days and water and change out the plants." He figured he should release her hand, but realized he liked holding on to it too much to let go just yet.

"Very cool." Turning to look at him, she held out her free hand. "Back to your mom. Does she like to read?"

He thought about her question. "Not really." There were books scattered all over the house, but if he ever spied his mother reading anything, it was a gardening magazine or seed catalog.

"Okay. Let's try something else. Over the years, has your mom mentioned anything—like a hobby or a skill or something she used to do when she was younger—that she wished she could take up again?"

He really had to think about this one. "I remember years ago her wanting to take a photography class. I don't remember why she didn't take it, but she once wanted to take professional-quality pictures."

Meghan nodded, fairly bouncing up and down with excitement. "Now we're getting somewhere. Does she have a good camera? Because if she does, you can get her a gift certificate with photography lessons."

"She has one of those small cameras. You know the one that's tinier than a cell phone?"

She waved away his words. "Well, that takes care of her gift. We need to get her a good camera."

"There's a store on the third level," he said, suddenly excited as well as relieved. He could imagine his mother's surprise when she opened her gift on Christmas morning. A camera. "Thanks so much, Meghan. I would never have thought of that."

Her shy smile had his blood heating again. "We're not done yet."

At the electronics store, he told the salesperson what he needed and was directed to a display case in the middle of the store. "These are perfect for a beginner," the older man said.

Gabe checked them out. He recognized the manufacturers: Nikon and Canon, as well as Pentax. Some of the others he knew made electronic products, but he decided to stick with the Nikon, since that was the best known. He bought her a model midway between a professional DSLR and a Point and Shoot. According to the salesman, it was called a digital bridge camera and came with an amazing 70x zoom lens. Along with that, Gabe purchased a camera case and spare battery. All in all, he'd finished with his mom for under five hundred dollars.

When they left the store, bag in tow, he watched Meghan cross his mom off the list. "One down. Now let's talk about your father."

Several hours later, he'd gotten something for everyone on the list. Something really good, too, not just random junk. In fact, he figured his entire family would love their gifts. All thanks to Meghan, a woman he barely knew. He felt a glow of warmth, the cynical side of him slightly surprised she hadn't asked for anything for herself. Of course, why would she? She could simply purchase whatever she needed.

Being with her had somehow made shopping, usually something he could barely tolerate, bearable. Even…fun. Because he liked her. Honestly liked her. In addition to being beautiful and talented, she was a pretty awesome human being, too.

"I couldn't have done this without your help," he told her. "Thank you, from the bottom of my heart."

Her pleased smile told him how much she appreciated the compliment.

"Let's get these bags up to my place and then we'll grab a bite to eat."

"I'll help you, but count me out on dinner." Once again, she'd surprised him. "I've got some phone calls I need to make."

He hid his disappointment. "What about later?" he asked. "You mentioned you wanted to try your luck at some slot machines. We could grab a drink and check those out."

Covering her yawn with her hand, she smiled politely. "Thanks, but not tonight. I'm really tired. If it's okay with you, I'd like to grab a rain check on that."

She'd just spent part of the morning and most of the afternoon in a crowded mall helping a near-stranger Christmas shop. Of course she was tired.

"A rain check it is," he promised. "I definitely owe you dinner and a drink. Just let me know when."

"I will." The relief flashing in her green eyes told him she'd expected him to try to persuade her to change her mind. Glad he hadn't, though that thought had occurred to him, he walked her to the elevator. Once inside, he set his shopping bags down and relieved her of hers.

"You don't have to do that," she protested. "I was going to help you carry them to your suite."

He couldn't help himself; he kissed her cheek. "I can manage." The elevator stopped at her floor, the one right below his and Rafe's. "You go and get some rest. Remember, if you get hungry and don't feel like going out, our room service is top-notch."

With an uncertain smile, she nodded and walked away.

He'd kissed her on the cheek. Just one, not both sides with the air-kiss the way everyone did in LA. All the way down the hall to her suite, Meghan pondered what to make of this development. Maybe she'd been wrong. Was it possible Gabe Stavros wasn't attracted to her at all? Men only kissed women's cheeks if they thought of them like a sister or friend. Perhaps…he was gay. This last thought made her laugh out loud. If he was, then the joke was on her. Her friends had told her this had happened before to them—meet a man too gorgeous for words and find out he played for the other team.

Except she just knew Gabe wasn't gay. He wasn't disinterested, either. The way he looked at her, like he could eat her up with his gaze, told her the attraction was mutual. Then what? Considering, she felt a stab of pain. Maybe it was her reputation, that fake and glittering persona her PR people felt was necessary for a pop star.

But really, would a man as confident and virile as Gabe let a little thing like a wild reputation scare him? For the first time in her life, she actually wanted to live up to her utterly false characterization, especially since all of this—her show as well as her stay in Vegas—was only temporary.

How ironic. She wanted to be wild, but he wasn't interested. Or was he? She'd have to be blind not to notice the way he looked at her. But then why the kiss on the cheek?

The only other alternative was that he didn't think someone like her—aka free, untamed and a little bit crazy—could possibly be interested in someone steady and stable like him. As an alternative possibility, he might not believe in a boss fraternizing with his employees.

Letting herself into her suite, she shook her head. Overthinking things was one of her specialties. She needed to let it go. Though a wonderful distraction, no doubt getting involved with the man who technically employed her would be a horrible idea. Since she couldn't have a distraction, she'd simply have to do what she always did and find a way to deal with her loneliness and sadness.

Buying Christmas presents for his family and then watching as the store clerks wrapped them in brightly colored paper and bows had made her once again yearn for something she could never have. No matter how much she wished it, her family would never be the type from a Norman Rockwell painting, gathered around the gaily decorated Christmas tree. There would be no Christmas feast, no mushy cards or hugs or holiday joy. No togetherness, no love.

They only cared about the hunt. Her destiny, they'd said, unable to understand how she could want to let such a horrible thing go. They'd never get that she'd had to. How could someone full of bloodlust and hate sing songs of beauty about love and peace? She couldn't be that person, the fierce and focused Hunter, constantly stalking a type of being that, if they even existed, had done nothing to deserve murderous rage.

Of course, there were the stories. Every now and then, a Hunter got close. One had even died here in Vegas recently, supposedly because he'd gotten too close on his hunt for a Helios.

Her family lived for the hunt. She'd wanted something different. And so they'd rewarded her by leaving her utterly and completely alone.

Wandering into the opulent bathroom with its floor-to-ceiling marble and huge Jacuzzi tub, she decided to take a bath. Usually a hot shower type of girl, she thought a luxurious soak just might be the perfect way to drain some of the tension from her. If all else failed, she had her choreographed dance routines for the upcoming show to practice. A perfectionist, she'd keep at that over and over again, until her body wilted from exhaustion.

But practicing alone wasn't the same as rehearsing with

her dancers. And she'd given her people two weeks off for the holiday. She couldn't very well rescind that and demand they show up in Vegas and begin rehearsal. After all, they'd gotten everything down perfect before she'd left LA. Once the special set she'd had built had been transported here, all it would take would be a few routine practices before they'd be ready to go live. She'd made sure of that. She'd never liked to leave anything so big to chance.

After getting all the brightly wrapped parcels to his suite, Gabe arranged them on the dining room table. For the first time ever, he found himself wishing he'd taken the time to put up a Christmas tree. Of course, he could call and have one of his employees take care of it, but it felt like the sort of thing he should do himself. He might even ask Meghan to help him decorate it.

The instant the thought occurred to him, he put on the breaks. What the hell was wrong with him? They weren't dating; they weren't even friends. He barely knew the woman, yet when he was with her he felt as if he'd known her forever. One thing for sure: he wanted to get to know her better, especially in a physical way. Someone like her could probably care less about a Christmas tree. She'd even told him her family wasn't big on the holiday.

If Meghan couldn't help him decorate, then he might as well have someone else do it. What fun would setting up a Christmas tree all by himself be? He picked up the phone, called the people who took care of the hotel decorations, and placed an order for a fully decorated tree to be brought to his suite. After being assured it would be done by the next day, he hung up and headed back downstairs to find his brother and see if Rafe wanted to grab a bite to eat.

But when he reached the office area, he saw his brother and Evangeline leaving together, arm in arm. She'd snuggled into Rafe's side and he gazed down at her, his expression tender. No way Gabe could interrupt that. It'd been a long time since he'd had a serious relationship. Lots of dates, but none had really clicked, and he'd grown tired of one-night stands. Feeling lonelier than he had in years, he headed for the buffet and a solitary evening meal.

Later, as he made his usual rounds checking out the blackjack tables, poker games and the satisfyingly crowded slot area, he found himself looking for Meghan. Just on the off chance that she'd decided to come and gamble, after all. He didn't spot her, but then again, he had no idea what disguise she might have chosen to wear. He had to admit, the intrigue of her various costumes intrigued him. He truly had no idea who the real Meghan Frost might be.

A shout near the blackjack area had him turn. "He's got a gun," someone yelled. A woman screamed. Then there was a loud pop—a gunshot. Instantly, Gabe began to scan the crowd, trying to determine the location of the shooter.

He had two concerns. Neutralize the shooter and get all of his guests immediately to safety. More shots, more screams. As panic spread like wildfire through the crowd, people abandoned their slot machines, stampeding for one of the three exits.

Luckily, Gabe and Rafe had trained their staff well. Hopefully, that training would hold up now.

Chapter 5

"Don't panic," one of the blackjack dealers ordered. "Everyone, please proceed in a calm and orderly fashion toward the exit."

No one listened. Glad no small children were allowed on the casino floor, Gabe directed two of his other employees, both cocktail waitresses and both clearly terrified, to help him get the guests outside.

"I've called 9-1-1," one of the women said, her eyes huge in her pale face. "LVPD should be on the way."

"Good job." Again he scanned the room, looking for the gunman. He saw nothing beyond the mad crush of panicked people rushing to get out. Across the melee, he caught sight of Rafe and Evangeline, both also herding people toward the exit. Gabe took off toward his brother.

"What the hell's going on?" he asked.

"Not sure." Mouth set in a grim line, Rafe grabbed an elderly woman in a wheelchair and began pushing her toward another employee. "Help get her out," he ordered.

He shot a look at Evangeline, who shepherded another old couple. "You'd better go outside, too."

"No." She balked. "Not until all of the patrons are safe."

Rafe cursed. He crossed to her and cupped her face in his hands. "Please," he said. "For me. I can't concentrate until I know you're safe."

Finally, she nodded. "I'll be right outside if you need me." Rafe watched until she'd disappeared through the double doors. When he turned to face Gabe, he took a deep breath.

"Any signs of the shooter?" Gabe asked.

"No. I've got the security team searching," Rafe informed Gabe. "Beyond that, I don't know who the actual target was or if there are any injuries or—gods forbid—any fatalities."

Feeling sick, Gabe nodded. The stampede had thinned and the cavernous casino floor appeared empty. The silence of the normally loud slot machines felt eerie.

"Time to head out," Gabe said.

"The police are here." No sooner had the words left Rafe's mouth, when three men wearing black vests proclaiming them SWAT burst through the door.

"Clear the room," one of them ordered. "That includes you two," he informed Gabe and Rafe.

"We're the owners," Rafe began.

"I don't care if you're a god," the SWAT guy said, his choice of words causing Gabe to give him a second glance. "You need to get out until we secure the site."

Gabe nodded and took Rafe's arm. "Come on." Though he practically had to drag his brother away, he got him through the door and outside.

The front of the Archangel, with its twin, tall, vengeful angel stone fountains and pavestone circular drive, normally bustled with taxis and limos, along with throngs of patrons coming and going from the Strip. Today, however, the police had roped off the front of the hotel with yellow crime scene tape. They'd posted several guards, turning away incoming vehicles and keeping people a good distance down the drive. Anyone needing to enter the hotel had been directed to wait. Even the employees' side entrance was being manned by uniformed police.

In effect, their entire operation had been shut down.

Meghan. His heart skipped a beat. He had no idea if she was safe, if she'd gotten out. Pulling out his phone, he called her. The call went straight to voice mail.

Glancing at the guards, he debated the difficulty of going back in and locating her.

"I swear by ancient Rome, if the Hunters are behind this..." Rafe began, distracting him.

"Do you think they are?" Eyes narrowed, Gabe glared at his brother. "With so many random, crazy humans in this world, why would the Hunters do such a thing?"

"To create chaos." Rafe's simple answer rang with truth. "Their specialty. And since I was attacked, I know they've been around here waiting for the winter solstice and hoping to witness a Rejuvenation."

"But gunshots?" Gabe wasn't convinced. "That would draw attention to them, maybe even get them arrested. I'd think that'd be the last thing they'd want."

Rafe pondered his words. Finally, he shrugged. "Who knows?" He jerked his head toward the front door. "Looks like we might just be about to find out."

One of the SWAT members, the one who'd done all the talking, strode toward them. "Kevin Kern," he said, holding out his hand. "You two said you own this hotel? We need to ask you a few questions."

Gabe nodded. "Fine. Tell me you caught the guy first."

The police officer paused. "We didn't find anyone. We've got several witnesses who claimed to have seen him, but none of their descriptions match."

"We've got security footage," Rafe chimed in. "Let's go take a look at those."

"Fire!" someone yelled, sending a shudder of foreboding up Gabe's spine. His body took the reaction a step further, attempting to force Rejuvenation. Right here, right now.

"Damn," Rafe cursed. "That's the last thing we need."

"Wait here," Kevin ordered, taking off running. Of course Gabe and Rafe followed him inside. A cloud of thick, black smoke billowed from an area near the poker tables. The two brothers exchanged glances. Gabe could see his own inner struggle mirrored in his brother's eyes. Fire called to fire. Though Rafe had already Rejuvenated early, Gabe had not. He was so close to the time. It took every ounce of self-control Gabe possessed to keep from bursting into flames.

"There's no doubt now," Gabe said through clenched teeth. "It has to be the Hunters."

Rafe nodded, clearly not wanting to use any of his energy to speak.

"Outside," one of the SWAT members barked, shepherding them away from the smoke. "No civilians here until we secure the area." Fire alarms sounded. "We're evacuating the entire hotel."

The entire hotel. Gabe swallowed and nodded. *Meghan.* Had she heard the alarms? Again, he tried her cell. Once more, straight to voice mail.

"You two. Out."

Rafe and Gabe looked at each other. "We can't," Rafe began. "We're the owners."

"That's irrelevant."

"It's not. Since we own this place, we have a responsibility to make sure all our employees and guests get out safely," Gabe countered. "We can't leave until we're certain of this." No matter what, he had to make sure Meghan Frost had made it out. Though surely she heard the alarms, even up in her isolated penthouse suite. Despite this, he needed to see her personally and make sure she was safe.

"No." A second man, this one wearing an LVPD uniform, stepped up to assist the first. "We've got personnel doing exactly that. Now please, step outside and let us do our jobs."

Gabe didn't move. "I've got a VIP guest staying in one of the penthouse suites. At least let me get up there and make sure she got out."

"No." The officer moved to block his path. "Let me make a call."

Gabe glanced at his brother. Rafe knew him, knew what he was thinking, and shook his head. "You're not charging past them to try and find her. There's no way."

"Why not?" Gabe muttered back. "You'd do the same if it was Evangeline in there."

Rafe didn't have an answer for that, as he knew Gabe was right. Shoulders tense, Gabe watched the officer on his radio, trying to formulate some sort of plan. He had to get to Meghan.

"My guys have cleared the top three floors," the officer said. "While they didn't find any celebrities, they were able to evacuate a woman staying alone on one of the floors."

Gabe's chest felt tight. "Did they get a name?"

The other man looked at him as if he'd lost his mind. "No, sir. But she's a very attractive young lady, according to my men."

"That had to be her." Rafe grabbed his arm. "Come on outside with me. Surely you have her number. Call her and make sure she's safe."

Gabe glowered, but finally nodded, aware Rafe had a point. Again, the nearby flames called to him. Rafe, too. Side by side, the two brothers moved quickly outside again. Once away from the tantalizing lure of the flames, they breathed identical sighs of relief.

"Damn Hunters. We've got to locate them," Gabe began.

"And then what?" Rafe countered, while scrolling through his contacts. "You know as well as I do that we can't hurt them unless they attack us first. We need to direct the human police toward them. If we can get them arrested for their very real crimes, that'll keep them away."

"I know you're methodical, but come on."

Expression thunderous, Rafe didn't immediately reply. Tamping down his mounting frustration, Gabe glowered while Rafe kept scrolling, aware his brother most likely was aware how badly Gabe still struggled with the urge to burst into flames.

"What's going on?" A petite woman with long blond hair and oversize sunglasses came up to them. If not for the husky purr of her voice and the smooth perfection of her skin, Gabe wouldn't have recognized her. When he did, he felt instant relief and then a thrum of pleasure.

"You made it out," he said.

"Exactly like the nice police officer told you she did," Rafe interjected, barely glancing up from his phone.

Gabe ignored him, unable to tear his gaze away from Meghan. "How many disguises do you have?" he asked.

Her slow smile started a different kind of heat simmering inside him. "Several," she replied. "I'm actually having fun playing dress-up. But you haven't answered my question. They're evacuating the entire hotel. Is the casino on fire?"

"It would appear so," Rafe answered glumly. "We're hoping to have answers soon."

Which would be the understatement of the year. Gabe checked his watch. They had two large company parties being held that night. Both firms had paid lavishly for the use of the two ballrooms. The hotel catering staff had been busy all day preparing food. They had brought in additional bartenders to handle the alcohol since each company wanted open bars set up. These types of things were always profitable. With the holiday season upon them, the Archangel was booked every single night.

"The fire's out." Kevin Kern strode toward them. "One of the card tables was set ablaze. You got lucky since it was contained and didn't spread. Most of the damage is smoke related."

Relieved, Gabe nodded. "We can cordon off that area until it can be cleaned up. The rest of the casino can go back to normal."

"The fire department will have to approve that," Kevin said. "Their investigator is in there now."

"I'll go talk to him," Rafe said immediately.

"And I'll take you to review the security footage," Gabe put in. "This way, please." As he led the way, he realized Meghan had decided to tag along.

"Ma'am." Kevin turned to face her. "I'm afraid this is a private matter. I'll have to ask you to move away."

"She's with me," Gabe heard himself say. Meghan rewarded him with her trademark brilliant grin.

"Employee?" Kevin asked.

"Friend." The no-nonsense tone in Gabe's voice warned the other man not to pursue it any further. After all, this was Gabe's hotel.

Gabe used his security key card to unlock the door. "In here." He stood aside, allowing Kevin and Meghan to precede him. "Let me introduce you to our head of security. He can cue up the video we need."

A short while later, they all clustered around a monitor, watching as a tall, thin man in a gray hoodie wandered up to the poker table, pulled a pistol from his pocket and shot the dealer point-blank in the chest. Then, while the man lay crumpled at his feet, he turned and fired a few shots up toward the ceiling.

Meghan gasped. "Did he kill that man?"

"He's been transported to the hospital." Kevin gave her a hard look. "Still alive, though obviously that could change."

Then the man in the hoodie pulled something from his pocket and tossed it on the poker table. He had unusually long and slender fingers. A flash occurred, a small explosion, knocking several people off their feet as they ran by.

Meanwhile, the perpetrator strode swiftly away, vanishing into the growing cloud of smoke.

"I can't get a look at his face." Frustration darkened Kevin's voice. "He seems to know where the cameras are, so he's making sure the hood keeps his face in shadow."

"I've got my men looking for him," the security head said. "As soon as we saw that go down, I radioed them and they converged on the casino. I'm pretty sure most of them were there when the explosion happened."

Gabe cast him a startled look. "Did they get out?"

"Yes." The terse response spoke of the other man's worry. "A little singed. One of my men can't hear out of his left ear. But they're alive. That's all that matters."

"That, and finding out who did this." Gabe couldn't let on that he had a pretty good idea. After all, how could he explain Hunters to humans? Especially since humans were not even aware of such things as Helios.

"Something about him looks familiar." Meghan mused. "Though I can't say where, I'd swear I've seen him before."

Kevin stared at her hard. "You seem familiar to me, too. Have we met?"

"Nope." Both Meghan and Gabe answered at the same time. They exchanged slight smiles before turning their attention back to the video.

"Play it again, this time in slow motion," Gabe ordered. They all watched intently, each struggling to see something that wasn't there.

"Maybe if we had another angle," his security chief said. "But we don't. We just need to catch that SOB."

"Agreed." Kevin shook his head before handing over a card. "I'll need a copy of that video, please."

"Sure. I'll have one of my guys prepare it immediately."

They left the room, this time with Kevin leading the way and Gabe and Meghan bringing up the rear.

"I'm going to go check on the progress," Kevin said. "Mr. Stavros, please stick around in case we have any more questions.'

Gabe nodded. "I'm always around. I not only work here, but I live here, too. So does my brother."

When they reached the common area, Rafe came hurrying over. "Anything?"

"Not yet." Kevin looked from one man to the other. "You have my card. Call me if you hear or see anything out of the ordinary. And you," he added, pinning Meghan with a measured stare. "If you remember where you saw that man before, you call me, okay?"

She nodded. They all watched silently as Kevin hurried off to rejoin his team.

Rafe cleared his throat. "What did he mean by that?" he asked.

"Meghan said the shooter looked familiar," Gabe supplied. "She thinks she might have seen him somewhere."

Rafe swore in their native Greek.

After a startled look, Meghan shrugged. "Sorry. I don't know why or where I might have seen him. I still wasn't able to be of any help."

"The important thing is that no one else was seriously hurt," Gabe said, shooting his brother a hard look. "We need to find out the identity of the man who was shot and make sure neither he nor his family want for anything."

Rafe's gaze narrowed as he looked from his brother to the pop superstar. "Agreed. But after those things are accomplished, I want every effort possible put into finding this man in the gray hoodie."

"Of course." Putting his hand on Meghan's shoulder, Gabe turned her to face him. "Are you going to be all right?"

Slowly she nodded. "Sure. I'll see you around later?"

"Of course." He kept his tone smooth. "Let me help Rafe deal with the cleanup and then I'll find you."

She nodded and left them, probably aware his gaze followed her until she was out of sight.

"Getting pretty involved there, aren't you?" Rafe asked, his tone serious.

"Weren't you worried about Evangeline?" Gabe countered.

"I was, but I just spoke with her. She's out back in the greenhouse, making sure the plants are okay. But that's beside the point. We're talking about you."

"I'm fine." Gabe realized his clipped response meant he was anything but. "Or I will be." He managed what he hoped was a cocky grin. "Once I get her out of my system."

Chapter 6

As she walked away, Meghan couldn't help but dwell on his words. *He'd find her.* She didn't know why this particular phrase affected her so strongly. The way he said the words sounded as if he was making her a promise.

Which was silly. They hadn't known each other long enough to promise each other anything.

More realistically, her feelings were heightened because when she was around him, she existed in a continual haze of sexual arousal.

Soon, she hoped the time would come to do something about that. Not right now, while the Archangel was in a state of chaos and upheaval. *Chaos.* Her family thrived on that. Supposedly, her people were descended from an ancient Greek god of Chaos.

Legends and stories. Because of their belief in them, her people belonged to a larger group who called themselves Hunters, with a capital *H.* As a teenager, she'd begun to wonder if they were a cult, especially since every single one she'd ever met, including her entire family, believed they'd been entrusted with a unique destiny. Bringing chaos to the modern world.

Personally, she figured everything was chaotic enough, without the help of any Hunters. But when she'd tried to voice these thoughts, she'd been treated as if she'd gone insane. If not for her musical success, she honestly thought they might have sent her away to one of their retreats, where information would have been pounded into her until she believed as strongly as them.

A shame really, because they were all nice people. Since she'd become a success, she took care of her entire family financially. She just wished, every once in a while, they'd take care of her emotionally.

Therapy had helped her come to grips with her lack of closeness with her family. She'd learned to understand that she alone was responsible for her happiness. That didn't mean she could make herself stop longing for something she couldn't have, especially around the holidays.

The next morning, when Meghan went downstairs, the hotel and casino seemed back to normal. When she walked past the area where the fire had occurred, despite the missing poker table and small, roped-off area, she smelled no smoke and didn't see any burn marks or even blood on the carpet. Whomever the Stavros brothers employed to do cleanup, they did a fabulous job.

The entire walk to the restaurant, she caught herself looking for Gabe. Foolish, maybe. She knew he'd have his hands full dealing with not only the police investigation, but the media and the hotel staff. He wouldn't have time for her today, she knew. But she thought if she could just catch a glimpse of him, exchanging a small, secret smile, then that would be enough to carry her through until they could reconnect. Somehow, just being in his presence was enough to keep the loneliness away.

She was given her usual seat near the window, a spot she liked. She'd never minded eating alone as long as she had a good book to read. This time, she had trouble focusing on the words. Her continuous searching for a glimpse of Gabe was too distracting.

As usual, the breakfast tasted delicious. She'd pushed her empty plate away, still sipping coffee, and forced herself to focus on at least finishing the chapter.

Since the story was engaging, this shouldn't be so difficult, but it was.

Finally, she abandoned the attempt. Her good mood had begun to fizzle and she knew she'd have to work hard to get it back. Loneliness sometimes affected her like that. This was one of the reasons she enjoyed being on tour, where people constantly surrounded her.

Her phone chimed, indicating she'd received a text message. Her brother Damon.

Thinking of you, he'd written.

Immensely cheered, she texted him back. She reminded him that she was already in Vegas, staying at the Archangel. He knew she was doing a resident show there for three months and had promised to attend opening night. Are you sure you haven't changed your mind about having Christmas dinner with me? She'd invited her entire family. They'd all declined, using the hunt as their excuse. If any of them were to change their minds, it would be Damon.

Of all her brothers, Damon was the one she was closest to. He'd been the only one who'd stood by her when she'd announced she'd no longer be participating in the quarterly hunts.

No can do, he responded. I'm gearing up for the hunt. Wish you were by my side. Despite his support of her choice, he'd never stopped hoping she'd change her mind.

They exchanged a few more texts, and then he said he had to go. But at least he'd made contact, which was more than she could say about her parents or any of her other brothers. Which brought her a constant sense of hurt, since when they weren't on an active hunt, except for constant practice, they lived ordinary lives. Though no one had said it out loud, it was like since she'd renounced her heritage, she no longer mattered.

On Christmas Day she'd call them, just like she always did. She knew none of them would be eagerly waiting by the phone to wish her a merry Christmas. She tried not to let it bother her, but she usually ended up in tears, vowing not to put herself through that again next year.

But she'd never been able to make herself lose hope. Hope that one day things would change, that her mother would tell her how much she missed her, that her father would beg her to come home.

Again, an impossible wish. They were what they were, and she loved them anyway.

After breakfast, she decided to wander the shopping mall by herself this time. In years past, she'd actually purchased Christmas gifts for her family, wrapped them up and mailed them. Finally, her mother had asked her to stop. Meghan had never forgotten the pain she'd felt upon hearing those words. She'd also never forgotten the lesson she'd learned.

That was why today, if she bought anything, it would be for herself.

The check came and she signed for it, adding a generous tip.

"There you are."

Gabe. His husky voice sent a pleasurable shiver through her. Brightening, she looked up and smiled, her previous great mood now entirely restored.

In his usual custom suit, he looked elegantly handsome. His dark hair gleamed in the lights and his unconscious air of authority impressed her. What she worked hard to achieve on stage, he came by naturally.

"Any news on the gunshot victim?" she asked.

"His condition has been upgraded from critical to serious. He made it through one surgery and I think there's another scheduled, though I'm not sure when."

"That's good."

His gaze darkened. "What are your plans for today?"

She shrugged, wishing she had the courage to say what had flashed in her mind—that she'd like to spend the rest of the day locked up in her suite with him. "Shopping, probably. After that, I'll play it by ear. What about you?"

"Work." His instant answer didn't surprise her. "I should finish up around noon or so, though I have to remain on call in case any sort of crisis erupts."

Gathering up all of her courage, she took a deep breath. "Are you free for lunch?" Though she kept her smile in place, she braced herself to keep it from slipping if he turned her down.

When he smiled, a sensuous flame danced in his dark eyes. "I am. How about I meet you by the front desk? There's a wonderful Italian place in the hotel next door I love."

Thrilled, she grinned back. "Helping out the competition?"

"We're all friends. We like to sample each other's menus."

She matched his casual tone. "Sounds great. I'll see you around noon?"

"Make it one, just to be safe."

After she agreed, he nodded and strode off. She couldn't tear her gaze away until he disappeared out of sight. His masculine self-confidence and rugged good looks drew many eyes as he passed.

At least she wouldn't be spending the afternoon alone.

She felt quite pleased that she'd mustered up the courage to ask for what she wanted. Now if she could just manage to take that one step further. With a sigh, she got up and headed toward the shops.

The crowds in the mall appeared to have increased, which she knew would happen the closer it got to Christmas. She browsed the purses in the Hermès store, toying with the idea of buying one, but aware to do so she'd have to use her credit card and reveal her true identity. Of course, according to Gabe, the salesclerks were all trained in the use of discretion.

As she examined the purse for the third time, a woman bumped her. "Excuse me, but aren't you Meghan Frost?"

Though Meghan's first instinct was to back away in horror, she forced herself to smile. "I wish. I get that sometimes. If I had her money, I could afford to buy this purse." She put the purse back on the shelf.

Usually, this comment was enough to defuse an overly zealous fan. Not this time. The woman, who had long pink hair, cocked her head and looked her up and down.

"You *are* her," she insisted.

With a wry smile, Meghan shook her head. "I'm really not. But I've been hearing that often enough that I'm thinking maybe I should enter one of those celebrity look-a-like contests. I bet I would win."

This statement finally appeared to work. The woman apologized, though she still cast several suspicious looks over her shoulder as she walked away.

"Are you still interested in that purse, Ms. Frost?" Speaking in a discreet murmur, the salesclerk appeared at her elbow. For a second, Meghan considered denying her identity again, then decided to let it go.

"I think I would," she finally said, unable to keep from glancing toward the door. "As long as that other woman doesn't see me getting it."

After buying the purse, she thought about retreating to her suite, but the new, brave Meghan refused to let the pink-haired woman unnerve her. Shopping bag in hand, she went from store to store, mostly looking, but occasionally making a small purchase here and there.

The prospect of meeting Gabe for lunch made her feel giddy, even if they did end up only discussing business. She couldn't help but wonder if he felt the same way.

Though he had a busy morning schedule, Gabe rushed through everything, anticipation and arousal making his blood simmer. Meghan Frost was not only exquisite, but her inner flame attracted him like a match to dry kindling.

Always honest with himself, he wanted her. But surprisingly, he wanted to get to know her better, too. To learn how to coax that animated smile from her, to bring that spark to her lovely eyes interested him nearly as much.

She'd be here three months, so he planned to take it slow. Or, he amended, as slow as his body would let him. Anticipation would only sweeten the impact when they finally came together.

After Rejuvenation, he knew he'd have a lot more control over both his mind and his body. The rebirth each Helios experienced was exactly that. When he took his turn, he'd burn to ash and rise again whole while the embers still smoldered. A completely new man, his powers restored.

Then, and only then, would he allow himself to make love to the delectable Ms. Frost.

For now, he'd continue his courting. The old-fashioned word made him smile. While Helios didn't live forever, they enjoyed extended life spans. As a result, he had an extensive and sometimes archaic vocabulary that he had to be careful not to use. Being alive for over a century could be confusing sometimes.

For lunch, he had the best plans. He'd changed his mind;

they could always eat Italian food for dinner. He had something else planned. No restaurant, not today. He'd phoned down to the kitchen and had the chef prepare a picnic lunch. Ham sandwiches on French baguettes, hot potato salad and a nice cheese selection. He also had some fresh fruit: strawberries, blueberries and raspberries. To that he'd added a bottle of wine and several pieces of chocolate.

"Where to?" she asked, her quiet, calm confidence seductive in its own way. He liked that she hadn't changed clothes, and her disguise only made him long to peel it off her.

"It's a surprise." He lifted up the picnic hamper.

Her brows rose. "A picnic? Here in the hotel?"

"You'll see. Come with me."

Though he probably should have questioned what he was doing, since he'd never brought an outsider here before, he didn't. He took her to the elevator marked Staff Only, and using his key, they ascended to the top floor. There, he and Rafe had built their own version of paradise. Since Evangeline was skilled with flowers and plants, Rafe had asked her design the layout. At her direction, at least once a day, hotel gardeners tended a massive plot of plants, native and otherwise, some shielded from the scorching Nevada sun by screens of black netting. The brothers had their own swimming pool, surrounded by artfully placed waterfalls, trees of all sizes and shapes, interspersed with blooming flowers of every color. They'd made a refreshing oasis of green in the midst of the desert.

Most important of all, they'd made a Rejuvenation area. Concrete walls on three sides, and a cement roof twenty feet up. As long as they were able to control the urge to Rejuvenate, they could come here at the appointed time and no one would ever see.

Meghan gasped, slowly turning in a circle, trying to take it all in. "This is amazing," she said.

Pleased, he grinned. "You should see it at night, under the stars."

Her eyelashes fluttered. "Is that an invitation?"

Was she flirting with him? His grin widened. "Definitely. But first, I wanted you to experience this during the day. It's private. Besides the gardeners, only Rafe and I can access it. The elevator will only come here if the right room key card is inserted."

"Wow. Definitely impressive." She wandered toward a beautiful blooming cactus. "This is huge."

"It's one of our most prized plants. A really old one, handed down from our grandparents to our parents and then to us."

"And someday you'll hand it down to your children," she said softly.

His children. Not something he'd really ever thought of, but hearing Meghan say the words in her wonderful voice sent a shiver up his spine.

Enchanted despite himself, he showed her the secluded courtyard where they often had family meals. A large stone table sat in the middle.

"You want to eat there?" she asked, glancing longingly at one of the many little grottós complete with waterfalls and koi ponds.

He got the hint. They sat on the slate pathway in one of the larger grottos, the waterfall separating them from the outside world. There, he spread out the meal.

Delight and wonder reflected in her ready laughter, the sparkle in her green eyes and her animated gestures. Though normally Gabe had a restless nature, he thought he could stay right here for hours with her. Even the food tasted better, each flavor heightened.

"My compliments to your chef," she drawled, once they'd finished the meal. "This was absolutely amazing. One of the best lunches I've ever had."

"Just one of the best?" he teased. "Where else have you had lunch that could rival this?"

At his question, her smile faded and some of the brilliance disappeared from her eyes. She looked away, her gaze shuttered.

About to apologize, to say it was none of his business, Gabe stood. Meghan rose, too, forestalling him.

"I'm sorry," she said. "I was thinking of my family. One time, when I was small, we took an actual vacation together. My parents rented a cabin near Lake Murray in Oklahoma. That week was one of the best times I've ever had. One day my mom packed a picnic lunch—sandwiches and chips, nothing like this—but I want to thank you for bringing back such a happy memory."

"You didn't look happy," he said before he could stop himself. Even now, sadness darkened her eyes, entrancing him.

"That's because times like those were few and far between. The older we children got, the less interest my parents had in spending quality time with us."

Not sure how to respond to that, he simply nodded.

"And that," she said, giving him a rueful smile, "is going to be the last time I bring up my family. Talk about ruining the mood."

"The mood?" he teased, hoping they could get back to lighthearted banter. "I wasn't aware there was one."

For an answer, she stood on her tiptoes and pressed her mouth to his.

Chapter 7

As kisses went, this one fell more in the category of chaste and friendly rather than passionate. Then why, Gabe wondered, did the soft touch of her mouth send his insides into a wild spiral of desire?

Trying to collect his thoughts and regain control over his aroused body, he contemplated crushing her to him and showing her exactly how a kiss between them should be. Instead, he held still while she stepped away.

"If you have time, I'd like to see the amphitheater," Meghan said, her hopeful and earnest expression letting him know the kiss hadn't affected her the same way at all. "Though I'm sure you know my people have already been out and drawn up all the plans and my construction crew is arriving the day after Christmas to get the set and props up, I'd still prefer to see it myself. I'd like to get a feel for the venue. Especially the acoustics. I'm dying to test out the sound in there."

Talk about a quick change in subject. And mood.

Inhaling deeply, he managed a nod. "I thought you were on vacation," he said, following her lead.

"I am. So what?" She lifted one shoulder in a delicate shrug. "Even if I was a tourist, I'd still want to see the venue where Meghan Frost was holding her no-doubt fabulous concerts." The flash of her perfect white teeth let him know she was teasing.

Though not about checking out the acoustics. He understood this instinctively.

Working while on vacation was something with which he was infinitely familiar. And her references to herself in the third person made him smile. "Sure. Come on. Let's go take a look."

Impulsively, he held out his hand. When she slipped her slender fingers into his, he felt like he'd won the lottery or a million dollars from a progressive slot machine.

"We built it to be in between the Colosseum at Caesars, which seats just under five thousand people, and the MGM Grand Arena, which holds a little over sixteen thousand."

"My paperwork says the Archangel seats thirteen thousand."

"Give or take a few, yes." Pleased that she'd actually read her contract, he led her past a gated-off area and used his key card to open a door marked Employees Only. "This way," he said, giving her hand a little tug. "I think you're going to be pretty darn impressed."

Laughing, she let him pull her down the hallway, going quiet as they stepped out onto the midlevel balcony. He clicked on his flashlight. "The light box is down below," he told her. "You can use this flashlight to see."

"Wow." Accepting the flashlight, which freed up her hand, she walked over to the railing and stared down at the still-dark stage. With one click, a perfect circle of light parted the darkness,

"It's amazing," she breathed. "Though it's brand-new,

it sort of reminds me of the Ryman in Nashville. I need to go down there and stand where I'll be performing so I can get a feel for the energy of the place."

"Careful," he cautioned, already missing the feel of her hand in his. "I don't need my star falling and breaking something. Why don't you wait here and let me go down and find the light box?"

"Why don't we go together?" Sidling up close to him, she bumped him with her slender hip, sending a sharp jab of lust through him. "We'll use this flashlight to show us the way." And then she laughed, the husky honesty of the sound making him yearn to capture that laugh with his mouth. This close, he could identify her scent, which was not what he would have expected. She smelled like vanilla rather than some smoky perfume. Like a homey kitchen instead of a seductive corner booth in a bluesy downtown bar.

Interesting. And fascinating. Evidently Meghan Frost was a woman of contradictions.

Moving down slowly, stair by stair, with Meghan hanging on to his elbow, they finally reached the floor area. "We'll have to go up on the stage," Gabe told her. "The switch is in back."

"Perfect. The stage is exactly where I want to be." Anticipation hummed in her voice. He had another flash of heat, of desire, strong enough to make him catch his breath.

Once they climbed up the short staircase leading to the stage, she released him. While he went to flip the switch that would turn on the lights, she moved across the platform, making little sounds of pleasure low in her throat. He wondered if those were the same sort of noises she made when making love, then gave himself a mental shake.

When the lights came on, so bright they temporarily blinded him, he blinked, trying to focus on Meghan.

She stood in the center, gazing out over the empty auditorium, her arms upraised as if about to take a sweeping bow. Or worship the sun. As he watched, she pirouetted, an impossibly graceful and sensuous move. And then she sang a few notes, running up and down the scales. The raw beauty of her voice sent a shiver up his spine. The sound seemed to carry and echo off all the empty seats, hang vibrating in the air before being swept up into unseen currents.

What the… With a sense of shock, he realized he'd never really heard her sing live. He'd seen her a few times on TV. Performing on the Grammys or the People's Choice Awards. But that was different. Not live, for sure.

He wanted to hear more. More than just a few notes. An entire song. But he didn't ask, not entirely sure how he'd do so without sounding like a starstruck fan. Instead he moved closer, as if by doing so he could absorb some of her heat.

Catching sight of him, she waved. "Thank you." She crossed the space between them, almost skipping. "This is absolutely perfect. I'm guessing you hired someone good to make sure the acoustics worked."

Nodding, he named the man he'd used, someone he'd been told was the best in the industry. Hearing the name, Meghan clapped. "Oh, he *is* good. Thanks again."

"Nothing but the best for the Archangel." He gave her a slow smile. "And you."

Then, as she gazed up at him, her entire being vibrating with so much life he felt dizzy, he pulled her to him and did what he'd been wanting to do since he first laid eyes on her. He kissed her. Not on the cheek this time, but right where he'd been longing to since the moment she'd seen her. Capturing her mouth with his, what he'd meant to be a slow and thorough exploration of her caught fire. Like lightning to dry kindling, like a wildfire racing across a prairie.

As they kissed, warm and wet, deeper and more passionate than any kiss that had ever come before, the dizzying current of his need for her nearly brought him to his knees.

Damn if he wasn't in trouble.

They both were breathing hard when he finally lifted his head. So was she.

Their gazes locked. Another prickle of awareness, like a breeze stirring banked embers, and he swallowed hard.

"I…" he began.

Her green eyes dark as a stormy sky, she shook her head. "Don't you dare apologize."

That coaxed a laugh from him. "I won't. Come on." He held out his hand. "Let's get out of here. We can walk up and down the Strip and check out the competition, maybe find a quiet bar where we can sit and listen to music."

She went still. "You have the rest of the day off?"

"Most of it. With the casino, I work odd hours. I'll have to check back in later tonight. There's more than enough time to show you around Vegas. If you don't want to walk, we can take my car."

Though he couldn't read her expression, she nodded. "I'd love to go for a drive. Away from the city, out into the desert. At heart, I'm a country girl."

This surprised him, making him realize he knew too little about her life before she'd become a big star. "Where did you grow up?"

Again that mask. "Here and there. Everywhere, it seemed. We moved a lot."

He knew he should leave it alone, but suddenly didn't want to. "Where was your favorite place?"

"Favorite place?" She made a face, but at least her frozen expression was gone. "None of them. We didn't ever stay in one place long enough for me to find out if I liked it."

Stark contrast to his family, who'd lived in the desert for generations.

"I'm sorry." He squeezed her shoulder. "I shouldn't have brought it up. I don't mean to dredge up unhappy memories."

Clearly relieved, she flashed a quick smile. "Let's talk about something else. This has been a phenomenal afternoon. I don't want to ruin it by discussing my childhood."

Or her family. From what little she'd said about them, they weren't a nurturing or loving bunch.

"Come on." He slung his arm around her shoulders, going for a casual embrace. "Let's get going. We'll take my car and do some driving. Later on, it'll be time for me to buy you that steak dinner I owe you."

Though she leaned into him readily enough, she appeared hesitant. "I'm not a big fan of steak."

"That's okay." He didn't really care what they ate, as long as they shared the meal together. "We can get something else. Like that Italian meal I mentioned."

Still she eyed him, almost as if there was something else she wanted to say, but was afraid to. "No," she finally said. "We just had this wonderful lunch. If you want steak, I'm sure I can find something else on the menu. After all, since you're a carnivore, I don't want to come between you and your sirloin." Again, a ghost of a smile hovered around her lips, letting him know she was attempting to lighten the mood. Maybe so, but her choice of words confounded him.

"Don't tell me you're a vegetarian."

"I'm not." She made a face. "That would be a sin in my family. They're all avid hunters."

Again with her family. Her use of the hated word startled him, although he knew she hadn't meant it the same way as the evil beings that were constantly after him and his kind. After the initial jolt of adrenaline, he pulled her toward him and kissed her again, aware he was courting ruin but unable to help himself.

Once again, the heat that blazed between them had fire arcing through his blood. This close to Rejuvenation made each time he touched her even more dangerous, though he couldn't help but thrill to the heady danger of simmering on the edge of losing control.

She reached up and cupped his face, her fingers searing his skin as she opened her mouth to him. Another second and he knew he'd go up in flames.

Pulling back, he rested his forehead on hers while they both struggled to find their breath.

Her wide eyes and dilated pupils told him the kiss had affected her as much as him. His body stirred, the embers constantly smoldering inside him needing just one more push to stroke them to life.

Aching to kiss her again, he tugged her toward the exit instead.

Both kisses had been… Meghan couldn't think, could barely walk as Gabe pulled her along with him. Another second longer and she'd have begged him to take her, right there, right then.

The first kiss had whetted her appetite. The second had sent all her inhibitions up in a blaze of fire and smoke.

Despite her carefully concocted reputation as a bad girl, no man had ever made her lose control the way Gabe just had. She swore she could still feel the heat of his lips on hers, and her entire body sizzled, craving more.

Evidently, she didn't affect him as intensely, even though his breathing had been as ragged as hers.

Desperately trying to regain her shattered control, she focused on the conversation they'd had just before he'd kissed her.

She didn't know why she'd told him what her family

truly was. Hunters. Of course, he would only think she meant they hunted animals—deer and hog and such. Not mythical beings named Helios, which he wouldn't have even heard of.

As to calling him a carnivore, truthfully she'd fall into this category, too. She'd given vegetarianism a shot a few years back, thinking it might be an easy way to stay thin. But three weeks into it and she'd found herself at an In-N-Out Burger, scarfing down two delicious hamburgers at once. That had ended her short-lived attempt.

The idea of watching Gabe devour a steak appealed to her. She found something sensual in watching a virile man consume red meat. She'd have to be careful not to reveal her carnal fascination with him, but other than that, dinner with Gabe sounded like fun.

Even better would be if he wanted to go up to his room for a nightcap later. His kiss had given her a taste of what making love with him might be like. She wanted more.

Patience had never been one of her strong suits.

Once they were back in the main lobby, he stopped. "I've sent for my car, but is steak later really okay?" he asked, brow furrowed. "I guess I should have asked if you like it. If not, we have lots of other choices. Seafood, Italian, even sushi."

"Steak is fine." She smiled, leaning in a little closer so she could inhale his virile scent.

One of the nearby slot machines caught her eyes. There were flying pigs, farmers with pitchforks and what appeared to be mini-tornados dancing on the horizon.

Still holding Gabe's hand, she moved over to check it out. "This looks fun," she said, smiling up at him. "Even better, it's a quarter machine. I'll have to remember where this is so I can play it later."

His gaze darkened. "Play it now." Reaching into his pocket, he pulled out a twenty and inserted it into the machine. "Go ahead. Make sure you play three quarters at once. The winnings are better that way."

Still, she hesitated. "Twenty dollars might take a while to go through."

At that, he laughed, the rich sound rolling through her like a sip of hot rum in the winter. "Trust me, it won't. And if it does, I don't mind waiting."

She took a seat on the chair and pushed the button. The reels spun and stopped. Nothing. She read the game description, seeing she needed to get a certain combination to get to activate the flying pig game in addition to the slot reels. She tried again. "Come on," she told the machine. "I really want to play that pig game."

Another spin, and this time three gold crests aligned. Bells went off, a siren sounded, and the little red light on top of the machine began flashing like a lighthouse beacon.

Chapter 8

"Wow." Gabe appeared stunned. "You won the progressive jackpot. Three million dollars."

"I did?" Her stomach lurched. "Did you do this?" she asked.

"What?"

"Did you somehow make it so I'd win? Since you own this casino and all?"

He chuckled. "That's not the way it works."

She gave him a suspicious look, half turning in her seat and noticing the small crowd rapidly gathering around them. Crud. If this kept up, someone would recognize her.

"We need to leave," she told Gabe, her breath catching in her throat. No amount of money was worth losing her privacy.

He looked at her as if he thought she'd lost her mind. "Let the attendant verify your winnings and then we'll go to the cashier's office. Everyone dreams of winning the jackpot. You just did. You might as well enjoy it."

He didn't get it. She fought to remain cool and calm as more and more people wandered over. Some cheered, others clapped. Several came up to her and offered hearty congratulations. This, she didn't mind. But there were a few in the growing crowd peering at her in puzzlement, as if they knew they should recognize her. She guessed it would just be a matter of time until they did. All it would take was one person saying her name and her cover would be blown.

Inwardly groaning, she prayed the attendant would hurry. She wished she'd taken a bit more time with her disguise this time. She wished she hadn't stopped to play this stupid slot machine. Of course, she'd had no way of knowing.

Finally, after what seemed an agonizingly long wait but was really only a few minutes, the casino cashier hurried over, key in hand. "Wow," she exclaimed, unlocking the front of the slot machine and turning the siren and flashing light off. "You really did hit the big one. Once we validate everything, you'll have to pose for us with a big check. We hang these on the winner's wall on the way in for promo for the casino."

This time, Meghan couldn't quite contain the flare of panic leaping inside her. She looked at Gabe, silently begging him to help her out.

"No photo this time," Gabe said, stepping forward.

The attendant jumped. "Oh, hi there, Mr. Stavros. I didn't see you. This lucky guest won our biggest jackpot."

"I see that," he drawled. "And once you've completed your validation process, I'll escort her to the main cashier office." A not-so-subtle hint to hurry up.

Finally, whatever process was completed and Gabe led Meghan away from the crowd. They'd begun dispersing rapidly, to her relief. She considered herself lucky as no one had appeared to recognize her.

Once in the back room, away from the public's eyes, Gabe sat with her across the desk from an elegant older woman wearing the casino uniform. She studied Meghan's ID with one brow arched before handing it back. "Amazing," she said, her slight smile cool. "A superstar winning the jackpot."

Meghan nodded. She didn't need the money. Her last album had gone triple platinum and the advance on the Vegas residency had been astronomical. "I'd like to donate it to charity," she said.

The woman frowned.

Gabe's brows rose. "Really?"

"Yes, really." Meghan smiled. "The local SPCA, I think. I love helping animals."

"I see." The frown cleared off the head cashier's face. "That'll not only be a great tax write-off but extremely good publicity for you. And us, as well."

"No publicity." Meghan's reply was instant and absolute. "I want the donation made anonymously."

After several assurances that yes, she was serious, Meghan signed the necessary paperwork and they were finally done. Gabe took her elbow as they moved toward the exit. Before they left, he turned and looked at his employee. "This is to be kept quiet," he ordered. "All of it. No one is to know Ms. Frost won or even that she's here yet. Understand?"

Slowly, the woman nodded. "Understood."

"Good."

Once they reached the casino floor again, Meghan exhaled. "Remind me not to play slot machines again."

"Oh, I will," he assured her. "Considering how much that twenty I put in actually cost me."

This made her laugh. "Come on," she said. "I'm dying to get out of the city. Let's go take that drive so I can see more of Las Vegas than the Strip."

* * *

Meghan Frost was like no other woman Gabe had ever met. From everything he'd read about her, he thought he'd known what to expect. A wild and crazy party animal, talented but shallow, gorgeous but vain. But she was none of these things. In the short time he'd known her, she'd taken every preconceived notion he'd had and turned it on its axis, which made him wonder if the people who wrote those articles actually even knew her.

A diva would have basked in the kind of adulation and attention that Meghan sought to avoid. He'd had a few stay as guests and there was nothing they appeared to like better than sweeping through the casino with their bodyguards and entourage, every gesture and movement calculated to draw attention.

And the money. He'd met plenty of wealthy stars, from both film and music. Most of them never seemed to have enough cash. Small wonder, since it seemed they blew it every chance they got.

While Meghan Frost seemed both low-key and humble. And she'd just given away three million to charity.

Of course, all of that would probably change once her show went live and she became the darling of Vegas. Right now, she was on hiatus and acting accordingly.

Outside, storm clouds hung low and ominous over the valley.

"Rain?" she asked, sounding surprised. "I read somewhere that Las Vegas only averaged around four inches of rain a year."

"Yep. And sometimes we get snow." He shrugged. "Though lately, it's been unusually warm for December, so if we get anything, it won't be frozen. When it actually rains here in the desert, it can be kind of dangerous. You can see it coming, as if someone ripped a hole in a storm cloud."

"Dangerous? How?"

"Flash floods and high winds. And amazing lightning. The water runs down from the mountains really fast. We definitely need to keep an eye on those clouds."

"Should I worry?" She glanced from him to the sky and back again.

"No. Most of the dangerous weather is from July to September. Since it's December, I think this will probably move on. Like you read, rain is really rare here."

Though she nodded, she cast one more glance at the dark sky. "If you say so."

"I do." Somehow, he restrained himself from kissing her.

They drove away from the Strip—not an easy feat with the ever-present traffic jam—and headed toward the suburbs.

"I'd like to see where people live," she said.

"People? Like regular people or the famous ones?"

She squirmed a little. "People like me."

People like Meghan Frost. He'd gotten pretty darn good at forgetting she was famous.

"Are you thinking of buying a place here?" He hoped not, at least not yet. Though her residency definitely could be extended, right now the contract was only for three months. Plus, if he were honest, he really liked having her living in the hotel.

Her shrug didn't really answer his question. "I'm really just curious," she finally said. "I just want to see where people like Celine Dion have their houses."

"Most of the true celebrities live in seclusion," he told her. "And we can't access their estates. But I can show you where some of the rich have their mansions."

She nodded, gazing out the window at the scenery. The dry dirt mountains weren't a spectacular as the Rockies, but they carried their own kind of beauty.

Since the storms usually came from the south or southeast, he took her west, to the Summerlin area. "Red Rock is my favorite." And also where his parents lived. "And not because of the two Arnold Palmer–designed golf courses or the huge clubhouse. But because the residents have access to the Red Rock National Park and Conservatory. It's amazing."

She regarded him curiously. "You sound like you've been there."

"I have." And that was all he wanted to say on the subject. "The community is gated, though. Most of the really nice ones are."

They drove to the area known as The Ridges next. He stopped at a local coffee shop and they sat outside on the patio and drank their lattes. No one even spared her a second glance. Gabe couldn't get over how ordinary she seemed. With the oversize glasses she wore today, only her high cheekbones and the perfect bow of her mouth gave testament to her amazing beauty.

He felt a flash of pride that she was with him.

After their coffee, they made a short visit to the edge of Red Rock. The storm clouds continued to gather, but so far he saw no sign of rain or lightning. Aware when it came on, it would be sudden, he wanted to keep watch just in case they needed to park and get out of the streets.

The gathering storm, though still far away, clearly made Meghan uneasy. She sat up straight, unable to resist constantly checking the sky. Sunny in the north and west, and gray in the south and east. A sight you only saw on the prairie or the desert.

Meghan sighed. Every time she shifted in her seat, he ached to pull the car over and kiss her. At one point, the setting sun reflected off a metal roof, making the rocks look as if they were on fire. Again, the urge to Rejuvenate stirred in him. He tamped it down, focusing instead on his desire for the beautiful woman next to him.

Unfortunately, at this point the two cravings mixed. Woman and flame, the desire for both, shot like lightning through his blood.

"Look," Meghan gasped. "The storm. It's closer. And moving quickly."

So it was.

"No worries." He kept his voice calm. "We're heading back now. I promise you, I'll keep you safe."

The storm kept advancing as they made their way back to the Archangel. He avoided the Strip as long as he could, weaving through back roads with the assurance of someone who knew all the shortcuts.

When they pulled up to the valet, he looked at her. "Here we are. All safe and sound."

She gave him a relieved smile as he took her arm and helped her out of the car.

They'd barely made it inside when the sky opened. Rain—not in drops, but a deluge—sheets of rain so heavy the visibility instantly became zero.

"Wow." Meghan stopped and stared. "It doesn't rain like that in LA."

He nodded. "It hardly ever rains like that here, too. Are you ready to grab dinner? I have a reservation at the steak house, but I can cancel that if you'd rather go elsewhere."

She swallowed, then lifted her chin and met his gaze. "I'd rather go up to your room," she said. Somehow she managed to sound bold and nervous and sexy all at once.

Meghan thought she might choke on the words, but she'd never wanted anything the way she wanted this. Him. Naked, with his body deep inside her.

His gaze darkened at her words. "Come on," he said, taking her arm as they rushed to the elevator. Once inside, the doors had barely closed before he hauled her up against him, letting her feel the proof of his arousal as he pressed against her. "Are you sure?" he growled.

Instead of answering, she pulled him down for an urgent and passionate kiss.

Somehow, they made it from the elevator to his room, still locked in an embrace. He fumbled with his key card, managing to get the door open. The second he kicked it shut behind him, he backed her up against the wall.

"This isn't going to be gentle or kind," he told her, his hands already underneath her shirt.

She tossed her head. Her grin felt as savage as her need. "Good. Because I want it hard, fast and deep. And now. Right now."

A bark of laughter escaped him. "Me, too."

His touch blazed a path of heat on her skin. A moan escaped her. "My clothes," she managed. "They're in the way."

"All in good time." With surprisingly gentle fingers, he tugged her shirt over her head before he eased the silky cups of her bra away. Once unbuckled, he let it fall to the floor.

She reached for him and he stilled her grasp. "I want to look at you," he rasped.

The sensuality in his voice banished her shyness. Head up, she stood still, her entire body aching, and let him look his fill.

"Now it's my turn," she said, her voice a husky echo of her own need. She let her hands slide across his muscular abdomen, tugging his shirt from his pants and fumbling with the buttons.

"Here," he said, yanking the shirt apart. He helped her undo his belt, the force of his arousal straining against his pants.

Throat dry, she carefully unzipped him, helping him out of his underwear so that he finally sprang free.

"Magnificent," she murmured, longing to take him in her mouth and taste him, all of him. When she bent to do just that, he stopped her.

"Not yet. Not the first time. I want inside you first." And then he captured her mouth with a kiss.

Openmouthed, she drank him in, showing him with her tongue what she wanted to do to the rest of him. Unbelievably, his body stirred and swelled even more.

"Now," she ordered, panting as she tried to catch her breath. She wanted him to push her up against the wall. "Take me now. Please."

Half laughing, half growling, he moved them both toward the bed. They fell together, side by side at first, as his hands and mouth and tongue sent currents of desire pulsing through her. She writhed against his touch, needing more than a finger inside her. Nearly mindless with need, she touched him, too, with her hands and her tongue, exploring all the parts of his body that she wanted—save one. That one, hard and huge, pressed into the side of her thigh.

The less he gave her, the more she wanted. Dizzy with need, she tried to climb on top, to settle herself over him and take him deep inside her slick, moist heat. Again he laughed, the deep sound of his masculine virility only making her want him more.

"Patience, little one," he drawled. "Don't rush things." He grabbed a condom and slid it over the engorged length of him. Ironically, this only increased her frantic craving.

"I'll show you patience," she gritted, twisting enough so the tip of him pressed close enough that one swift move would have him inside her.

His laughter died. His gaze glittered dark heat. Rising above her, he used his large hands to pin her down. Moaning, she arched her back, and he took her nipple into his mouth, suckling until she thought she would die if he didn't…

Then. And then, with one swift move he entered her, filling her. She gasped at the sheer size of him, and gasped again as he slowly began to move.

Her body throbbed. With each thrust, she met him halfway until the movements became a dance of explosive harmony.

The flames built, higher and higher, until she shuddered and shattered into a fiery flare of ecstasy. A second later, he followed her.

They held on to each other while their pleasure ebbed. She sighed, loving the sound of his heartbeat slowing against her ear.

She felt reborn, a new woman who'd risen from the ashes of her former self. About to voice this, she reconsidered and said nothing.

Outside, the torrential rain continued. Water roaring and wind howling provided the perfect excuse to snuggle under the sheet in Gabe's muscular arms. Sated, she let her eyes drift closed.

His phone buzzed. They both glanced at it. It buzzed again and Gabe groaned and reached for it. "It's Rafe," he said. "He knows I'm spending time with you, so he wouldn't be calling me if it wasn't urgent."

With a sleepy yawn, she snuggled under the sheet and shamelessly eavesdropped as he spoke to his brother. The short conversation had Gabe climbing out of bed and searching for his clothes.

"What's happened?" she asked, sitting up but keeping the sheet pulled up to cover her nakedness.

"A flash flood. Water filled the lowest level of our parking garage. Some people were trapped. Rescue operations are under way. Las Vegas PD and the fire department are on-site now."

Chapter 9

"What?" Meghan stared. "Here? How is that possible?"

"It's rare, but does happen." Gabe shot her a look, his expression unreadable. "Rafe says he's been trying to call me for a good while now, but I wouldn't answer my phone. I turned it to Vibrate, but I still should have heard it."

Of course neither of them had. They'd been kind of busy. Still… His clipped words and tense jaw told her he blamed himself for not being there.

"Is there anything I can do to help?" she asked, already knowing the answer.

"No." Eyeing her, he softened his bleak tone. "I'm sorry. I'd much rather spend the rest of the evening with you."

She nodded. "If you'd like, I can wait here until you get back."

"That's up to you." He headed toward the bathroom, made a quick stop to clean up and check his appearance, then went for the door. "I'm not sure how long this will take. I might be gone a few hours or until the morning. There's no way to know."

"I understand." Instead of blowing him a kiss, which would have been corny, she smiled. "If I'm asleep when you return, just wake me up." The huskiness in her voice left no doubt as to how.

"I will," he said. And he was gone.

The instant the door closed behind him, Meghan knew she wouldn't be able to nap, not now. All traces of sated sleepiness had vanished. Instead, she located the remote control on the nightstand and clicked on the large, flat-screen TV he'd hung on the wall.

Sure enough, the news had picked up the story. Propping herself up with two pillows, she settled in to watch. Startled, she realized the lower level of the parking garage was where she and Gabe had left his car with the valet when they'd arrived back. As the reporter talked about a white van with occupants still trapped inside, she realized but for a matter of timing, this could easily have been them.

Gabe mentally chastised himself all the way to the elevator. Once inside, he forced himself to let it go, aware if he kept this up, he'd ruin this potentially beautiful thing that had started between him and Meghan.

Instead, he emptied his mind, aware he'd need to focus on the current crisis. When the elevator let him out at the lowest level, he sprinted toward the parking garage area.

Turning the first corner, a small crowd of people blocked him. Shouldering his way through, he looked for Rafe's tall form.

"There you are." His brother spotted him first and grabbed his arm, moving him past the police who were keeping the gawkers back.

"How bad is it?"

"We got them out," Rafe assured him, the glad news not matching the darkness in his gaze.

"And? What are you not telling me?"

"There were three of them. All men. They declined medical attention." Rafe swallowed tightly. "While everyone was busy checking to make sure there weren't any other people trapped, those three from the van disappeared."

"Disappeared? That doesn't make sense. They left their vehicle?"

Rafe nodded. "It was a rental. The police are checking now to see who rented it. It's what we found inside that worries me."

Somehow, Gabe thought he knew what Rafe's next words would be before he said them.

"Weapons."

Gabe swore. "Guns?"

"Some, yes. But there were also crossbows and containers of metal-tipped arrows."

In other words, Hunters.

"We've got to find those men," he said. "Did you get a good look at any of them?"

"Not really. Everything happened so fast. I was more concerned that no one was killed than getting an ID on the victims." Rafe swallowed hard, a muscle working in his jaw. "I've got people reviewing the security footage now, but we may have no luck. The flood waters shorted out some of the cameras."

Gabe squeezed his brother's shoulder. "Don't worry. You know they're still here somewhere, lurking around. It's almost the solstice. They'll come out in force then."

"Which definitely means we both need to be extra careful."

"Agreed." Every year, Rafe worried. And, given the sheer numbers of Hunters who showed up in Vegas every three months, he had good reason. This was why they'd built the cement bunker in their private garden to begin with. To protect them from alert Hunters. Though the hunt was centuries old, Gabe often wondered if a Hunter would know what to do with a Helios if they were lucky enough to catch one. Would they kill them? Or just try to torture information out of them? He hadn't ever heard of such a thing actually happening, so he wasn't sure. The gateway to the world of the Ancients remained safe.

"Looks like the rain has stopped." Rafe pointed. Now, instead of sheets of windblown precipitation, they could actually see more than a few feet.

"Hopefully the water will go down."

As quickly as it had come, it receded. The fire truck that blocked the street entrance to the garage moved off, lights still flashing. While Gabe and Rafe stood watching things return to a semblance of normality, a uniformed police officer came over.

"We've learned the guy that rented the van used an alias and fake ID. We can't find any info on him, though we did get some photos from the car rental place's security cameras. ATF has been called and we're confiscating the weapons for them. They'll likely run serial numbers on the guns to see if they're registered to anyone. We've been talking to witnesses, including the rescue team, to try and get a description of the three men, but so far we don't have a whole lot."

"There was too much going on," Rafe put in, his expression glum. "We're hoping we might have some security camera footage."

"If you do, please notify us." The officer shrugged. "We're going to keep a few of the barricades up until all of the water has run off. Just count your blessings. It could have been worse. At least no one was injured or killed."

Yet, Gabe thought. The presence of Hunters in large

numbers virtually guaranteed an incident of some sort would happen on the twenty-first. In their desperate attempt to find a living, breathing Helios, the Hunters sometimes latched onto an unsuspecting human. The Archangel always discreetly upped their security force on those four special days each year. So far, they'd managed to stave off anything truly serious.

After the policeman had walked off, Gabe studied his brother. Rafe's frown had deepened.

"It's going to be all right," Gabe said. "It always is. We go through this four times a year."

"I know." The determined tilt of Rafe's chin lightened Gabe's heart. "It just seems like Mother Nature is cooperating with them this time."

"Or the opposite. Think about it. The flood almost ended them. While they managed to escape, they not only lost all their weaponry, but we now know for sure they're here."

"And how many there are."

Gabe nodded. "True. Unless there's more than one pod at our hotel. You know how Hunters are always competing with each other."

His statement made his brother groan, which in turn had Gabe trying to hold in his mirth.

They both finally chuckled and the last remnant of tension dissipated.

"Where were you?" Rafe asked. "Why didn't you answer your phone?"

"With Meghan." Gabe put a wealth of emotion in those two words.

Rafe grimaced. "I'm sorry, man. I hope this didn't completely total your day."

"Nothing, and I mean nothing, could ruin this day. Even this." Gabe couldn't help but give a quick flash of a grin.

"Wow." After a second, Rafe grinned back. "It's about freaking time."

"Yeah." Gabe took a deep breath. "I think this might be the start of something great."

For whatever reason, Rafe's laugh sort of irritated him. "Three months of something great, if you play it right."

Though Gabe nodded, he realized Rafe didn't really understand. When it came to Meghan, Gabe wanted more than just fun and games. Actually, he might be in trouble. Because Meghan Frost was a delicious puzzle he wanted to explore, piece by fascinating piece. Three months suddenly didn't seem nearly long enough.

For the next several hours, both Gabe and Rafe handled damage control. The press, the customers, even the employees were shaken by what had just happened. Flash floods, though an ever-present danger in a parched desert like Vegas, were still rare enough that people were always shocked when they occurred.

They'd gotten lucky this time. There'd been other times when lives had been lost.

Finally exhausted, both men ended up in Gabe's office. "You know what?" Gabe commented as he sank down into his desk chair. "Just once, I'd like to be able to hunt the Hunters. I'm sick and tired of having to hide from them."

"Yeah, but that's the way it always is. They hunt, we stay alive long enough to Rejuvenate and do our job of guarding the entrance into the world of the gods. As long as no Hunters were able to gain access and free Chaos, Earth was safe.

Gabe snorted, earning a surprised glance from his brother. "Have you ever really thought about that? How long has it been since you've seen a god or goddess? In fact, have you ever even seen one?"

"Well..." Rafe had to think about it, which underscored Gabe's point. "What are you trying to say? That the ancient gods and all their secrets have vanished?"

"No. Not at all. You know as well as I do that as long

as someone believes in them, they exist. As long as there are Helios to believe in them and protect them, they live."

"And as long as we keep the two worlds separate, Chaos is banished," Rafe recited the words taught to every young Helios before he or she could walk.

"But where is it decreed that we can't try to stop the Hunters?"

At Gabe's words, Rafe chuckled. Then, when he realized his brother wasn't kidding, he slowly shook his head. "Don't you see? If we started something like that, it would be the beginning of chaos. The proper order of everything would be in turmoil. The Hunters would win without even trying." Lowering his brows, he frowned. "And in addition, going after them would reveal exactly who we are. It would put our entire family in jeopardy."

"You're right." Gabe shifted in his chair. "Though I hate it. Each year, every equinox or solstice, the necessity of hiding grates on my last nerves."

"Mine, too. But we Rejuvenate. Once that's over, we're new and all that goes away."

"For another three months." Gabe knew he should stop, but he couldn't just let it go.

"Time to change the subject." Spinning in his chair, Rafe stopped and faced Gabe. He appeared oddly hesitant, which in itself was unusual enough to give Gabe pause. "I do have a bit of good news."

"Okay."

"I've asked Evangeline to marry me. She said yes."

Dumbfounded, Gabe stared. Finally, collecting himself, he jumped to his feet and clapped his brother on the back. "Congratulations! When's the wedding going to be?"

Rafe grinned. "That's where I stepped back, per her instructions. Evangeline is planning everything. You know how good she is at that. She says she'll let me know the date and all I need to do is show up."

"Lucky you." They'd both had friends whose fiancées had turned into bridezillas. "If she holds to that promise, that is."

"She will." He checked his phone. "Speaking of Ev, she just texted me. I promised to take her out for an early breakfast tomorrow. After that, I plan to be busy the rest of the morning."

Gabe envied Rafe his happiness. Despite his current fascination with Meghan, he doubted he'd ever attain that level of commitment in a relationship. When he'd been younger, he'd fallen in love, only to have his girlfriend's true colors come out when they'd gotten engaged. She'd cheated on him with his best friend and after that, he'd had trouble trusting. "Have fun."

Rafe left. Gabe put his feet up on the desk, thinking about Meghan. He'd had fun today. If she hadn't been a famous performer, he would have thought her the most down-to-earth woman he'd ever dated. That, combined with her exquisite beauty, made an irresistible combination.

But he knew better. She had a reputation as a diva, just like most female superstars, at least as they were portrayed in the media. He just hadn't known her long enough to see that side of her.

Which was good. He had enough on his plate without trying to deal with something like that.

His stomach growled, reminding him he hadn't eaten, either. He checked his watch, glad most of the restaurants in the Archangel kept later hours to cater to the ever-present nightlife. He made a phone call, confirmed he'd have a table, and hurried upstairs to see if Meghan wanted to join him for that elusive steak dinner.

Entering his suite and finding her still naked in his bed nearly abolished any thought of leaving for nourishment. Her emerald eyes lit up at the sight of him.

"How'd it go? Is everything all right?"

He nodded, momentarily unable to speak. She looked beautiful and sexy and...*his*.

No. A quick stab of panic had him sucking in his breath. Not his. Not by a long shot.

"Are you hungry?" he asked, reminding her of the plans they'd made earlier.

"Sure." Was that disappointment or confusion that darkened her eyes? "Give me ten minutes to put on some clothes and mascara and lip gloss." She jumped up and, keeping the sheet wrapped around her, hurried into the bathroom.

True to her word, she emerged ten minutes later, once again dressed in her disguise. "I'm starving."

He held out his arm. "Let's go eat.

The Flame Steak House, long his favorite restaurant not only in his hotel but the entire Vegas Strip, had won several awards as the most romantic place to bring a date. Gabe took full advantage of this by taking Meghan there. Since he'd phoned ahead and given a generous tip to his hard-working hostess, they had a wonderful seat near the window, looking out over the fountain. Of course, being one of the owners of the place didn't hurt, either. He watched Meghan carefully, still in awe of her beauty and wondering if and when the prima donna that had to be inside her would rear its head. There'd been lots of stories, on entertainment television and in gossip magazines, of her unreasonable demands and expectations. While he knew enough to question the factuality of some of the stories, there had to be a grain of truth in there somewhere.

But, no. They had a nice quiet dinner, during which he spent entirely too much time looking at her mouth and aching to kiss her one more time. To his surprise, she ordered a filet mignon and he had his usual rib eye.

"Steak?" he asked, raising a brow.

Her response was a grin and a shrug. "What can I say? The more I thought about it, the better it sounded."

They shared a bottle of good red wine and talked about everything and nothing. Every time he tried to get more personal, Meghan deflected and moved the conversation to a more general topic. Which only served to frustrate him as well as pique his interest even more. He knew every single inch of her body. He wanted to learn more about what made her tick.

The chef—his cousin Rocco, who also was the restaurant's owner—came out to speak with him after the meal, accepting Gabe's compliments with a little bow and claiming it had been an honor to serve his boss. Since Gabe ate in the steak house on a regular basis, and this little exact same ritual occurred every single time, he smiled but kept from laughing out loud.

"Now what would you like to do?" he asked Meghan as he escorted her from the restaurant. "The night's still young and is just getting started. We have several excellent clubs here at the Archangel."

Shaking her head, she laughed. "I'm sure you do. And I promise I'll check them out eventually. But if I were to go dancing now, someone for sure would recognize me. I'd rather stay incognito for as long as possible. It's really nice to be able to go somewhere without paparazzi jumping out from behind bushes."

Again, not at all diva-like.

"Then what would you like to do?" Part of him—okay, most of him—hoped she would say go back to his room and make love again.

She thought about it for a moment. "Maybe see a show. Or find a bar and listen to some music."

"Since I know for a fact all this evening's shows are sold out, we'll have to go with the second option."

"Okay." Once again she lifted her shoulder in a delicate shrug. "That sounds great. Though I have to say, I'm surprised." The flash of mischief in her eyes made them sparkle. One corner of her mouth quirked, as if she was struggling not to laugh.

It took him a minute to be able to focus enough to get the words out. "Surprised about what?"

"That the owner of the casino can't pull a few strings and get us into a sold-out show."

Aha. There it was. *Diva.* Rafe had warned him. He squashed down the rush of disappointment, because he shouldn't have expected any different. She laughed, as if she'd made a joke, but once she caught sight of his expression, her mirth faded away to nothing.

"I'm sorry, I can't. Doing something like that would mean paying patrons would lose their seats." His wooden voice sounded stiff, even to him.

Of course she noticed. "I was kidding," she said. "Seriously. Just joking. I laughed—didn't you hear me? I would never expect you to throw your weight around for me."

Which was ridiculous. She was a superstar. Any casino owner worth his salt would fall all over himself to give Meghan Frost every single thing she needed.

And even a few things she didn't. He waited for her to point that out. When she didn't, he wasn't sure what to think.

He wasn't sure if he felt like a fool or if she really had been toying with him. Whichever it was, evidently his silence stretched out too long.

"You know what," she said, speaking carefully and avoiding looking at him. "I'm really tired. I think it's time to call it a night. Thank you again for your time. I'll give you a call if I need anything in the future." And then, having dismissed him, she turned and strode off without a backward glance.

Chapter 10

Gabe didn't follow her, even though he hadn't been ready for the evening to end. He'd enjoyed her company and until now, he'd thought the feeling was mutual. In fact, he'd even begun entertaining hopes they could end the night up in his penthouse with a nightcap.

And more. Much, much more.

Instead he found himself in the high-limits salon, surrounded by a select few others willing to play twenty-dollar slots. He chose a machine in the dark corner and played until he'd run out of twenties. One of his cocktail waitresses kept him supplied with drinks, but after a few hours had passed he didn't feel any different other than a few hundred dollars poorer.

With a sigh, he got up and made his way to his suite and his bed.

His black mood hadn't improved by the morning. Not only had he lost quite a bit of money gambling, but he'd missed Meghan with an ache that felt way too strong, considering the short amount of time he'd known her. He'd even considered a booty call in the middle of the night, but Meghan had made it quite clear she wanted to be on her own. He knew he hadn't made it clear enough how much he wanted to be with her.

In fact, he hadn't been fair. He'd let his past experiences with women who only wanted to date a casino owner for what he could get them—the perks and jewelry and attention—make her into something she wasn't. After all, she hadn't demanded anything. She'd claimed to be joking and in retrospect, she probably had been. Meghan Frost was the most un-diva-like woman he'd ever met.

He wanted to spend the entire day making it up to her. He shook his head. He actually couldn't. He had a hotel to run, after all. There were back-to-back meetings scheduled for that afternoon and enough paperwork to keep him busy all morning.

So he went through the steps, workout, shower, breakfast, and then donning his suit and tie and heading to the office in the business area of the hotel. Once there, he focused on his job, trying really hard not to snap at anyone. He didn't always succeed. He felt grumpy and out of sorts and couldn't seem to get himself out of his rotten mood.

After he'd been hard at work in his office for a couple of hours, his brother came in and closed the door.

"What's going on with you?" Rafe flashed him a look of annoyance. "I get that it's close to time to Rejuvenate, but you act like you're about to jump out of your skin."

Swallowing hard, Gabe shook his head. "You're one to talk. Unlike you," he teased, "I'm sure I can wait until the solstice."

"Then what's wrong? The entire staff is walking on eggshells around you."

"It's..." Gabe swallowed. He and Rafe weren't in the habit of keeping things from each other, so he didn't see any reason to start now. "It's *her*. Meghan Frost."

"I see." Rafe didn't seem surprised. "But I don't actually see the problem. Didn't you two have dinner last night?"

"We did." Abandoning all attempts at focusing on the reports in his screen, Gabe leaned back in his chair and crossed his arms. "And then I acted like an ass and the night ended way earlier than it should have."

"You? Act like an ass?" The pointed statement wasn't lost on Gabe. "Wow. What a shock."

"Come on, Rafe. I'm not usually that bad."

Rafe nodded. "No, you're not. So what gives? I thought you'd decided to enjoy a brief, three-month affair with her and then each of you go your own separate ways."

"I did." For a few heartbeats, Gabe debated telling his brother the truth. After all, Rafe had found happiness with Evangeline. He might actually understand.

"I feel differently about her." The confession felt as if it had been torn from him. "I don't want to. Sex this good should be enough. More than enough." He swallowed, hard. "But it's not. With her, I want…*more.*"

Under any other circumstances, the long look his brother directed at him would have made him laugh. Not now. Not today.

"More what? Sex?"

Unable to articulate, especially since nothing he said would make sense, Gabe nodded. "Maybe that's it. Evidently I haven't gotten her out of my system yet."

"Are you worried she's done with you? Because of whatever you fought about yesterday?"

The thought hadn't really occurred to him until now. "It wasn't a fight," he protested. "We had a minor misunderstanding and she stalked off. I'm thinking I might need to apologize."

"So do what you have to do. Judging from the smoldering looks you two have been exchanging, she won't need too much persuading to take you back, bro."

Startled, Gabe titled his head. "Do you really think so?"

"I do." Rafe's firm tone left no room for argument. "But remember who she is. You've read the same articles I did. Our pop superstar is kind of a wild child. As long as you spell out the rules ahead of time, no one gets hurt."

Touched by his brother's concern, Gabe nodded. "She's not really like that, you know. At least not from what I've seen. I bet a lot of it is her public persona, dreamed up by her PR people. It has to be. But I do appreciate your warning. I have no plans on getting too emotionally involved. You know that."

"It wasn't you I was worried about," Rafe said drily. "The last thing we need is a brokenhearted superstar refusing to honor her contract."

After a second of shocked silence, Gabe threw back his head and laughed. A moment later, Rafe joined him.

"Good point. Although I don't see that happening."

"Hopefully not. But all kidding aside, I still don't see what you're agonizing over. What's the problem?" Rafe asked. "You're both healthy and unattached. The attraction appears mutual and neither of you are the type to expect long-term commitment. If she's mad, kiss her and I bet she gets over it. Why beat yourself up?"

"I don't know." Though he did. Even the blood pumping through his veins tingled at the thought of touching her again. Despite his confusion, he knew there was more to his complicated feelings than that. He felt foolish even attempting to articulate them.

Staring Gabe down, Rafe shook his head. "So what's the problem? I don't know what's wrong with you. You're not usually this wishy-washy."

"Wishy-washy?" Gabe raised one brow, eyeing his brother. "Really? You couldn't think of a better word?"

"No." Rafe gave him a small shove, right in the middle of his back. "Since you've been increasingly more and more difficult to deal with, go. Find her, kiss and make up, and take her to bed. Don't come back until you're in a better mood."

He might be right. For all he knew, they could easily smooth this over. Maybe Meghan would even have forgotten all about the fact that they'd parted awkwardly the day before. Though he kind of doubted it.

Suddenly, all the work he'd planned to do today seemed unimportant. Most of it was checking his employees' work—he'd long ago learned to delegate.

"You know, you're right. I think I will." Halfway to the door, Gabe couldn't resist one final parting shot, delivered over his shoulder. "Okay, bro. Since you want me out of here so bad, I guess I can assume that you don't mind picking up the two appointments I have with vendors this afternoon. They can't be rescheduled. I'm sure my assistant can fill you in on the details."

He took off without waiting for an answer. Rafe would juggle his schedule to make sure he could accommodate Gabe's appointments, or more likely, he'd try to have them rescheduled. While Gabe was off wining and dining the beautiful Meghan Frost in the hopes of making up for lost time.

The morning after she'd sent Gabe packing, Meghan tried to figure out how things had gone south so fast. Inherently shy, she knew well that her people skills were admittedly abysmal. This was why she had an entire team of PR people and a manager, to smooth out the messes her rough edges could conjure up. This was also why she hadn't had a genuine relationship in ages. Every single date or supposed boyfriend had been something set up by either her people or his. It wouldn't look good, they claimed, for a star with a reputation as wild as hers to be known as celibate. Even though she basically was. And had been, for a really long time. Until now, when she felt positive her dry spell was finally over.

Still, she'd gone on dates and pretended to enjoy them. Most of these were with other celebrities. Several men had made it clear they were interested in more, but none of them had the patience for a woman with old-fashioned values who wanted to take things slow.

She'd tried—oh, how she'd tried—but there hadn't been a single man with whom she'd felt even the tiniest spark. Until she'd met Gabe Stavros. That spark had been more like a blazing inferno. Interesting how quickly she'd managed to initiate things with him. Because she'd wanted to. Her people would be amused, if they knew.

She knew they talked behind her back, though they took care to make sure she never heard. Still, the occasional gossip managed to drift its way toward her—was she gay, asexual or secretly married to a much older man? The truth, that her awkward social graces and bone-crushing shyness nixed relationships before they began, would be completely unpalatable to these people. So she let them think what they wanted.

Her job as a performer was all that saved her. Music brought her reprieve, allowing her to push away the shyness. When she lost herself in the melody and the words, the songs carried her outside of herself and transported her to a place where she became one with the music and her awkwardness no longer mattered.

Mostly, she knew she had a good life, that she was lucky to be able to live out the fantasy, what so many musicians could only dream of. Despite the loneliness of her estrangement from her family and her lack of close friends, as long as she focused on the music, she was okay.

Except when she wasn't. She'd been at a low point when she came to Vegas. Christmas usually was a miserable time for her, spent wishing for what she couldn't have. And then Gabe Stavros had come along, and the days before the actual holiday suddenly didn't seem as bleak.

Her stomach clenched. She actually liked Gabe Stavros.

Hopefully, whatever wrong impression she'd made could be smoothed over. In addition to being attracted to him, she realized she actually wanted to get to know him better. In addition to continuing to have mind-blowing sex with him. The thought made her grin.

And it wasn't just because she couldn't bear to be alone.

Most of the time, she could handle her loneliness. But from Thanksgiving until New Year's Day, she'd learned it was better to keep herself as busy as possible. This was partly why she'd come out to Vegas early. She should have known she'd never be able to escape herself. Even worse, everywhere she looked, all she saw was happy couples. Feeding each other fruit, strolling hand in hand. Shopping, like she and Gabe had done.

Gabe. Even thinking of him brought a fresh jolt of pain. He didn't know her well enough to realize she'd been teasing. He truly believed she was being a diva.

Except she hadn't made a single demand. Not really.

Wandering to the balcony, she opened the sliding glass door and walked outside. Below, the sun rose, dulling the glittering lights of the Strip, humanizing the place.

Usually, there were people as far as the eye could see. Tourists mostly, strolling the sidewalks. This early, the streets were deserted. Even the notorious traffic had died out, leaving the place looking like a bit of a ghost town. The sight, as captivating as it might be, only intensified her feelings of solitude.

Turning, she went back inside, figuring she'd hurry and get her workout out of the way earlier today. She shivered with a chill she couldn't seem to shake, which meant it was more in her mind than an actual physical thing. She thought of Gabe's touch, how being close to him set her on fire, and hoped later today they could talk things out and get back to the good stuff.

Hurriedly pulling on her workout clothes, she did ten minutes on the treadmill and then thirty minutes of weights and body exercises, before finishing up with twenty minutes of flat-out running.

Though jumpy, she kept an eye on the door the entire time, both relieved and disappointed when she saw no sign of Gabe. Of course she didn't. It was well before his usual time to hit the hotel gym.

Finished, she hurried up to her suite to take a shower. The exercise had calmed her and she felt centered and once again in control.

After she'd showered and dressed, she made a protein smoothie for breakfast and drank it on the patio while watching the town begin to come alive. Since she had to keep busy today, she decided she'd go back and see the amphitheater—*her* amphitheater. Even though her set designer and her team had already visited so everything could be mapped out and built to spec, Meghan wanted to envision where everything would be.

Plus, she needed to sing. By herself, with no other ears to listen but her own. She felt she needed to get a feel for her stage so that when the time came for her to actually perform, the amphitheater would feel like a beloved friend.

Cheered, she checked her watch. Still early. If Gabe followed a schedule, and she imagined he did, he'd be done working out now. No doubt he'd soon have to go to work, though she had no idea what hours casino owners kept. Maybe later, they could run into each other and…

She shut the thought down.

The room phone rang, startling her. Instantly, her heart started pounding. Instead of Gabe, a friendly female voice informed Meghan that her manager had booked her a much-needed spa day as an early Christmas gift. If her schedule permitted, she was due for a massage at 8:00 a.m. After, she'd have a facial, get her hair done, followed by a mani-pedi, a body wrap and more. Meghan stopped listening after the seventh or eighth item. The entire thing would take six hours.

Hanging up the phone, she smiled. This was even better. After all, she was supposed to be on vacation. A little pampering would be good for her soul. She'd sing later.

Still smiling, she left her room and headed for the spa.

The Archangel's spa, appropriately named Heaven, had rapidly become known for taking beauty treatments to the upper stratosphere. During her time touring when in concert, Meghan had visited numerous spas, but by the end of the day, she could honestly say Heaven took top prize.

She'd never felt more relaxed. They'd taken an hour break in the middle of her treatment and served her a gourmet lunch, complete with fresh fruit and a tuna tartare she thought would melt in her mouth.

By the time the spa day had ended, she truly felt like she'd died and gone to Heaven. After leaving a more than generous tip, she sailed out energized and revitalized.

On the way back to her room, she even stopped to play a slot machine. This time, she didn't win and her twenty disappeared fast.

Absurdly, this capped off the perfect day, increasing her happiness. The only thing that would make it better would be to run into Gabe. But at this time in the day, he would still be at work. So she headed up to her room.

Once in her retreat, she opened her laptop and checked her email. She also anonymously posted a five-star review for Heaven. Still feeling ridiculously relaxed, she debated changing into her pajamas, but decided it was much too early at three in the afternoon.

Who knew, she might gather up her courage and call Gabe. She spent a pleasurable few minutes imagining all the things she'd like to do with him, if only she could. A soft knock on her door startled her out of her reverie. "Who is it?" she asked as she moved toward the door.

"Room service." Gabe's voice.

Chapter 11

Joy and anticipation flooded through her. Proof positive now that this was a perfect day. "I didn't order anything," Meghan said, playing along. "It's too late for lunch and too early for dinner. Though I'd love a bottle of red wine."

His laughter warmed her. "You got it."

Smiling, she opened the door, stunned to see he actually had brought a bottle of wine, along with two long-stemmed glasses. "Wow. Are you a mind reader?"

"Not at all. It's my peace offering. It's white, though," he said, lifting it up. He looked devilish and handsome, like a dark angel who'd fallen from heaven. She'd never seen a man who looked so good in a suit. "If you'd rather have red, I can go and switch it out."

It took her a moment to realize he'd spoken. Was this a peace offering? Did he want to talk about that moment of awkwardness from yesterday? Deciding to let that statement go, she stepped aside and motioned him in. "White is fine. Thanks for bringing wine at all."

"No problem." His intense gaze banished her earlier chill. The perfectly proportioned outlines of his shoulders strained against the well-cut fabric. "How about we go out on the patio? The Strip is always fascinating, even in daylight. I can't think of a better place to sit and sip wine."

Pleased, she nodded. The restless energy in his movements aroused her. "I don't know if I have a corkscrew here or not."

"I'm sure you do. I asked them to make this a very well-equipped suite. Do you mind if I look?"

Touched that he'd even asked, she swept her hand toward the kitchen. "Go right ahead."

She watched as he rummaged, opening and closing drawers. Despite his suit and tie, he appeared perfectly at home in her kitchen. "Aha," he said, holding up a corkscrew, his brown eyes sparkling. "Victory!"

Once the bottle had been opened, he poured two glasses and handed one to her. "After you."

Conscious of his gaze on her, she led the way outside and took a seat in one of the chairs. Aching to touch him, she took a sip instead, pleasantly surprised at the taste of the wine. "Perfect. Not too dry and not too sweet. I'll have to get the name and make note of this one."

Every time she looked up, she found his gaze on her, his caramel eyes dark and unreadable. She fought the urge to fidget, to wonder if she had something on her face or her clothes. This man had hired her and was paying her an astronomical amount of money to perform in his hotel. He definitely wouldn't be examining her critically.

"You look relaxed," he said, reaching out to lightly finger a strand of her short, spiky hair.

She hid her shiver. "Oh, I am. Compliments of your wonderful spa." She proceeded to tell him about her day, taking care to mention the attendants by name, hoping this would give them additional recognition.

When he actually made notes in his phone, she knew it would. "They all deserve a raise," she told him, meaning it. "I've been to spas all over the world. Heaven beats them all, bar none."

Grinning, he looked even sexier. "I'll check into that. To be honest, I already make sure all hotel employees are very well compensated for their efforts."

Even his voice, silky and sensual, sent a ripple of desire through her. How this man affected her so strongly, she didn't know. But she liked it.

Taking a deep breath, she tilted her head, drinking him in with her gaze. "I should have known you would. Your entire operation here is first-class. Thank you for bringing me on board."

"You're a very confident woman, aren't you?" he asked, admiration and amusement flickering in his eyes.

This patently wrong statement made her laugh. "Only when I sing," she told him. "The rest of the time, I'm bumbling and unsure, just like everyone else."

He looked so incredulous she laughed again, shaking her head.

"Sorry, but I don't buy it." Leaning back in his chair, his gaze raked over her, making her skin heat. "I've never met a woman as comfortable with herself as you. Not only are you beautiful, but you're talented. Seems to me like that would give you all the confidence in the world."

Those were all superficial things. Okay, not her talent, but still… Maybe they would be enough for some people, but not for her.

"Would it?" She kept her tone light, sipping on the wine and gazing out at what seemed to be a constant traffic jam out on the Strip. No one knew about her childhood, or what it was like living with a family obsessed with their hunt. And for good reason. People—regular people—had no idea there were even a race of beings called Hunters. And the mythical beings the Hunters chased? The so-called Helios were even more elusive. If they truly even existed. She wouldn't be surprised to learn that the Hunters' constant stalking had led to them being eradicated centuries ago or something.

"Any more news on the guy in the gray hoodie?" she asked, needing to change the subject to something not so personal.

"No." He made a slight face. Even frowning, his chiseled features attracted her. "I wish you could remember where you might have seen him," he added.

"Me, too. But it could have been anywhere. All I know is a quick feeling of familiarity. Not why or when or even how." She sighed. "I wish I could be of more help."

"If you remember, please let me know."

She nodded. "I will." Every time his gaze met hers, her heart turned over. She wasn't sure what to make of the handsome Gabe Stavros. She'd seen the fiery look of desire in other men's eyes, but none with as much intensity. Everything about the darkly handsome casino owner was intense, as if he burned like too-hot embers, from the inside out.

This drew her to him like a moth to a flame.

The clichéd analogy made her grimace. Everyone knew it hadn't ended well for the poor moth. What did that say about her damaged psyche that she still wanted to be with him?

"Yesterday, I—" They both starting speaking at once, with almost identical words.

Stopping, she grinned. He grinned back. Now, she thought. Now he would kiss her.

Instead, he chuckled, dragging his hand across his chin. "How about we just agree to forget what happened before?" he suggested. "I was way too serious and took what you said the wrong way."

Heart in her throat, she nodded. "That sounds great. I promise you, I'm not a diva."

"Not even the tiniest bit?"

It took her half a second to realize he was kidding. Though she smiled, her response was serious. "Not even the tiniest bit. If you ever see me acting even remotely diva-like, call me on it."

Again he boldly raked his gaze over her, as if he could see through her clothing. Her entire body tingled in response. "Agreed." He cleared his throat. "So, what do you say to hanging out with me the rest of the afternoon and into the evening? We can't catch a show, though I have reserved tickets for us next week. Tonight we can grab a bite to eat and then go listen to some music, like you'd mentioned yesterday."

Stunned, she gazed up at him, struggling to formulate a response. He'd reserved tickets for next week, like a real date… In the future. She knew she shouldn't be so surprised, but she was.

Then again, why did it matter? He wanted to spend time with her and she—well, she definitely wanted to get to know him better. A lot better.

Talk about a distraction. She glanced at him. His gaze smoldered when he looked at her. Even the thought of his hands on her skin made her knees weak.

Maybe the time had finally come for her to break out of her shell. Just once, perhaps she could actually become the bad girl everyone already believed her to be.

"Sounds great," she said, curling her toes inside her sneakers. She wished desperately she could summon the nerve to kiss him. Or that he'd correctly interpret the longing in her gaze and kiss her.

"You know what," she heard herself say, moving closer. "I have a better idea, if you want to hang out." When she reached him, she grabbed hold of his jacket and pulled him close. His quick intake of breath and the darkening of his eyes told her he wasn't any more immune than he'd been before.

Confident, huh? Actually, in this moment, with him, she was. Taking a deep breath, she reached up and pulled his face down to hers. The instant their lips connected, that familiar heat blazed between them. She wanted more. The rapid-fire thunder of his heartbeat told her he did, too.

Suit and tie. Darkly handsome and sexy, but she wanted it off him immediately. While she pondered how to accomplish this, he pulled back, his expression hooded.

"I think your idea is an excellent one," he rasped. "Your place or mine?"

As she was about to answer, his phone rang. Of course he glanced at it.

"My brother," he said, holding up a finger. "Hold that thought." He didn't do much talking—after the initial hello he simply listened, his expression growing blacker the more Rafe talked. "On my way," he finally said, and ended the call.

"I've—"

"Got to go." She nodded. "I heard."

Clearly distracted, still his gaze smoldered, as if a banked, internal fire burned inside him. "Another work crisis. Let's continue this conversation later, all right?"

Though she nodded again, she secretly doubted that. She wondered for the first time if they were jinxed. Something always seemed to happen when they got together physically.

She kept smiling as he hurried away and let himself out. Once the door had swung closed behind him, she poured herself another glass of wine and carried it out onto the patio. She'd barely taken a sip before she set it down. This wasn't what she needed. Sitting alone and drinking wine wouldn't make her feel any better. Only one thing—besides music—could do that.

Gabe.

"You've got to take a look at this." Rafe couldn't contain his excitement. Laptop open in front of him, he'd paused a video on YouTube.

"What is it?" Gabe pulled up a chair and sat down next to him. "Looks like one of Meghan Frost's concert videos."

"It is."

Gabe suppressed a flash of irritation. "You said this was urgent. You have no idea what you just interrupted. This better be good."

"Just watch." Rafe punched the play button.

Of course Gabe found his gaze immediately drawn to Meghan, who danced in a skimpy outfit. Her body looked even more toned than he'd imagined, and her moves were guaranteed to set any man on fire.

"Not at her." Rafe tapped the screen. "Look at him."

A man in a gray hoodie sat on one side of the stage, his face in shadows. With his height and slender build, he looked very similar to the man the witnesses had described.

"It's him," Rafe said. "That's why she thought he looked familiar. He's either part of her show or a superfan."

"I don't know." Gabe didn't bother to hide his doubt. "There are lots of people with light-colored hoodies."

"But this guy is tall and slender. And look at his hands. On top of that, he's with Meghan's crew."

"She gave all of them two weeks off for Christmas. None of them traveled with her."

Expression determined, Rafe refused to give up. "That she knows of. What if one of her guys decided to come out on his own?"

"Okay, I'll play along." Clenching his jaw as he thought

of what he'd just walked away from to hear this, Gabe paused the video. "Following that line of thought, say one of Meghan's employees came out to Vegas. He doesn't check in with her, just comes on out and shoots one of our blackjack dealers and sets a poker table on fire. Because...?"

Judging from the muscle working in Rafe's jaw, now his brother was equally pissed. "Because he's a Hunter."

"Look." The last shreds of Gabe's patience vanished. "I agree there's a possibility this guy is a Hunter. I disagree that he's part of Meghan's crew or attached to her in any way."

"Because you're not thinking with your head," Rafe protested fiercely. "At least not the right one."

"What are you saying? That you think Meghan is somehow involved in all this?"

Rafe took a deep breath. "No. Not at all. I doubt she even knows what a Hunter is or that one of them is part of her entourage." He frowned. "And it's possible that guy is some sort of stalker fan. Has she mentioned anything like that to you?"

"No. But I can ask her." After he made sweet love to her one more time.

"You do that." Rafe's attention had already gone back to the video, which he replayed over and over, continually stopping on the frame with the man who might or might not be linked to the Hunters. "And when you're in the casino, keep your eyes out for that guy in the gray hoodie. Or anyone resembling him—tall, thin, with unusually long fingers and dusky skin."

"Will do." Anticipation coursing through his blood, he hurried to the elevator. Even the thought of making love to her again made him burn with an inner fire that had little to do with his upcoming Rejuvenation and everything to do with Meghan.

All the way to her floor, his heart pounded. His blood ran thick and heavy as he contemplated the things they'd do to each other this time.

When he reached her suite, he tapped lightly on the door. No answer. Waiting a second, he used his master key to get inside.

She wasn't there. Not curled up on the sofa, or lounging on the bed, or even out on the patio where she'd left a half-full glass of wine.

After the first crush of disappointment, he turned and went to look for her. He figured he knew where to find her.

Casino or auditorium? If he were a betting man—and he'd been known to place a large wager a time or two—he'd take the auditorium. After he'd shown it to her, he'd made sure she had her own key card so she could have access whenever she needed. She'd been itching to get back there.

Decision made, he headed toward the amphitheater. Huge posters announcing her upcoming shows flanked the main entrance. He stopped for a moment to admire them. With makeup and false eyelashes, her beauty transcended reality. But he found he much preferred the real Meghan, with little or no makeup, wearing her baseball cap and faded jeans.

Gabe went around back, down the long hallway and through the door marked Employees Only.

Once he'd slipped inside, he saw the stage lights were on. Moving quietly, he headed that way. A sound stopped him. Meghan, singing a cappella. Her crystal clear voice rang out, soaring from the rafters, magical and sensual and full of hope and joy. An entire song this time. Something about love and loss and hope.

Though the sentiments were unusual for him, he couldn't move. Stunned, he stood frozen, listening. Her voice reached deep inside him, grabbed him by the heart and wouldn't let go.

Though a Helios, he'd never been prone to flights of fancy like some of his kind. Both he and his brother were more down-to-earth, analytical types, Rafe especially. Gabe tended to be a bit brasher, but rationally so. But then he'd never met anyone like Meghan.

As she finished the song, drawing out the final note before letting it fade away in a husky murmur, he felt a shudder move through his entire body, expanding his heart so much he thought it might burst.

She was something, this Meghan Frost. From soft and warm to sultry and seductive, she was unlike any other woman in the world.

Chapter 12

Taking a moment to get his raw emotions back under control, Gabe moved closer to the stage. He felt he should make his presence known, since the very act of listening to her intimate, personal performance felt like an invasion of her privacy. Far too familiar for two people who still danced on the edge of real intimacy.

"Sounds great," he called out, long before he reached the edge of the shadows. "I can't wait to hear it with your live band."

If he'd startled her, by the time he rounded the last corner, she showed no sign. Tiny and strong, sexy and powerful, she pivoted on her toes to face him. Instead of surprise, an amused smile hovered around her lush lips. "Thanks. I just had to check out the acoustics again. So far, I'm very pleased. I'll know more once my full crew arrives."

Which wouldn't be until after the holidays.

"You're a workaholic, aren't you?"

Her smile widened. "You say that like it's a bad thing."

A jolt of lust slammed him, right in the gut. He looked down to try and collect himself. "It's not. I can relate. How much longer are you going to be here working?" He eyed her, trying like hell to keep his voice casual.

She cocked her head. "Why? What did you have in mind?"

Though he wanted to answer her by stating he wanted to finish up where they'd left off, he didn't. Even though every cell in his body screamed desire. She deserved more than that. He wanted to take her out, show her around and spend some real time learning more about the woman who fascinated him on so many levels.

"I thought we could go out on the Strip and check out my competition. You know, act like tourists. We can play some slots or poker, wander from casino to casino and grab a drink here and there, maybe even a bite to eat."

Her smile morphed into a huge grin. "I'd love that."

"Then later tonight, if you're up for it, we could hit out the Fallen Angel or Spark, here in the hotel. They're two of the trendiest nightclubs on the Strip. We've had lots of celebrities party in both of them already." Because truth be told, he wanted to see a little bit of her wild side.

Just like that, the animation vanished from her expression. She shook her head, her green eyes flashing. "Thanks, but no thanks. I'm afraid I'll have to take a pass on that."

Curious, he studied her. "Why? Are you worried you'll be recognized?"

"That, too, but I'm not much for the club scene, actually."

"Really?" He thought of every tabloid article he'd read, the photographs showing her on the dance floor. She'd been on gossip blogs too many times to count, always getting in or out of someone's car after partying all night. When she didn't respond, he couldn't help but ask. "Is that because you don't want to hang out with the casino owner when you party?"

"No." She sighed, dragging her fingers through her hair, making the short strands stand up even more. "It's because I don't really like to party."

Stopping, he crossed his arms and studied her. Sexy as hell. And so many contradictions. She fascinated him. "Then why—"

"Is every tabloid filled with my partying antics? And the blogosphere always seems to catch me living it up?"

"Exactly."

She exhaled wearily. "Most stars' lives aren't really what they're made out to be. When I first made it big, my publicist and the label decided my sales would be stronger if I came off as a bad girl."

He wasn't sure whether to be disappointed or relieved. Some of his thoughts must have shown in his face because she laughed. "I'm sorry. But I'll tell you what. At some point, my PR team is going to make me do something wild and crazy. Just so I can be photographed and make the entertainment shows. When that happens, I promise you can come along with me."

This made him chuckle. "That sounds like a plan."

"So for now, no to the nightclubs." She smiled up at him. "But the rest of what you suggested sounds like fun. I'll need a little bit to get ready."

"How long do you need?"

"Twenty minutes."

He mustn't have done a good job hiding his skeptical shock, because she laughed. "Look at you. You must be used to women who need a couple of hours to do their makeup and hair."

"And to choose exactly the right outfit." He didn't bother denying it.

"Well, since I'm trying to disguise myself, I don't have to worry about that. As long as you don't mind me looking kind of raw, it's all good."

What she called "kind of raw" on her was better than any other woman. He almost didn't tell her that, guessing she had a pretty good idea of her own beauty, but at the last minute he did. To his amazement, she blushed, pink transforming her dusky complexion.

"Thank you." Glancing at her watch, she rocked up on her toes. "Let me run up to my room and put on my disguise. Do you want to meet in the lobby in twenty minutes?"

"I'll just come to your room." He hadn't meant the words to sound so suggestive—or maybe he subconsciously had. Meghan's blush deepened, making her dusky skin take on a rosy hue, odd since earlier she'd propositioned him.

Again he felt a tug of lust, which he pushed away. They'd gone fast once, nearly twice. This time, he was determined to woo her.

"Sounds good," she said easily. "See you in twenty."

She hurried off, her hips swaying. Heaven help him, he watched until he could see no more.

He had it bad. This kind of craving was a definite distraction. The sooner he got her out of his system, the better. Years ago, one of his previous girlfriends had told him angrily that he was all about the chase. Once he captured his quarry, his intense interest faded into boredom. He'd disagreed at the time, but now he hoped that statement had actually been accurate. Though he couldn't imagine anyone growing bored with a woman as fascinating as Meghan Frost.

Yep. He definitely had it bad.

Meghan couldn't recall the last time she'd had more fun. Gabe taught her to play poker, and she learned she had a knack for keeping her expression impassive so as not to give away her hand.

She won a small jackpot before deciding she'd had enough.

"You're a natural," he said, his expression proud. "You should have kept playing. You might have cleaned up."

"I think," she reminded him gently, "I've already won enough."

This made him laugh.

They ended up in a smoky piano bar where a husband and wife sang Christmas carols. The bar had been decorated for the holiday, from the red-and-gold-trimmed Christmas tree to the poinsettia plants on several tables.

This time, thinking about the holiday didn't make her sad. Instead, for the first time in a long while, she felt almost…festive.

Keeping her voice low, she sang along to "White Christmas." After a second, Gabe joined her, his low voice hitting the notes just right. She leaned into him, content.

"Since your family doesn't celebrate, what are your plans for Christmas Day?" he asked.

Too happy to let the bleak prospect of the actual day blacken her mood, she shrugged. "Sleep in, have a nice breakfast, maybe watch some TV. What about you?"

Though he eyed her with what might have been compassion, she refused to acknowledge the need for any such thing.

"My brother, Rafe, and I have a Christmas Eve tradition," he told her, his tone light. "We play some high stakes poker, knock back a few drinks and grill steak in our private rooftop garden. On Christmas Day, we either have the entire family over to eat a huge meal, potluck style, or we go to our parents' house out in Red Rock. This year it's our turn to host."

She felt a twinge of envy. "That sounds lovely."

"It is." Twining his fingers with hers, he kissed the back of her hand. "But this year, Rafe is engaged. He'll naturally want to spend the holiday with his fiancée. So I think everything is going to change."

Bemused, she studied his face. "You don't seem too sad about it."

"I'm not. Change is inevitable." He nuzzled her, his lips searing a path up her neck to her ear. A shiver of raw need rocked her. She held her breath, waiting to see what he'd do next.

But he released her and leaned forward, taking a long pull on his bourbon. "You know what?" he asked, his tone musing. "I'd really like it if you would spend Christmas Eve with me."

"What?" Though her heart leaped at the idea, she didn't want to be anyone's charity case. "There's no way I'm crashing your and Rafe's traditional celebration."

"You won't be. He's either doing something else entirely or he's bringing his fiancée, Evangeline. You should meet her. I think you'll like her."

Unsettled, she shifted in her seat and turned to face him. "Gabe, you have a big heart. I appreciate you thinking about me. But we've only known each other less than a week. I'm not sure this is a good idea." Which she honestly wasn't, even if she wanted it so very badly.

The intensity in his gaze made her ache. "It feels like longer."

She hoped he didn't notice that her short laugh contained a hint of pain. "I'm not sure if that's a compliment or an insult."

He kissed her then, right there in the bar. A slow, lingering kiss that left no doubt about his comment. "Please spend Christmas Eve with me," he murmured. "Otherwise, Rafe will feel guilty about leaving me alone, so he and Ev will take pains to include me in their plans. I'll be the proverbial third wheel."

Hope flared in her, though she took care not to let it show. She shook her head. "So you're wanting me to make up the foursome."

"Either that, or it'll just be the two of us. I don't know if Rafe and Evangeline need to have this, their first Christmas Eve, alone together. I don't see any reason why you and I can't find something to do."

Christmas Eve. A few times, when the loneliness had grown unbearable, she'd gotten in her car and tried to make an annual tradition of driving around the neighborhoods and looking at Christmas lights. While the outdoor displays had been breathtaking, she'd been witness to so many family gatherings displayed through huge picture windows lit up from inside, that this had become her own peculiar form of torture. She'd finally stopped the practice because it made her too conscious of what she was missing.

"Christmas is a joyful time," Gabe said, squeezing her hand. "I'm happy when I'm with you."

Warmth spread through her at his words. Too fast? Maybe. But he was right. She needed to seize the chance for happiness while it existed. After all, she knew from personal experience how fleeting such moments could be.

"You talked me into it," she finally said, trying for casual. "I love your patio and garden. I can't think of a better place to spend Christmas Eve."

He watched her, his eyes still molten. "I'd love it if you'd consider coming up on Christmas Day, too. My family would love to meet you. One of my nieces idolizes you. She has every album you've ever made and can recite the words to all of your songs."

She loved how he managed to make even this, asking her to meet his family after only knowing her a few days, seem like it wasn't such a big deal. Who knew, maybe to him it wasn't.

This would have to be one of the first times ever she would gladly use her celebrity status in exchange for not feeling like an intruder.

"I'll think about it," she said, not wanting to seem too eager.

"Don't think about it too long. We're only five days out."

Which meant tomorrow was the twenty-first. Winter solstice. The night of the big hunt. When legend had it the Helios Rejuvenated, their earthly bodies engulfed in flames. Supposedly, they survived this, emerging from the ashes cleansed and whole.

She'd never understood how so many could believe so much nonsense.

"You know what," she said, deciding, "I'm in. I'd love to spend both days with you, on one condition. If you change your mind, you promise to tell me right away. There'll be no hard feelings, I promise."

Instead of agreeing, he lowered his brows in a frown. "What kind of person would do something like that? Cancel at the last minute, right before the holidays?"

She could list numerous people right off the top of her head, all show-business types. She'd learned loyalties didn't run deep among the party crowd.

"Thank you," she said instead, smiling up at him, her heart full. "You're a kind and generous man."

"I hate to interrupt this lovefest," a voice said to the left of them. "But do you mind if I join you?"

Rafe.

"Of course not." Gabe grinned. "Order a drink and take a seat. Where's your lovely fiancée tonight?"

"Working." Rafe sounded glum. "We have lots of holiday parties, and she's overseeing all the florists who are doing the decorations. I haven't seen much of her today at all."

"It's almost over," Gabe said. Under the table, he nudged Meghan with his thigh, sending heat through her.

Rafe got his drink, a dark beer, and sat. They made small talk, all the while Gabe worked his hand up Meghan's thigh. Finally, she grabbed his fingers and stopped him, unable to bear the embarrassment if his brother learned what he was doing.

The talk turned to the ongoing investigation about the shooter. "The police still have no leads," Rafe said. "Have you given any thought as to where you might have seen that guy before?"

Meghan shook her head, glancing up in time to see Gabe shoot his brother a warning glare. "What?" she asked, looking from one man to the other. "Is there something you're not telling me?"

Gabe sighed. "Rafe watched one of your music videos and saw a man in a gray hoodie sitting in the wings. It was hard to get a good look at his face."

"Which video?"

"'Melancholy Reset.'"

"Seriously?" This time, she had to laugh. "You didn't recognize the guy wearing the hoodie? He's even more famous than I am. He performed later in the video."

"No." Rafe shrugged. "I didn't watch the entire thing and I'm not really familiar with your kind of music. Who was it?"

"Leoculous. He's a popular rapper."

After a second of stunned silence, Gabe laughed. "Well, I guess that proves there are a lot of men who own gray hoodies, bro. Just like I told you."

Rafe gave them both a sheepish smile. "Sorry. But when you said that guy looked familiar, and I saw someone in a similar outfit in the video, I thought maybe I'd found the connection."

"Good try." Still chuckling, Gabe put his arm around Meghan's shoulders and pulled her closer. "I feel reasonably confident that he wasn't here at the Archangel, setting fire to our poker table."

Chapter 13

After his brother left, Gabe and Meghan wasted no time hurrying up to his room. This time, he resolved to go slower. Every time they touched, he rapidly lost control. And with tomorrow night being the solstice and his Rejuvenation, he'd have to maintain restraint over his passion more than ever. He felt confident he could control himself until the Rejuvenation. Helios knew, he'd done it often enough.

But Meghan? He was powerless to resist her.

Once inside, they came together like a blazing inferno. They shed their clothes, each of them with a craving too urgent to be denied. Though initially, Gabe tried to stick to his resolve to go slower, when his skin touched hers he lost all restraint.

Together, they were explosive. When he and Meghan made love, the act felt like a form of rebirth in its own way.

He could love this woman, he realized. His insides flip-flopped as he realized this truth. He might already love her, not the fleeting, heady love of initial intoxication, but a deep, abiding and unshakable emotion.

With that thought, he fell asleep holding her in his arms.

The morning of the solstice he woke up ready, every nerve ending tingling. Aware. Being so physical with Meghan had helped calm the innate restlessness that usually intensified on that morning, right up until he actually Rejuvenated.

Still, a sense of nervous anticipation had him wanting to pace. Instead, he lay in his bed next to her and watched her sleep, his chest tight with affection.

When she stirred, her breath catching as her amazing green eyes flew open, he couldn't help but smile. "Good morning."

"Mmm." Propping herself up on her elbows, she squinted at him. "I don't suppose you have coffee?"

"Not yet."

Her groan made him laugh out loud. "What do you have planned for today?" He wanted to make sure she stayed busy. The one thing he couldn't do was let anyone interrupt or interfere with his Rejuvenation. The event didn't take long, though when in the midst of burning his body to ash it felt like it took hours.

After, he always felt a little sore, his newborn skin pink and tender until he'd gotten a good night's sleep.

"You ask me that this early?" She wrinkled up her cute little nose and considered his question. "My plans? Well, they're sort of fluid. Work out, maybe. I might go check out the amphitheater again, test out the acoustics once more." A quick smile made her eyes sparkle. "At some point, I'm even thinking of giving the slot machines another whirl."

"Because we can't all win the jackpot every time," he teased.

"Oh, sometimes we can," she breathed, trailing kisses down his chest and skimming over his abdomen. And she proceeded to show him how they'd both won the jackpot just right then.

Later, after showering and getting dressed, he took her downstairs for a late breakfast. His restlessness increased the longer he waited to Rejuvenate, but he was determined to make sure Meghan didn't suspect anything was different about this day. "We have a champagne brunch today," he told her. She rewarded him with an impish grin as they went into the restaurant. He'd called ahead and made a quick reservation. They were given the table he'd asked for, a small, very secluded spot. Once she'd taken her seat, she ordered a mimosa and coffee. He admired the graceful lines of her neck while she drank.

"This is nice," she told him, smiling as she caught him watching her. "The rosy afterglow from earlier, now food and champagne. It doesn't get much better than this."

He laughed out loud, because she was right. Impulsively, he leaned across the table and kissed her, a lingering kiss that might have turned into more if they weren't out in public. He couldn't seem to stop touching her. Even now, when normally all he could only think of was fire.

"Stop," she said halfheartedly. And then giggled as she took another sip of her drink. "People are going to stare, and you know how I feel about attention."

"No one can see us," he pointed out. "I asked for this table on purpose. Not only are we behind a pillar, but that huge potted plant blocks us from view."

"Oh." Leaning forward, she scooted her chair over and nibbled on his lips. "In that case…"

Laughing, he shook his head. "Let's eat first. We need fuel to give us energy if we're going to go another round."

A dusky blush spread across her cheeks. "You know, at the risk of scaring you off, you make me happy. I can't stop smiling," she said. "Thank you for that."

He smiled back, taking her hand from across the table and twining his fingers in hers. "Right back atcha."

"This might just be the best Christmas ever," she began,

glancing around the crowded restaurant at the other diners as if needing to see if anyone noticed her joy. "Oh, no!" Her smile vanished and she pulled her hand free. Looking down and swallowing hard, she doubled over slightly, looking as if she'd been punched in the gut.

"What's wrong? Are you ill?" Instantly concerned, he reached across the table to try and recapture her hand. This time, she avoided his touch.

"No." She shook her head as she straightened, her eyes bleak. "Nothing like that. It's just… See that man over there in the buffet line?"

Following the direction of her gaze, he spotted a tall, lanky man with short, curly black hair. "Him?"

"Yes." She took a deep, shaky breath. "That's my brother Damon. I just texted him a few days ago and let him know where I was. More than anyone else, he's aware how badly I want to be with family during the holidays. I can't believe he's in Vegas and didn't even bother to let me know."

Tears shimmered in her eyes. With jerky, angry motions, she swiped at them using the back of her hand. "It's Christmas," she said, her voice unsteady. "He could have at least tried to pop in and say hello. Or something."

Stunned, Gabe glanced from her to her brother and back again. He could see the family resemblance, especially in the high cheekbones and sculpted features. Definitely her brother. Which boggled his mind. Gabe's family—loud, demonstrative and close-knit—would never have done something like this. In fact, it was so out of the realm of rational behavior that he wasn't sure what would be the right words to say. "Maybe he doesn't know you're here?" he tried, watching as the man walked to his seat.

She shook her head violently. "Oh, he knows where I am. They all do. I invited them all to share a meal with me on Christmas Day. I'd planned to make reservations at one of the restaurants. But every single member of my family, including Damon, let me know they had other plans."

Though this time she managed to keep her voice level, he couldn't help but see the pain in her eyes. For one second, he felt a flash of violence. He wanted to go over to her brother and haul him up out of his seat and shake him.

"Are you going to let him know you've seen him?" he asked quietly, since that's what he would have done.

"No."

Their breakfast arrived, but Meghan had clearly lost her desire for food. She picked at her omelet, and while he felt terrible for devouring his corned beef hash and eggs, he'd worked up quite an appetite.

"You've got to eat," he pointed out. "Especially if you plan on working out the way you do. Your muscles need protein."

Relieved to see a tiny smile lifting the corner of her lips, he continued eating. Finally, she picked up the fork and ate a bite. Then, studiously avoiding looking anywhere else, she demolished her omelet with a methodical intensity before starting on the toast.

Looking past her shoulder, Gabe saw the man she'd identified as her brother grab his jacket and leave. The jacket appeared to be a gray hoodie.

Meghan knew she should have been used to the way her family acted and shouldn't let their actions hurt her. But of all her siblings, she and Damon had always been closest. She couldn't understand why he'd come to Vegas and not even make an attempt to seek her out.

Damon. Her throat ached as she fought to keep from doubling over at the pain of her own brother's complete and utter betrayal. He knew where to find her but simply hadn't cared enough to contact her. Unless maybe he planned to surprise her on Christmas itself.

Possibly, she thought, at first desperately clinging to a tiny thread of hope, he would after the winter solstice, after the hunt. In fact, what if he wanted to spend Christmas together for the first time ever?

Just as quickly as she'd allowed herself to consider this possibility, she squashed it. While she loved him, she knew all too well Damon's flaws. The hunt came first. Always had, always would.

The hunt. The damn, stupid hunt. If Damon was in Vegas, that meant he'd brought others and they were hunting here. Here? In the land of glitter and sin? Why would they think one of their mythical Helios would be here? No doubt this was the reason her brother was here. If she remembered right, there'd been a news story a while back about some guy bursting into flames, which would have drawn all kinds of crazy talk about Helios. She knew such things had happened before.

She didn't get it, but then she never had. And she'd let her seeing Damon ruin the magical morning she and Gabe had shared. Being with Gabe made her feel blissfully alive. Beautiful, both inside and out.

After breakfast, she'd come back to her room, telling Gabe she needed some time alone. Clearly preoccupied, he'd readily agreed, explaining that he had quite a bit of work to catch up on and would also be unavailable the rest of the day.

"What about tonight?" she'd teased.

Instead of answering, he'd kissed her until her head spun and she forgot what she'd asked.

Gabe had turned out to be more than a welcome distraction. They'd clicked instantly, and the chemistry between them was unbelievable. Initially, she'd sort of thought once they'd gotten the sex out of their systems, the insistent craving would fade, but it hadn't. Instead every touch, every kiss, every smile only made her want him more.

Even stranger, he seemed to feel the same way. Could she possibly have found love?

As usual, even in her private thoughts, she shied away from the word. It was too soon, too fast. They'd only known each other five days. Real love, true love, took time to nurture, to grow. It didn't burst into one's life like a lightning strike setting a lone tree on fire. Or did it? She wasn't really sure. In truth, she had no way of knowing since she'd never been in love before.

Shaking her head at her own odd observation, she listened as Christmas music piped in from somewhere drifted up to her balcony. Usually, holiday music made her sad. Now, mingled with the grief over her brother's betrayal, she had hope. Instead of feeling nostalgic for something she'd never had, Gabe had ensured that this Christmas, she'd no longer be alone. That certainty brought her great joy and a feeling of optimism about the future.

It was hard to believe that Christmas was right around the corner. Just four more days until families would gather together for church and opening gifts, seeing what Santa had brought the children, a huge meal with everyone gathered around a well-decorated table. At least she thought that's what the rest of the world did. She'd always felt like a stray dog with her nose pressed against the window, watching the well-fed warmth and laughter inside and wishing she'd be welcomed.

Shaking off her melancholy, she couldn't help think of her family. It still hurt to know they wouldn't be thinking of her. Not on this date.

Today was the winter solstice. A big day for Hunters. Instead of planning the Christmas celebration, her family would all be gearing up for the hunt.

Random Rejuvenation was part of the lore, though legend had it that true Helios only burst into flame four times a year.

No. She wouldn't think of her family and their all-encompassing traditions that they valued more than her.

Still full from the huge breakfast, she yawned. A nap seemed like a good idea. Grabbing the do-not-disturb sign and hanging it on her door, she crawled beneath the covers and tried to fall asleep.

Though usually when she napped, she slept a couple of hours before rising and going in search of food. Today, maybe worn out from all the energetic sex, when she finally raised her head from her pillow to glance at her clock, she was stunned to see six hours had passed. Lunchtime had come and gone.

Stretching, she yawned. Her body must have needed the rest. Barefoot, she padded into the kitchen, scarfed down a bag of trail mix and headed into the shower. On her way there, she detoured and made a quick call to room service, ordering a grilled chicken salad and iced tea, along with a bottle of that same white wine Gabe had brought earlier. She asked that it be left unopened so she could keep it chilled in her mini-fridge to enjoy whenever she wanted.

Later, cleaned up and wearing fresh clothes, she ate her meal and wondered what Gabe might be up to. She'd checked her phone a couple times and he hadn't called. He hadn't even texted, which was unusual. She figured he must really be busy at work.

Wandering out onto her balcony, which had rapidly become her favorite part of her suite, she thought she'd sit awhile and maybe even watch the sun go down.

Below, the noise and bustle of the Strip made her feel hollow. She thought longingly of Gabe's private garden, wondering if he'd mind if she retreated there for a while. When he finished up with work, they could share the bottle of wine.

Cheered, she grabbed her wine, a corkscrew and a couple of glasses and rode the elevator up one floor to his, using her room key to grant access as she'd seen Gabe do before. She wasn't sure it would work, but when the elevator started moving, she shrugged. Apparently he'd either granted her access or his floor wasn't as well secured as he'd thought.

Once there, she stepped off the elevator and took a deep breath. She'd seen a lot of fantastic things hanging out with other rich and famous stars. Even other stars' Bahamian estates paled in beauty compared to this. A peaceful green oasis in the middle of concrete and neon. Already feeling better, she walked around the well-tended gardens, smelling the riot of beautiful flowers, wondering about the man who could arrange something like this here in the desert.

When she came across the hidden grotto where she and Gabe had shared their picnic meal, she went inside. She'd never experienced anything like this place. Just being here brought her a sense of calm akin to meditation.

Pouring herself a glass of wine, she sat back, enchanted by her surroundings, happier than she'd been in a long time.

Movement in the direction of the elevator caught her eye. When Gabe stepped out of the building, she smiled but remained hidden. She'd wait to surprise him once he got a little bit closer.

But instead of heading toward her, he headed around to the back of the garden, toward an area she'd glanced at but skipped, assuming it was where they kept supplies or trash.

Curious, she set down her wineglass and followed. If he turned and saw her, she'd simply smile and wave. Her entire body tingled at the thought of how he'd react. A kiss would only be the beginning.

As she rounded the corner of the building, she saw Gabe step into a three-sided concrete structure. Before she could call out, he raised both arms to the sky and instantaneously burst into flames.

Chapter 14

Meghan gasped out loud and staggered backward, torn between horror and the desire to help him, save him. Except she knew he didn't need assistance. This was what he did. Today was the solstice and Gabe was Rejuvenating. He was a Helios, and what she'd just seen meant all the old legends were true. Her family truly were Hunters and Helios existed in more than their collective imaginations.

Instinctively, she pulled out her phone and snapped a few photos. Then, realizing what she'd done, she jammed her cell back into her pocket, appalled.

What now? She had to move, had to hide before he saw her. She had no idea what would happen if he saw her, if he realized she'd watched him catch on fire.

Nauseated, she ran back in the direction she'd come, her bottle of wine forgotten. Looking up, she realized there were security cameras, like everywhere else in the casino. Everywhere except that concrete fortress area where Gabe had burst into flame. If he reviewed the footage, he'd know she'd been there and realize she'd likely seen.

Though panic had her heart pounding, she tried to maintain her composure, at least on the outside. Inside, she was a jittery mess of nerves.

When she reached the elevator, she jabbed the down button, praying it would hurry and arrive. A moment later, the doors slid open and she stepped inside.

Once inside the elevator, she began to shake. All these years, she'd considered her family, with their absolute devotion to the hunt and belief in the Helios, wrong. She'd been hurt, angry and finally indifferent to their passionate quest. Now, it turned out she was the one who was wrong. Helios *were* real. She'd just watched one go up in flames. Rejuvenation. The archaic term suddenly took on life. She even had photos to prove it.

She had generations of Hunters in her blood. Even though it had been years since she'd participated in the hunt, she had a duty to find Damon and let him know what she'd just witnessed.

Or did she? Because this particular Helios was the man she'd halfway fallen in love with. Gabe.

What to do, what to do? She'd already once turned her back on her heritage, but that had been before she'd realized that they were truly after a being that actually existed.

Her family lived to hunt. Nothing else mattered more to them.

But then what? With an inward groan, she realized she had no idea what they would do once they caught a Helios, probably some sort of horrible torture in an attempt to get information out of him before they killed him. That was how things worked, at least according to the lore that had been pounded into her as a child.

But beyond that, she had no idea. She'd actually stopped

paying attention to their rantings and ravings when she'd become a teenager.

The elevator doors opened and she hurried to her room. Hands shaking, she slid her key card into the slot in her door. But the light stayed red. Her room key wouldn't work. She couldn't get into her suite. Though she had a spare, she'd left it on her kitchen counter.

Turning the key card over in her hands, she realized what must have happened. Somehow, her key and Gabe's must have gotten switched. That would explain why the elevator had allowed her to go to his private access area.

Now what? She assumed she could go down to the front desk and get another, but that would involve making her true identity known. Too much risk and one she'd rather not take, especially now.

She could contact Gabe, assuming he'd finished his Rejuvenation. But how could she act normally around him, knowing she and he were sworn blood enemies? Even if she didn't want to be. No, that idea wouldn't work, either.

Until she figured something out, she'd simply walk. The casino, the mall, the streets. She'd lose herself in the crowds and hope a solution came to her.

She pulled out her phone and eyed the text messages she'd exchanged with her brother. While she might have renounced her status as a Hunter, her duty to her family seemed clear.

As mud. Clicking off her phone and placing it on the counter beside the elevators, she knew she couldn't. Not now, not yet, maybe not ever.

As he let the flames consume him, Gabe raised his arms above his head. An instant before the blackness took him, he muttered a quick prayer to the ancient gods, aware it would be at their whim if he was to awaken in one piece, refreshed and new.

Sometime later—seconds, minutes, or more—he stood whole again amid smoldering embers, the scent of burning flesh lingering.

Again, he'd been reborn. A new earthly body for his Helios spirit. Though in appearance he looked identical, he'd been given back his waning powers. A clean slate, the better to defend against the Hunters, though none had ever even managed to get close to him, though one had attacked Rafe recently.

Rejuvenated, he always felt as weak as a newborn baby. With unsteady legs, he walked from the bunker out into his private garden. It worried him that he'd somehow lost one of his room keys. Good thing he always kept a spare.

Later, he'd have to have them recoded, but right now, he needed to shower off any ashy residue and take the rest of the night easy. Over the next several hours, his powers would continue to build. By this time tomorrow, he'd have regained his full strength, plus more.

This was why the Hunters always tried to catch a Helios either mid-flame or right after, because this was when they were most vulnerable.

About to step into the shower, he went back outside instead, intending to cool off just a little more. He toyed with the idea of contacting Meghan, but knew he wouldn't be up to another night of intense lovemaking. Unbelievably, his body stirred at the thought, making him grin. How she could always have this effect on him he didn't know, but he sure as hell liked it.

His cell rang. Rafe. "The Hunters are here," Rafe said. "Security just alerted me. The cameras picked up the guy in the gray hoodie."

"Where?"

"Meghan's room." Even Rafe sounded worried. "He's with two others. They appear to be looking for something. They're in her suite."

Gabe swore. "Do you have a security team on the way?"

"Not yet. I thought I'd check with you first."

"Good call." Shaking off the lingering weakness, Gabe pulled on his slacks.

"Have you...?" Rafe asked.

"Yes. I'm all done. A bit weak. If we're going to confront them, I'll need your help."

"I'm on my way. Wait for me there. Don't do anything until I arrive." After barking this out, Rafe ended the call.

Dressing hurriedly, Gabe hurried out into the hallway. He took the stairs instead of the elevator, figuring this would give him an additional element of surprise. While he couldn't lead a direct attack, he could still defend himself. All he needed to do was goad the other men into making the first move.

As he rushed down the stairs, willing strength into his rubbery legs, it occurred to him that maybe Damon had intended to surprise Meghan for Christmas. But then why wreck her suite?

When he arrived to find her door slightly ajar, he didn't even consider waiting for his brother. He stepped quietly inside, stopping short at the sight of three men all staring at a cell phone.

"A Helios," one said. Meghan's brother caught sight of him then and made a gesture for silence.

They knew. How?

"What are you doing in this room?" Gabe asked, putting on his hotel owner/manager persona. "This suite is reserved for a VIP. Security has been alerted and are on the way to remove you."

"I'm her brother," Damon Frost said. "She's expecting me." The other two men stayed silent, though alert.

"Is she?" Gabe pulled out his cell. "Let me call her and make sure." He pulled up his contacts and hit her number.

The phone in Damon's hands rang.

"You have her phone?" While Gabe wasn't sure what that meant, he knew it wasn't good. "Is Meghan in danger?"

Instead of answering, Damon advanced on him, eyes narrowed. "You," he said, holding up the phone. "You're the guy I've been seeing around with my sister. I found this by the elevators. Where is she? I need to ask her about a couple of pictures she took an hour or two ago."

A chill snaked up Gabe's spine, though he was careful not to reveal anything. An hour or two ago would have been around the time he'd Rejuvenated. What if Meghan had his missing room key card? Was it possible she had seen?

"Let me see." He held out his hand for the phone.

Instead of handing it over, Damon took a step back and slid the phone into his back pocket. He glanced at his two associates, then spoke two words that set Gabe's blood ablaze. "We hunt." And then Damon lowered his head and charged.

Hunters. This was what Gabe had been waiting for. Damon had attacked first, which meant Gabe could fight to defend himself.

Gabe met the other man full on, knocking him back with ease, despite his weakened state. With a roar, Damon attacked again. This time, his two cohorts attacked with him.

Luckily, at that moment Rafe and two armed security guards burst through the door, weapons drawn.

At the sight of the guns, Damon backed away, hands up. His helpers did the same. "We're unarmed," Damon said. He glanced at Gabe, his lip curling. "I have a message for you to deliver to my sister. Since clearly she's seen our quarry, tell her not to try to take down the Helios herself. If she can't reach us, there are others."

Though his new blood turned to ice, Gabe pretended

not to understand. "What does that even mean?" he asked, his voice as harsh as the pain inside.

"None of your business." Damon met his gaze with a show of defiance. "Just tell her. She'll know."

Careful not to look at his brother, Gabe slowly nodded. "Let me have her phone."

The other man didn't move.

"Now!" Gabe held out his hand.

Reluctantly, Damon handed over Meghan's cell.

"Take them down to my office," Rafe ordered. "We already have a call in to the police."

As the security guards moved to do as he asked, the three men moved as if synchronized. Two of them twisted and knocked the pistols from the guards' hands while Damon headed for the door. The others were right on his heels.

By the time the stunned security officers dove for their weapons and gave chase, the three were way ahead of them.

Gabe and Rafe didn't move.

"Do you think they'll catch them?" Rafe asked.

"I doubt it." Staring down at Meghan's phone, Gabe cleared his throat.

"Are you going to look at it?" Rafe came closer. "I'm guessing it's not password protected, otherwise Meghan's brother wouldn't have been able to view any photos."

Gabe pushed the on button. "No password. As a matter of fact, this is an older model."

"That's weird. You'd think a superstar like her would have the latest and best phone."

"Actually, it's just like her." Again Gabe felt the crush of grief, as if someone had died. Not someone, he thought. But something. The bright and shiny future he'd thought he and Meghan had ahead of them. All gone. Not once had it even remotely occurred to him that she might be a Hunter.

Touching the icon for photos, Gabe swallowed hard. The first picture to come up showed an inferno in the shape of a human body. Him. Rejuvenating.

"She knows." Until he spoke the words, he hadn't realized how much he'd hoped that she hadn't. "Though her brother doesn't."

"It's only a matter of time."

Aware his brother was right, Gabe turned the phone off and placed it on the kitchen counter. "What a mess."

"I agree. What are we going to do about this?"

"I don't know." Briefly, Gabe let his shoulders sag. "I refuse to battle Meghan. I just can't."

"Then what? Do you plan to let her win? You know Hunters. Once they locate what they want, they don't give up unless they die. It's either them or us."

Crossing his arms, Gabe glared at his brother. "I'm definitely not going to kill her."

"Someone has to."

"No. No, they don't." The thought of Meghan, beautiful, vibrant Meghan dead made Gabe feel like a huge chunk had been ripped out of his heart. "Damn." He closed his eyes. "I can't believe this."

"Me, either." Rafe's eyes narrowed. "Her show."

"What about it?"

"We've got to find a way to break that contract."

Suddenly exhausted, Gabe shrugged. "She can still do it. It's business."

"That doesn't make sense," Rafe argued. "She knows you're a Helios. Tradition dictates—"

"Screw tradition. You know there's an alternative. We'll have to erase her memory." Which would also erase him, and them, from her mind. A stab of wild grief made him want to double over. Instead, he cursed again.

"That might work." Rafe watched him closely. "But what about you? Are you going to be all right?"

All right? When even breathing hurt?

"I'll be fine," Gabe said. "But I'm going to have to leave." Gabe didn't think he could stand another lecture about tradition and ancient rivalries. Rafe loved to talk about history and could go on for hours if he got wound up.

"You'll what?" Rafe gaped at him, clearly unable to understand Gabe's level of pain.

"Leave. I'm due a vacation." Gabe bit out the words. "It's been a long time since I've traveled anywhere. I can go to Australia or New Zealand. Canada or Mexico, even. Hell, I might just go back to Greece and visit family."

"For the three entire months?" Though Rafe rarely raised his voice, he did now. "You plan to abandon the Archangel—and me—for ninety days? How can you possibly think that's fair?"

Fair? Life wasn't fair. Though Gabe knew he was acting childishly, he'd never had to cope with this level of betrayal and grief. Rafe didn't know how close he'd come to giving Meghan Frost his heart. Seeing her every day, knowing she'd betrayed him, not only by being a Hunter, but not telling him the truth.

"Why not?" The more he thought about it, the more reasonable it sounded. "You can handle it. If you have to, bring in more staff to pick up the slack."

"No." Rafe crossed his arms. "I refuse to let you do this."

From somewhere, somehow, Gabe summoned up something close to a laugh. "You refuse? Just try and stop me."

And then, before he broke down completely, he turned around and strode out of the room.

Chapter 15

Several months ago, one of Meghan's crew had given her an exercise tracker. She wore it around her wrist diligently, but rarely thought of it except when the thing vibrated to tell her that she'd reached ten thousand steps.

This winter solstice, as she strode through the crowds heading up and down the Las Vegas Strip, the display showed she'd logged more steps than she'd gotten since she'd first put it on.

Gabe. She went for her phone, wondering if he'd texted her. With a sense of shock, she realized she'd left it in her room. Just great. One more oddity in a world that hours ago had felt full of promise. Without her phone, she felt naked, oddly detached from the rest of the world.

Detachment. Her ever-present suit of armor. All she'd ever wanted for most of her life was her family. And now, she had a chance to do the one thing that would guarantee her acceptance and admiration by the very people who ostracized her.

She could capture a Helios. A real, live Helios.

Who also happened to be the man she honestly thought she might be in love with.

Finally, after hours of aimless wandering, she found herself back in front of the Archangel. Taking a deep breath, she pushed through the double doors and entered the lobby. She didn't want to go up to her room, not yet. And she couldn't really go to Gabe's, since her intrusion earlier had nearly cost her everything that mattered.

That left her amphitheater. The one place where, beyond question, she felt as if she belonged.

As she used his key card to enter, she thought of the man who'd made all this possible. Correction, the Helios. How she wished she hadn't seen, didn't know. She'd give anything if things could go back to the way they were before she'd decided to trespass in Gabe's private garden.

Their relationship could never, ever work. Despite her disallowance of her heritage, it was her sworn destiny to kill him. Not that she could. Yet that alone would be a river too big to cross.

Groping blindly in the dark, she made her way to the stage. Though she needed to find the light switch, for now it was enough to be here, breathing in the scent of new construction and listening to the solid sound her feet made on the wood. Familiar scents and sounds, bringing her comfort.

The lights came on, making her jump. Just the backdrop lights, not the main spotlight, but enough so that she could see.

"I thought I might find you here." Gabe, stepping from the shadows into her sight. His beloved voice made her ache.

Her heartbeat skipped. "I…" Stunned to realize she hovered on the verge of tears, she choked on whatever else she might have been about to say. He didn't know she knew, she reminded herself. He had no idea that her entire world had changed.

He came closer, his movements both sure and oddly hesitant. "Here," he said, holding out his large hand. "Your phone."

She froze. "Where did you get that?" Had he seen the pictures she'd snapped?

Instead of answering, he cocked his head. The shadows made it difficult to read his expression.

A loud, clanking sound near the door had them both spinning around. Someone had disabled the lock.

"Meghan." Damon's voice. "Are you here? We need to talk." He burst onto the stage, stopping when he caught sight of Gabe standing back in the shadows. "You," he growled.

Trying to understand, Meghan looked from her brother to Gabe. "Do you two know each other?"

Before anyone could reply, Damon lunged at Meghan, yanking her close. "Don't move," he snarled. She felt the press of cold metal against her skin.

"A gun? Is that a gun? Damon? What are you doing? This doesn't make sense."

"I need information. Who is it?" Damon demanded, holding his gun close to Meghan's temple. "The Helios you saw Rejuvenate. You have photos on your phone. Give me his name so I can be the one to hunt him and bring him down."

Somehow, her brother had seen the pics on her phone. Now more than ever, she regretted the impulse that had made her take them.

"Tell me," Damon demanded, giving her a little shake.

And now he'd force her into making the choice she hadn't wanted to make.

Fury flashed across Gabe's rugged countenance, but he didn't move. Meghan briefly closed her eyes, unwilling to let him see her pain. "I don't know," she answered. "I was so shocked when I realized that Helios were actually real, that I ran away. I didn't see him before or after. I have no idea."

"You're lying." Damon sounded so positive, so certain. "Now give me the name."

Slowly, she shook her head. "No." Would she die at the hand of her own brother? Had Damon become such a monster that he could put a bullet in her head without remorse?

"Why are you protecting him?" Damon asked, shaking her again. "You know your duty. Reveal his identity."

"No. I can't." Meghan took a deep breath. "I won't."

"Then I'm going to have to kill you."

The pain of this betrayal, though only the latest in many, cut sharp and deep. "What's wrong with you, Damon?" she asked, hating the quiver in her voice. "We're family. How can you value your stupid hunt over your own sister?"

"Give. Me. The. Name." Damon acted as if he hadn't heard her plea. "Now. Before you force me to do something so horrible I don't know I can ever come back from it."

His words made her shudder. Still, she kept her mouth closed.

"It's me," Gabe said, stepping forward, his hands clenched into fists. "I'm the Helios. She saw me Rejuvenate a few hours ago. Now let Meghan go and drop your weapon. If you have any honor, then fight me like a man."

Damon laughed, a harsh sound, though he didn't lower the gun. "I'm more than just a man. Much more. I'm a Hunter," he boasted. "And you're about to go down."

Now he pushed Meghan away, spinning to face off with Gabe. Instead of lowering his gun, he brought it up to bear on Gabe.

"Meghan," Damon ordered. "You have one chance to redeem yourself. Help me bring this monster to his knees.

I'll even share the glory of this hunt with you. You'll be revered far and wide. We both will."

As if she cared. Instead, Meghan ran for Gabe. "I'll help you fight him," she promised, meeting his gaze to let him see how much she meant every single word. "I've got your back."

He stared at her, not moving, not speaking. For one awful moment, she thought he might actually refuse. Instead, he jerked his chin in a nod and pushed her behind him. "Keep your back to my back," he ordered. Then, focusing on her brother, Gabe flexed his powerful shoulders and spread his legs in a warrior's battle stance.

"Come on, Hunter," he told Damon, his voice slicing through the silence. "Let's see if you have the guts to take on both of us."

Damon cursed, his eyes wild. "Meghan? What the hell? Do you realize if you side with him, you no longer have the right to call yourself Hunter?"

Lifting her chin, she glanced around Gabe's muscular chest. All the holidays she'd spent alone, all the mocking words and not-so-subtle attempts by her family to make her feel small. For years, they'd festered like a thorn in her spirit. Until she'd finally let them dissolve. "I gave up that right a long time ago. Now, either fight us or go."

To her surprise, Damon kept his gun trained on them, then bolted for the door. "I'll be back with reinforcements," he shouted, disappearing into the shadows. Right after he did, they heard a metallic racket, as if he'd run into equipment and gotten tangled.

"Got him." Rafe. "He's disarmed and they're putting him in handcuffs. I'll hold him in security until we decide what to do with him."

He popped his head around the corner, grinning. "Glad you two are safe."

"He held a gun to Meghan's head," Gabe said, wrapping her in his arms and pulling her close. "That should result in at least one more charge."

Rafe glanced from one to the other. "I'll leave you alone for now. But at some point, the LVPD will need your statement."

"Just give us a few minutes," Gabe said, his gaze locked on hers.

"Can do." Rafe backed away. "Come to my office when you're done." And he left.

Even though Gabe held her tightly, Meghan couldn't seem to stop shaking.

"Shh," Gabe murmured, smoothing back her hair. "It's all right. You're safe."

Though she didn't want to, she forced herself to move away. "And you're a Helios."

His gaze sharp, he assessed her. "I am. And you're a Hunter."

"I was," she corrected. "I'm not now, nor will I ever be. I gave that up years ago."

"Despite that, it's your heritage, your blood. You were born a Hunter, brought into this world to hunt Helios and bring chaos to mankind."

"None of that matters to me."

"It should."

She made a snorting sound. "Now you're scaring me. You sound just like them."

A glint of wonder blazed in his eyes. "Why didn't you tell him the truth? He had a gun to your head and still you didn't let on that you knew I was the one he wanted."

Looking down, she tried to play it off. "It wasn't a big deal. I'm his sister. He wouldn't have shot me."

"Wouldn't he? I'm thinking you're not a hundred percent sure of that."

The fact that he was right sent a sharp jolt of pain through her heart. "That's so messed up. It shouldn't be like this. He's my brother—they're my family. Yet they'd gladly trade me in for one Helios, Rejuvenated or not."

At her words, he laughed. The rich, masculine sound coaxed an answering smile from her.

"What's going to happen to him now?"

"Well, I think he might be due some jail time. Not only did he break into your suite, but he held a gun to your head and threatened you. And me."

Disheartened, she grimaced. "I don't suppose there's any other alternative? I hate to think of my brother in prison."

"Well, considering he knows I'm a Helios, there is one other alternative."

When he didn't elaborate, she prodded. "Which is?"

"Instead of calling the police on him, we erase part of his memory. The part where he learned what I am."

She held her breath, finally exhaling. "You can do that?"

"Yes. We can." He tightened his arms around her, as if afraid to let her go. "It's rarely done. I'll need to discuss this with Rafe."

She didn't really want to know, but she also did, so she asked anyway. "How? How do you erase someone's memory?"

"With fire. Precisely targeted fire."

He spoke so casually, reminding her that Helios and flame were intimately interchangeable. "It won't actually hurt him—oh, maybe for a moment—but afterward he'll have forgotten all about it."

Relieved, she managed a smile. "That sounds better than actual prison time. Plus, it removes the possibility he might tell someone what he's learned."

"Exactly." He lowered his head and kissed her, long and slow and deep. When they finally came up for air, he released her. "We need to go talk to Rafe and the police. Come on."

Though she wanted to ask several questions, she nodded. Time enough for discussions about the status of their relationship later. She knew one thing for sure. If Gabe wanted to try and make this work—Helios and Hunter or not—she was all for it.

Christmas Eve. The magical night celebrated the world over with peace and joy and awe. On the solstice, her brother had been released to her custody, since neither she nor Gabe pressed charges. She'd left the room when Rafe and Gabe did whatever was required to make him forget, and when they called her back in, Damon looked and acted normal. He knew he needed to get back to hunting, but had no recollection of what he'd already found.

Which was good. Meghan sent him off with a fond smile and an aching heart. She knew she'd gradually have to accept that they'd never be a family, at least not the way she wanted.

But at least she had Gabe.

She and Gabe had rarely been apart since, except when he had to work. Since the solstice and his Rejuvenation, Gabe hadn't appeared to want to let her out of his sight. Which she loved.

With all the craziness, she hadn't been certain his Christmas invitation still stood, but he'd assured her it did. She'd promised Gabe she'd never turn on him, explained to him that she no longer considered herself a Hunter and wanted nothing to do with their hunt. Ever. She hadn't for years. She'd held her breath, not really sure if he'd believe her. So she'd also confessed her growing feelings, how easily she believed they could blossom into love. And while it might be too early to talk about forever, she honestly thought they had a real chance.

He did, too. And he'd told her he not only felt the same,

but he trusted her. She'd found his quiet masculine confidence sexy and let him know in no uncertain terms.

Now here they were, on Christmas Eve.

As Gabe led her to his rooftop garden, she stopped short at the sight of thousands of twinkling white lights.

"That's beautiful," she said, turning in a circle and trying to take it all in.

So many lights. And a tree. A tall and slender Christmas tree lit up so brightly the sight of it made her catch her breath. Next to it, he'd set up a small table, complete with white linens and gleaming china.

"Here you are," he said, pulling out her chair.

Though she sat, she couldn't stop looking around. Tears pricked at her eyes as she took in the magical fairyland he'd created just for her.

He cleared his throat. "Are you okay?"

Blinking hard, she nodded. The last thing she wanted to do was cry. "Where's your grill?" she asked.

"What?" His brow creased. "It's on the other side, closer to my sliding glass doors. But I'm not using it tonight."

"Oh. I thought you'd said your Christmas Eve tradition was to grill a couple of steaks."

His gaze soft as a caress, he studied her. "That's the old tradition. Tonight, we're starting a new one."

Happiness filled her as she nodded. "I like that idea."

"Good." He poured them each a glass of wine from a bottle nestled in an ice bucket on a stand next to them. "I took the liberty of ordering us both dinner. They'll bring it up soon."

She nodded. The tenderness in his gaze matched what was in her heart.

"Are you ready to meet the folks tomorrow?" His relaxed tone told her he thought it would be no big deal.

"Quite honestly, I'm terrified."

"Don't be. They'll love you, I promise."

She shook her head, her throat tight. "Why do you think that? They don't even know me."

"They'll love you because I do."

Her heart lurched. "What did you say?"

"I love you, Meghan Frost." With his large hand, he cupped her face, making her skin tingle where he touched her. "Growing feelings be damned, let's dive headfirst. I don't know where this might lead, but I have a feeling it'll be somewhere good."

A warm glow flowed through her. He was right. Nothing this big should be done in small measures. "I love you, too, Gabe Stavros. And I'm up for whatever the future might hold."

He raised his glass. "To us. And our first Christmas together."

As she touched her glass to his, the clinking sound reminded her of sleigh bells. Instinctively, she looked up, not sure why.

"Looking for Santa Claus?" he teased.

"Why not? If Helios are real, there very well might be a jolly man in a red suit riding around in a flying sleigh pulled by eight tiny reindeer."

His bark of laughter made her respond in kind. And when he reached across the table and kissed her, she knew this would be the best Christmas ever, full of joy and hope, and love. Especially love.

* * * * *